REDEEMING THE ROGUISH RAKE

Liz Tyner

MILLS & BOON

Published in Great Britain 2018
by Mills & Boon, an imprint of HarperCollins*Publishers*
1 London Bridge Street, London, SE1 9GF

ISBN: 978-0-263-93267-6

MIX
Paper from
responsible sources
FSC™ C007454

This book is produced from independently certified FSC™ paper
to ensure responsible forest management.
For more information visit www.harpercollins.co.uk/green.

Printed and bound in Spain
by CPI, Barcelona

Liz Tyner [illegible] a
acreage she imagines [illegible] the
children's book [illegible]. Her lifestyle
is a blend of old and new, and is sometimes comparable
to the way people lived long ago. Liz is a member
of various writing groups and has been writing since
childhood. For more about her visit liztyner.com.

Also by Liz Tyner

The Notorious Countess
The Wallflower Duchess

English Rogues and Grecian Goddesses miniseries

Safe in the Earl's Arms
A Captain and a Rogue
Forbidden to the Duke

The Governess Tales miniseries

The Runaway Governess

Dedicated to Ann Leslie Tuttle

Chapter One

Thumps sounded on the stairs outside the bedchamber. Foxworthy sat straight, covers falling to his waist, just as the door swung open. He looked at the visitor's hands first. No weapons. He raised his glance to his cousin's face. Andrew wore one of those grim-lipped spectacled looks even though he didn't wear spectacles.

'Stop swearing,' Foxworthy said. 'I do not abide such language.'

'If so, that's your only virtue and it's one more than you had last week.' Andrew paused.

'I'm on an improvement regimen.'

'About time. You look ghastly. As though you've not slept a night this week.'

'A bit of tiredness on my face and the ladies

flutter about with suggestions on how to make me feel better. I can't complain.'

'I just heard about your little escapade.'

Foxworthy nodded his head. 'A priceless moment I will not forget.' And he doubted anyone would let him from the look on his cousin's face. However, at the moment, he simply could not recall it. He'd danced a lot at the soirée—*that* he remembered. He'd decided to take a turn with every woman in attendance and in the short time of the dance, discover what was most endearing about her. Then Lady Havisham, all of elbow high to him and feisty as a tavern wench, had told him she could drink more than he. Since he'd started much earlier than her it was a difficult competition. She'd conceded defeat and he'd placed a kiss right on the top of the knot of her grey hair and she'd said she wished she had a grandson just like him, only smart and handsome.

He put a hand on his head. 'The woman must have been pouring it into her reticule.'

'You proposed.'

'I did?' He checked his cousin's eyes to see if he told the truth. 'To Lady Havisham? I can't imagine she'd be foolish enough to say yes.'

'You don't remember?' Andrew snorted. He kicked the base of the bedpost, but the frame didn't move. *'You don't remember?'*

'Not at the moment.' Fox pushed himself from the bed. Pain shot through his knee. He moved to the mirror, favouring the leg.

'Millicent Peabody,' Andrew continued. 'Bended knee, in front of six witnesses.'

Fox smiled, remembering. 'Yes. It was quite romantic. I only wished I'd had a red rose, but the proposal was unplanned.' And he was going to pay for the rather dramatic crash to one knee. It played to the group well, but he wasn't sure if the pain was worth it.

Andrew choked and swung around on one foot, looking away from Fox. 'So why must you do it?'

In the mirror, Fox examined his face. 'I do look like I could use a drink.'

'Why did you propose to Mrs Peabody in front of everyone?'

Andrew moved closer, eyes tightened. He expected an answer.

'Millicent Peabody's husband was being such a toad.' Fox tossed the words out. 'Earlier, he told everyone in the card room that he could not abide how frumpy she's grown since the children arrived. Mrs Peabody is lovely and her husband is too daft to know what a treasure she is because he's chasing every tart in town.'

'Nonsense.' Andrew's eyes darkened. 'You do it so you'll be mentioned in publication. Your sodden brain believes you must rival Lord Byron for attention.'

'Exceed. *Exceed* Byron,' Fox said, lips turning up. 'This proposal even put tears in one debutante's eyes.'

'Fox,' Andrew spoke softly, crossed his arm across his waist, rested an elbow on his other arm and tapped his fingertips against his lips. 'How many times have you proposed to a married woman?'

'It is not the quantity, it is the quality of proposals.'

'How many times now have you publicly proposed to a married woman?' Andrew repeated, voice rising.

'I can't very well propose to an unmarried woman. Might distress her when I don't show up at the wedding. Proposing to a married woman is more sensible.'

'To everyone except the husband.'

Fox quickly pulled on a shirt. 'That may have entered my mind, but I discounted it. Too minor to concern myself with.'

'I see your point. Mr Peabody is feeling disgraced and is planning to kill you. If he succeeds you will be in the papers again. Good plan. You should have thought of it years ago.'

Fox looked over his shoulder. 'I assure you, my demise would be on the *front* page and not only for one day or two. They would devote considerable space to the event.'

'I could get my wife to draw up a caricature of your passing on as well, and proposing again.'

'Assuming there are married women in the hereafter. Which is an immense leap of faith.' Fox poured water into the basin and wet a flannel before pressing it to his face. 'Make sure Beatrice gets my smile just right. I do want to be remembered as I am.'

'Including the wrinkles?'

Foxworthy patted his face clean and reached for the comb, but he spared another glance for the mirror. Not a line. Nothing. Not even at the eyes. His movements stopped and he stared into his reflection. Nothing. A caricature of a person. He flicked the comb against the glass, hearing the clink as he turned away.

'You've moved through the *ton*, gathering the ladies about you,' Andrew said. 'It's as if you wish to say to the husbands that had you asked the wife first, she would have chosen you.'

Fox snapped around, his eyes on his cousin. 'She would have. Nothing to do with me, though. The advantage of inheritance.' His voice roughened. 'The heir's advantage. None of it matters. Not to the women. Not to their husbands. Not to me.'

'No less than three men in this town have

threatened publicly to kill you. You'll hardly be laughing if one decides it's worth the noose to put you in the ground.'

'They only say it because it is required of them. They must bluster and spout. They don't care either.' Fox shut his eyes. The women were fickle. The husbands—cowards. He opened his eyes. The *ton* had become as boring as the country, only with more elaborate planning going into the staleness.

'You've not forgotten that woman who nearly chased you to the altar when you were a child.' Andrew grabbed the waistcoat the valet had left draped over the lacquered clothing stand and tossed the garment at Fox.

Fox caught it. His lips curled up. 'Best thing that ever happened to me was when she lost interest.'

'True. At the time. But not now.'

'I assure you I've no feelings for her at all. I wish her only the best her husband's money can buy. And if you think of it, I'm as good as married to half the women in London. I see them once in a while and don't live with them. The same as my parents do and they are quite happily wed.'

Andrew watched him without speaking for a moment. 'There are decent women out there. You just don't deserve one.'

'I must agree.' He looked at his cousin. 'I'd drown in annoyance.'

The knocking at the door interrupted them. 'Enter,' Fox called out. A footman, hair close cropped at the sides, walked in with a tray holding two notes. He held the salver out to Fox.

Fox stood, picked up one paper, flicked it open, saw that it was from Lady Havisham and read her warning that Peabody was incensed about the proposal.

Then he saw the script on the other page. His father's pen. He opened it. The man would be visiting. He claimed he wanted to see Fox's new horse.

'I am truly going on a health regime,' Foxworthy muttered as he read. 'I'll pay a surprise visit to my father's house in the country—since he's at Bath, searching for a new vicar, and will be in London soon. There's a tavern near my father's country estate that I miss.' He tossed the paper back onto the tray. 'Put it with the others.' He motioned the servant away, and the man nodded.

It would be best for all involved. His father didn't see the humour in marriage proposals, or anything else.

He shook his head. 'It's a sad day when Lady Havisham can handle her spirits better than I can. That tavern ale should put some iron in my stomach.'

Andrew nodded, pushing himself up from the chair. 'I'll tell everyone at White's that you're going to the country estate. Perhaps someone else will divert their attention before you return.' He paused. 'Peabody isn't the straightest arrow and everyone knows he's vengeful.'

Fox waved the words away and checked the mirror again. His blasted eyes looked soulless. As though they didn't care about anyone or anything. His cousin was wrong. He wasn't soured on marriage. He was soured on the world and there wasn't one better anywhere. He'd travelled just enough to know that.

'Don't get yourself killed by proposing to anyone in the country,' Andrew said.

'You have my word,' Fox said. 'I'm leaving London. I will stay from public view for a time. I am not proposing again…' he paused, thinking '…unless it is to Lady Havisham. I rather like her.' He chuckled to himself. 'I doubt she'd take her vows seriously.'

'Would you?'

'Do I take anything seriously?'

'Perhaps the taste of brandy.'

Fox gave an upward tilt of his head, and Andrew stepped out the door, closing it behind him. Fox stared at the wood for a moment.

He didn't even feel much for Andrew. They'd grown up together and had their fair share of adventures. But now they were men and Andrew had married, and his thoughts always seemed somewhere else. Not that Fox didn't understand. His own thoughts only half-attended the revelry around him. That last proposal had been a performance and a stale one at that.

Fox had to leave London. The stench of all the hypocrisy was flooding into him. Particularly his own hypocrisy of the easy smile and the game of getting his name mentioned in the newspaper.

He felt as if he had a bit of sand inside his boot all the time.

The tomb-like walls of his father's house would fit him well. Particularly since his father wasn't there. But first, he would have a crate of brandy sent ahead. Maybe two, since his father wouldn't be there to share. Or three. His father would not see the humour in returning home with a new vicar and finding all the servants with sotted smiles.

The next morning, Foxworthy ignored the superfine silk coat the valet had left out and went to the dressing chamber. He found the half-rag brown garment that suited the country better. He and his father agreed on that one thing. Just as Fox wasn't suited to the country life, neither were the clothes he preferred.

He didn't wait for the carriage. He wanted the power of the horse at his command.

Foxworthy left the house, taking a bite from the apple in his hand. The groom handed the reins to Fox, and he took Rusty's reins, moving to hold his palm flat at the animal's face. The horse nibbled with his lips and then crunched the fruit. The beast looked at Fox and then Fox reached out and gave him a scratch under the chin.

In moments, they were headed to the countryside. Fox leaned forward, giving Rusty a pat on the neck. Rusty's ear twitched his response.

Foxworthy looked around him as he rode. The sunbeams warmed his face. Servants with baskets under their arms walked along the road. A few carriages here and there.

He'd just been in a mood when he was at home. Probably from all the soirées and all the nonsensical talk he did. Damn. He got tired of his own voice sometimes. All the pretty words and all the right things to say. The ladies would flutter and he'd continue and he'd wonder why they didn't slap his face. And they'd chuckle and brush up against him, and he'd spout even more nonsense.

* * *

The saddle was getting a bit smaller and Rusty's ears had lost their *joie de vivre* when the horse stepped onto the road that would take him only one turn from his father's estate, leaving the commerce of London behind them. He had to be thankful the road wasn't mud soaked. The clouds had darkened and he hoped the weather wouldn't trap him at his father's house. The chilled air bit into his face.

He noticed the tracks in the road. Definitely well travelled. More so than usual. When he raised his head, he saw a man with an old, wide-brimmed hat that flopped over his face, standing, holding the reins of a horse in one hand and a cane in the other.

'Ahoy.' The man spoke. His clothes… His clothes were sewn by a fine tailor. Fox recognised the gold buttons. He'd seen them before.

Hooves thundered from the woods and, before he could turn his horse, a club thwacked at the animal's rump. Rusty bolted forward. The man in front raised the cane. The horse surged to the gold-buttoned man and the man stepped aside, swinging the stick. He knocked Fox backward, breaking the club. Another stick caught Fox as he tumbled from the horse. When he slammed into the ground, he noted the face of the man who'd been behind him and the other one charging forward with both fists gripping the broken club.

It wasn't a good sign that they didn't have their faces covered.

Rebecca pinched the frond of the thorn bush, moving the long strand aside carefully so it didn't prick her fingers. She stepped forward on the trail, then released the briar, and one thorn scraped along her skin as the stem swung back into place. The handle of her basket slid on her arm and the eggs she carried jostled, but barely moved, cushioned by the cloth. She checked her arm for blood, but only a white scratch marked the skin.

She continued along the path, listening to the chaffinch and knowing Mrs Berryfield would appreciate the eggs. She imagined Mrs Berryfield's children, chirping like hungry baby birds, their dirty hands reaching for her basket to see what she'd brought. Eggs. They'd be disappointed. But one did the best one could. And the eggs would surely gain her a promise from Mrs Berryfield to attend Sunday Services.

Eggs were not as plentiful now that the weather had chilled. In fact, she moved to the trees lining the road so she'd be out of the wind. The dark clouds threatened, and she hoped to make it back home before the rain.

Stepping up to the road, she crossed, planning to take the short path to the woods to reach the furthermost tenant on the old earl's land.

Then she saw a bundle of clothing lying on the ground. No one tossed the wash about like that. She moved one step closer, staring.

Brown. Brown hair. Still looking fresh from a morning comb. But it couldn't be, because the rest of him—the rest of him splayed about. His head was face down. And blood, brown. Dried.

She couldn't move.

Another funeral for her father to perform. Another widow needing courage and someone to listen to her pain. Rebecca didn't want to walk forward. Then she'd discover if it was Mr Greaves or Mr Able. They were the only two men with a head of hair that colour, except theirs always stuck ragged from their hats. She needed to know who it was. The family would have to know.

The dead man groaned, just the tiniest bit, and she dropped her basket.

'Mr Greaves? Mr Able?' she called out, voice screeching into her own ears.

He didn't move.

She took a step forward. No answer. Oh, my. She'd forgotten about Mr Renfro and he had *eight* children. 'Mr Renfro?' The words wobbled from her mouth.

He was quiet as a tomb. She was going to have to turn him over and she hated the thought of touching Mr Renfro, even dead. He smelled worse than a sweat-soaked draught horse. She didn't know how Mrs Renfro did it.

She clamped her teeth together. Putting her boot solidly on the ground, she stepped forward.

His big bare feet tangled in the grass. His boots had been stolen. Shivering, she darted her eyes to the trail, fearing the thought of someone watching her.

The birds still sang and a breeze wafted through the air.

Moving forward, she nudged her own boot against the muddied toe. 'Pardon.'

She was going to have to touch him. It wasn't good for a man to touch a woman unless they were married, but women were granted no such favours where men were concerned.

She knelt on the ground, took in a deep breath and pushed at his shoulder to move him over. He didn't budge. She tried again and then looked the length of him. He wasn't Mr Greaves or Mr Able. Mr Renfro overshot the door frame and had to duck when he stepped inside, but the stranger looked too precise for Mr Renfro.

She leaned in. He didn't smell like Mr Renfro. Even covered in dirt and mud, this one didn't have an odour. She touched the one bit of skin she could see, near his neck. Cold.

Instead of pushing, she reached across his back. She grabbed his shirt shoulder in one hand and the waist in the other and pulled. He flopped over onto his back, and she plopped to her bottom. She shut her eyes when she saw his face. She took two deep breaths before she could look at him again. His nose was to the side and so was his jaw. His eyes—she didn't know if he could even open them or not. His face could have once belonged to Mr Renfro, Mr Greaves or Mr Able. Then she looked him over again. He only wore a lawn shirt and his trousers. His clothing had been stolen. Or, it had been taken so he would freeze to death.

His eyelid fluttered and one eye opened a slit. She didn't know if he could really see her. Then his hand reached up and touched her wrist.

She didn't know what to do. She clasped his fingers. He squeezed, then relaxed his grasp.

'I must get you help,' she said. 'I must. I'll only be gone a moment. I can find a cart.'

He squeezed again. She hated to leave. But she had to. Both his eyes opened now. And she could have sworn he winked at her before shutting his eyes again.

But she didn't want him to die in the brambles. She didn't really want him to die in the vicarage either, but it wouldn't be the first time someone had.

She stood, took off her coat, put it around him and ran, whispering prayers under her breath.

Mr Renfro's house would be her best choice. He could carry the man to the vicarage and he'd have no trouble straightening the man's nose back in place, something her father could never do. One of Mr Renfro's sons could help. The stranger needed to be straightened out before they buried him and Mr Renfro would have plenty of help to hold the man down if he fought.

Chapter Two

He wasn't sure if he lay in a bed or a coffin.

Buzzing. Bees or flies. No, a woman's voice. An upset woman. Fox didn't open his eyes at the noise. Everything hurt too much for him to care. If they were going to kill him, he just hoped for them to hurry.

The woman's voice again and then a man's. But the man's voice softened. Concerned. Not angry. Not violent.

'I did find out who he is.' The male again. 'I spoke with the servants at the earl's house, letting them know we have criminals on the loose, and I have the victim here.'

'Who is he?' she asked.

'Well, Mrs Pritchett didn't want me to know, but the earl sent them a letter telling them to brighten up a room for…a new vicar. Said to expect him any day now.'

'Oh, Father…' The word ended in despair.

'Now, Rebecca. The earl only wants the best. Don't look so upset.'

'I'm not.'

The room was silent. Nothing. Then the rustle of clothing, someone moving, stopping at his side. He tried to open his eyes.

'Are you the new vicar?' the soft voice asked. Even in the blackness surrounding him, he could tell she leaned over him. The perfume of lilacs and just-cooked porridge touched his nose. She wasn't anyone he knew.

But even the scent of his favourite flower didn't ease the pain in his face. His eyes hurt and they wouldn't open properly. He couldn't open his blasted eyes.

He just wanted to rest. Rest. He needed to tell her.

He parted his lips to speak. Pain hobbled his words. His breath rushed from his lungs to throat and even thinking ached his head. He clenched his fist, barely trapping bedclothes in his hands. *Rest.*

But the first part of the word was too hard to speak. He couldn't talk with her. The feeling of bones crashing together tensed his body.

'Are you the new vicar?' she asked again.

Rest. He wanted to rest, but it hurt too badly. He pushed out as much of the word as he could. '...esss...'

The woman spoke. 'He said yes'

He didn't care who she thought he was. He hurt worse than he'd ever hurt when he awoke after going twenty-four hours with nothing to sustain him but brandy. *That* hadn't been this bad. He wanted to ask for brandy. He really did. He wanted to tell them he'd pay a hundred pounds for a good brandy to wash the taste of blood from his mouth. Or at least make him forget it.

'His lordship has been saying for quite some time I should take a pension. We knew he was hoping to find a new vicar, Becca.' A man's voice. The man's voice rumbled again. 'He said that was part of the reason he was travelling. It's to be expected.'

'I know,' she said.

The woman leaned in again, touching the bed, jostling Fox. Pain shot through the top of his head. She was going to kill him if she didn't stop moving him. They'd already stripped him and cleaned him and dressed him in a sack. Whatever they'd given him to drink had left a bitter taste in his mouth and mixed with the other tastes. He needed a shipload of brandy.

He'd heard the crack when the club hit his

face before the blackness had overtaken him. The breaking noise had been the same as when someone strong took a dried branch and snapped it. He'd not known a face could make such a sound.

The memory of the cracking noise warred with the pain.

'Do you think I should give him some milk, Father?'

No, he wanted to scream. *Brandy*.

'Put some on a flannel and drip it into his mouth.'

He raised his hand an inch, fingers spread, palm out. *No milk*.

'I think that's what he wants,' she said. 'Look. He's clasping his fingers for the glass.'

Forcing the effort, he lifted his hand and put it up, over the area of his mouth.

'He's not thirsty,' the male said.

'But he should drink something.'

'Leave him be. He probably can't get it down anyway. He said no, so let's give him some quiet.'

'He'd probably like it if I read from the prayer book to him.'

The male voice sounded from further away. 'Yes.'

Clothes rustled and the lilacs touched him again. Without opening his eyes, he reached for her. His fingers closed around something else. A book.

'Oh, Father. He wants the prayer book.' The words lingered in the air, floating, and wafted outwards, awe colouring them with praise. Much the same as his voice would have been if he'd been able to thank her for some brandy.

'Scriptures have always given me comfort in my time of need,' the gruff voice stated.

The sound of bustling clothing and a chair being moved close to the bed. 'I think I should start with the January ones until I get to this month,' the soft voice said. 'And I'll read the best parts slowly.'

It was autumn.

He was in hell.

And if he was going to be punished for all the wrongs he'd done…he would not be leaving for a while.

The old man interrupted the woman. 'He's not struggling and if he…doesn't make it…well, he'll be in a better place.'

No. No. He preferred London. It was good enough. It was wonderful, in fact. The best of everything the world could offer was at his fingertips. He'd been mistaken to leave it.

His hand slid sideways, and he clasped at the bedcovers to keep the feeling of floating from overtaking him.

'I'd best go spread the word that we've got some cutthroats in the area.' The gruff voice spoke again.

'Did you let the earl's servants know…he's here?'

The man let out a deep sigh. 'Yes. I told them it's best not to move him and that you're giving him the best care there is. You know as much as an apothecary does about treatments.'

'I learned from Mother.'

'Did you notice…?' The male's words faded. 'In his time of need, he reached for comfort. A sainted heart lives inside that battered body. At least I can rest easier knowing a man who appreciates goodness is replacing me. I just think I have a lot of Sunday Services left in me.'

'You do, Father. And you can teach the new vicar, too. You can help him.'

No one spoke for a few moments.

'Well, Vicar,' the older voice said from near Fox's elbow, 'I will look forward to hearing one of your first services.'

Fox, eyes still shut, breathed in and out. He could do that. He could give quite the sermon on why you shouldn't covet your neighbour's wife.

Shuffling noises sounded. 'Latch the door behind me,' the man said. 'I don't want any of those evil-doers coming back to finish what's left of him.'

The door closed, and a bolt sounded, being moved into place.

Chapter Three

Fox dozed and words pulled him from his stupor. More reading from that book. Voice gentle, but sounding more asleep than awake. The book shut with a snap.

This was as much enjoyment as reading his father's letters. The same type of admonishments. Mostly. Although, the voice wasn't telling him the additional commandment to wed a virtuous woman and put a blindfold on.

A scraping noise. A chair on a rough floor. Clothing moving against skin as someone moved. A female. The air she disturbed swirled around him, trailing the lilac scent.

He tried to turn towards her. But his head was too heavy for his neck to move. She leaned over him and brushed a lock of his hair from his forehead, her fingertip trailing cool across his skin. 'You look better than you did before I washed the blood from your face.'

His eyes remained closed. He remembered a rough rag brushing over his skin, shooting pain into him.

She stroked the skin in front of his ear, feather-light. His whole being followed the movement of her hand against his face, sending sparks of warmth. She pulled away. 'You've slept for a full day. Over a day.' She brushed a lock of hair from by his ear, but her hand remained, barely there. She stilled. 'Nothing since you reached for the prayer book.'

He waited. Why didn't she move again?

'I think you should wake up.'

He wanted to hear her speak again. Now.

'If you don't wake up soon, I'm afraid you'll never wake up. That won't be good.'

It's not my choice.

'You'll need to be shaved. I suppose Father can do that. But his hand trembles so.'

He imagined the razor at his throat and heard a guttural noise. Spears stabbed from inside his neck.

He couldn't force his eyes open.

'Quiet now,' she said. 'Don't hurt yourself. But at least you're talking now.'

Talking? He had no strength to agree or disagree.

She touched the cloth at his neck and tugged, loosening something. 'I wasn't thinking. You've jostled yourself and tightened the nightshirt strings over your bruise.'

The covers moved around him.

'Oh. I didn't mean to hurt you. I do beg your pardon.' Again, fingertips brushed at the side of his face. She smoothed across his eyebrows, first one and then the other. Her fingers didn't stop. 'The only part of your face that isn't bruised,' she said.

He relaxed into her caresses.

Then her cool lips pressed at his forehead, bringing the scent of a woman's softness. 'I hope you're sleeping comfortably.'

No. I never sleep comfortably.

He moved his feet and nothing new hurt. Then he moved his left hand. He tried to make a fist with his right hand, but he couldn't. He remembered deflecting a blow.

He was fairly certain he could walk. His legs moved fine, but he didn't think he could speak. He tried. But his throat ached and pain seared. Too much effort.

If she'd put a pen in his hand, surely he could write something without seeing. A haze of light seeped from under one lash. If he concentrated, he could make out the outline of the covers over his chest.

He tried to make a swirling motion with his hand to indicate writing, but she grasped it and he let her hold it still.

'Don't be uneasy.'

He could pen instructions for them to take him to his father's estate.

The rough nightshirt they'd put on him would definitely please his father. But surely the servants could find something that didn't bind him so tight.

Then he forced his eyes wider. He couldn't get them open enough to see much more than shadows. And a bosom.

He pushed against the puffed skin that wanted to defeat him. He could see very little of the world except a very delightful view. Two delectable beauties right in front of him. Oh, this was not so terrible. And then they moved. Not in the preferred way, but whisked from his vision.

'Praises be,' she said, and clasped her hands together, moving so rapidly he could not follow. 'Your eyes are open.'

Blast. His lids closed. *Blast.*

Then he imagined the sight he'd just seen. The faded and washed fabric, pliable from much use, and exactly the sight he wanted to wake up to. His whole body wanted to wake up to it and did.

He couldn't smile. It hurt too much. But if he'd had to be separated into two parts and only one portion functioned, his head or his manhood, well, it had worked out for the best.

Relief flooded through him, dancing around the memory of the breasts.

'Oh.' She slid on to the chair at his bedside and reached for a cloth. She daubed it around his face. 'Don't let it concern you that your eye twitches. You've done that almost every time I speak to you. That's how I know you hear me.'

He turned enough that he could see the book in her hands. He lifted his left hand, reaching for it.

She moved the volume into his grasp and helped him guide it against his body. He clasped it at his side, keeping it in his hand. She'd have to finish the job the cutthroats started to get that book back again. He would not hear one more saintly syllable from it.

Becca watched him. He grasped the book so tight. Her chest fluttered. His discoloured face had made her cringe at first, but now she was used to all the marks and bruises. Her mother had once told her a tale of a woman falling in love with gargoyles and now she could understand how the ladies of the village could tolerate the touches of their rough husbands. They saw through the appearance to the heart underneath.

She looked at him, clutching the prayer book to his side, holding close what was dear to him.

Biting her lip, she reached out. She patted his hand and then let her fingers stop over his knuckles. Strong hands, but not roughened with work because he spent his time tending people instead of livestock or fields.

He kept the book against his side, yet he moved his grasp so that he covered her hand with his, holding their hands resting on the volume. She'd never...been this close to a man before. Well, she had, but this made her breath shaky.

She took in a gulp of air.

'Are you comfortable?' she asked, leaning closer.

He moved his head and didn't squeeze her hand. The blink of his eyes was a bit long to be anything positive. 'Well, I guess you couldn't be. Not with all the injuries.'

His grasp tightened in agreement and her heart double-thumped. It was just the gratefulness of not having to watch him die. She'd not looked forward to that.

She moved closer. 'Do you mind if I talk to you?'

He pressed her hand, softly.

This time she couldn't help giving a return squeeze to his fingers. His hand felt so big compared to hers. She liked that. She put her free hand over their clasp and gently rubbed over his knuckles. The tension in his grip lessened. It didn't seem like they were strangers any more.

'I'm Rebecca Whitelow. I'm twenty-three. Mother died when I was twenty. I still miss her every day.' She shrugged the words, almost laughing at herself. 'Good works. I try to do her good works now. One for each day of the week, except Sunday,' she whispered. 'A day of rest.'

Smoothing the pillow covering at the side of his head, she said, 'No one knows about my good works, or my day of rest from them. They can't, or it could hurt their feelings to think it is a duty.'

She touched the pillow again. 'I like doing the nice things but I like resting on Sunday, too. It's my good works for myself.' Her hand was so near his head that she couldn't stop herself from smoothing his hair, although truly, it didn't need to be combed.

His grip had loosened. She peered at him. He wasn't asleep, though. He watched her. 'Father says most people spend so much time waiting for a chance to do something especially wonderful that they overlook little things, like the weeds that might need to be pulled from an elderly neighbour's garden.' She wrinkled her nose.

He listened. She moved closer to his face. He could see her. She could tell. Each time she bent near him his eyes followed her. She could see the tension. The concentration. The struggle.

'Don't you think it was wise of Father to help me understand the value of small efforts? To show me that goodness is not something to be saved for the biggest battles, but to be used every day?'

She asked the question to see if the man could give a response.

His eyes shut.

One quick pulse of movement at her hand rewarded her. But she didn't think he quite agreed. 'Oh, please understand that I'm not trying to ignore the bigger needs.'

He tapped her knuckles. A reassuring pat, but slow between movements. Much in the same way someone would agree who didn't really or didn't at all. Perhaps the way her father might when he wasn't listening, but wanted to show her he cared about her anyway.

She ducked her head. 'I'm not boasting. Forgive me if it sounds that way.'

She pulled her hand away, but his grip tightened, firm, keeping her in his grasp, but not forcing. His eyes flickered to her.

A sliding rub down her fingers told her he was pleased. Her heart grew, spreading itself throughout her body, warming it.

She kept the blossoming hope inside. She'd planned not to marry, ever, unless it was that once with Samuel Wilson. Not that she had a fondness for Sam. But he was sturdy and always attended Sunday Services and was her best choice in the village. And then he'd up and married the bar maid—not that Trudy wasn't a nice woman, if you liked a certain coarseness and the fact she never laced her boots properly. And she wore her skirts just short enough for it to be noticed. Men seemed to find those unlaced boots quite fetching.

Rebecca looked at where her own feet were concealed under the folds of her skirt. She'd accepted that her choices in the village were rather dismal for a husband and after Samuel got married they had become almost non-existent. The men were always respectful to her, but they kept their distance, as if she might scold them for speaking roughly. And there weren't a lot of them of marriageable age who weren't already married.

She'd been tending her mother when other people were courting.

She'd overheard her parents speaking of marriage many times. Her mother had complained to her father that finding a man of good quality was difficult for the young women of the village, particularly with the number of men who'd died fighting Napoleon.

So many times her mother had cautioned her that in order to continue her good works she must find a man who appreciated the time she spent on giving to others. Only a man devoted to goodness would understand.

But, well, now she wasn't certain that her future husband hadn't been delivered to her doorstep.

A vicar certainly needed a wife to administer to the women of the village.

But one shouldn't put the plates on the table before the vegetables had been planted.

She opened her mouth, relaxed her voice, then asked, 'Is there anyone special that we should send for who might need to know of your accident?'

No tug at her hand.

She leaned nearer, studying his face for the barest movement. 'Anyone?'

For a half-second, she thought he might have died. Everything stopped. His breathing. His movement. The awareness in his face. His eyes shut, but then he opened them. Something cold peered out.

'I may have overstepped,' she said.

Then his hand moved over hers, caressing, touching each finger as if to reassure himself of her. And she could feel the touch, bursting inside her, warming enough that even a day without sunshine would feel golden. A teardrop of emotion grew to a whole flood of feelings inside her, and ended on a trickle of guilt.

He could be all alone in the world and she'd reminded him.

Perhaps no woman had ever looked his way because he'd not found a parish yet and couldn't support her.

And now that he was going to have a way to care for a wife, his face had been mashed beyond recognition.

She was certain he would look better when he healed, but she doubted much about his features could be appealing, except his hair.

She took the comb at the bedside. His hair didn't need to be combed. It never seemed to. But brushing through it, letting the locks trickle over her fingers, soothed her.

What would it be like to be a wife cutting her husband's hair? she wondered. They could take a chair outside for the light and he could turn it so that he sat astraddle, and his arms crossed over the back. She'd comb the strands, in the same way she did now. They'd talk about… everything. Neither alone any more.

Perhaps, if she tried very, very hard, he would love her by the time he recovered. She'd let him know that his appearance did not matter to her. It didn't matter at all. His charitable ways were more important than anything else. She could learn to love his misshapen face.

She scrutinised him, realisation dawning.

'I don't even know your name,' she said.

His jaw moved slightly, but then his hand tightened on hers and he winced. She reached out, placing a palm on the covers above his heart. 'It doesn't matter,' she said. 'You can tell me later, Vicar.'

His eyes trapped hers, and she instinctively pulled her hand from him. She'd overstepped once again. She didn't know how, but she had.

Chapter Four

Rebecca sat at the bedside, knitting in her hands, but she'd hardly managed more than a few stitches the past few days.

His eyes were shut, but he didn't sleep. He'd move an arm, or stretch his leg or move a shoulder every few moments as if the very act of being still pained him.

He looked so much better. His eyes could open now and the bluish marks didn't quite reach his ears. The swelling in his nose had diminished some.

She took in his appearance again. Perhaps he didn't really look better. Perhaps she'd just grown used to the mottled appearance. But it didn't matter. He was mending.

Her father stood at the side of the bed, his

shoulders stooped and his face a reflection of studied thinking.

'I've never seen someone gain so much comfort from just the Prayer Book.' He spoke to the still form. 'But I must borrow it for Sunday Services.'

Instantly, and without opening his eyes, the man thrust out the book. Her father took it. Now he turned his studied look on Rebecca.

'Walk with me a few steps, Becca.'

Rebecca put her knitting on the floor and stood. She took one look at the bed, reassuring herself he'd be fine for the moments until she returned. She and her father had both fallen into their usual routine of caring for someone very ill. One of them stayed with him at all times, even though they both expected him to live. Without his ability to open his eyes more than a sliver, it seemed cruel to leave him to his own devices.

She slipped out the doorway with her father, pulling the latch closed behind her. 'Are you going to check if anyone has found the culprits?'

'No need. They'd rush here first if they had. I told the new vicar this morning that a horse without a saddle was found and it was taken to the earl's stables. Figure the men took the saddle and sold it.'

He snugged the book under his arm and

turned to her, taking both her hands. Concern wreathed his eyes. 'Rebecca. I've been worried about you. And I've thought about it a lot. This man may have been sent to us. To you.'

She ducked her head so he wouldn't see her eyes. She'd thought the same thing.

'It's true, Rebecca. I'm not going to live for ever and I know the earl would see that you're taken care of. But he's not going to live for ever either and his son will inherit… We don't know…what to…expect from him.'

'The heir can't be all bad, Father. After all, he's the earl's son.'

'I know. But the earl confided that he is worried about his son. It seems the boy has become more and more reckless.' Her father's eyes increased their concern. 'He's nothing like his father.'

'You don't have to tell me. Mr and Mrs Able brought a newspaper back from their visit to see her sister in London. She showed me the part about the proposals.' Rebecca sighed. 'Or at least she tried. I made her put it away. Mrs Able and her sister must write to each other with every post. The earl does not share the newspaper when mention of his son is made.'

Mrs Able was the villagers' prime source of London news, a status that made her preen and gave Rebecca's father trials on how to present sermons about talebearers without being judgemental.

Most people only told the vicar of all the goodness in the world, sheltering their words from any tales of idleness or revelry except when asking for help with a trial too big to handle, but Mrs Able never concerned herself in such a way. She wanted to let Rebecca and her father know they still had much work to do.

He pulled his hands from hers and took the book from under his arm. He smiled, but his eyes remained saddened. 'Before the earl came to his senses and saw what a decadent life he lived, he gave the boy too much. He knows that. The earl blames himself for the error of his son's ways.'

'Well, he shouldn't. His son is a grown man and he avoids the village as if we are plague ridden. When he's visited his father in the past, it's said he spends more time at the tavern than at the estate. And he's never once attended Sunday Services with the earl.'

'A parent has responsibility and only a short time to guide the child before the child becomes its own person. The earl feels badly that he left the boy with his mother after their daughter died, but she grieved so and the boy was the only reason she lived.'

'A good wife would have moved with her husband.'

The vicar shook his head. 'We shouldn't judge her, Rebecca. Perhaps he should have stayed with her. They were both swathed in grief and each blamed the other for the loss.'

'No one can blame someone because of a loss such as that.'

'The daughter was always sickly and the countess blamed the earl for encouraging the marriage. The earl thought his wife shouldn't have let their daughter go about so close to her time and the cough she caught weakened her in childbed. And he still feels the burden of his daughter's death.'

Her father sighed. 'The earl has promised me that you will be cared for should anything happen to me. When he said he was to look about for someone to take on the responsibilities of the church, I did ask…' His voice trailed to nothing and then he began speaking again. 'I did ask that he might look for an unwed vicar. One near your age.' His eyes met hers and then he turned, walking the path to the church.

Rebecca gulped in air. She didn't really like having her life planned for her.

'He reassured me you'd be taken care of, Becca.'

Emotions stilled her body, but her thoughts

exploded inside her. She must put aside her irritation at the matchmaking. To be able to remain in the village and continue her duties would be her greatest wish.

The new vicar had been chosen with her in mind. She was certain of it. If she and the new vicar were to wed, though, she would be able to remain in the home she'd lived her whole life and with the ladies who'd been like mothers to her as well.

She wouldn't have to worry about what might happen if her father passed on. She'd have a home somewhere and good works to do.

'Of course, you know I'd never wish you to do anything that might bring you unhappiness,' her father said. 'I just want you to have the happiness of a marriage such as your mother and I had.'

She went back inside. The man slept. She knew he did. He made the little whistle now—the one that reminded her of a kitten's purr.

She returned to take up her knitting. When she sat, she accidentally kicked her toe on the chair leg. 'Dash it.'

His eyes opened completely and stared into hers. Her heart pounded and she couldn't move.

'My apologies. I didn't mean to speak so roughly,' she said.

He didn't look at her eyes. He looked into them. She dropped her needles and took a cloth from the table at her side, relishing movement. She dotted the cloth over his forehead. He flinched. Then she slowed, taking her time, just as she would have with a newborn.

One eyelid drooped and one corner of his lip turned up. He winked. He shouldn't have. He really shouldn't have.

She winked back.

Nothing happened. No thunder ripped through the air. No violent wind shook the house. It was just an ordinary, calm moment. Not a butterflies-in-the-stomach moment, but butterflies around the heart.

This was what it would feel like to be married. She'd not realised. She'd not realised how much she truly wanted to be married. To have someone to cherish her and to hold her and share quiet moments with. She'd thought she didn't really care. That marriage wasn't important except as a duty and to provide a roof over her head.

But now he watched her. She looked past the marred countenance and into the blue eyes. She could see his kind spirit. The compassion for others that they both shared.

He touched her hand, and she dropped the cloth. Their fingers interlaced and it was as if their hearts connected.

* * *

He'd fallen asleep, and so had her arm. She slipped out of his grasp and noted the cracks on his lips. She moved for a plate of butter and with her forefinger dotted it on his chapped lips. His eyes opened and he watched her. She peered closer, observing him. She held one finger in front of his face and moved right, then left.

His eyes didn't follow the movement.

She tried again. Left to right this time.

He looked at her and then lifted a forefinger and moved it right, then left. And then he touched her nose. Then without moving his upper torso, he took the butter dish from her hand, their fingers brushed and she froze.

He touched the butter to the tip of his finger, reached up and traced her lips.

She couldn't move for a moment, locked in place by some experience that didn't quite fit in her life.

She jumped back, knocking the chair aside, reeling with the touch.

'Vicar.' Her cheeks burned. 'We don't do that.' But she'd done it for him. She righted the chair and stood behind it, hands grasping the top rung. Who knew how much of his mind remained?

The poor man had probably lost all his senses and was just following her movements. And she'd been so daft as to imagine a person behind the eyes, even though she had no reason to. Her own secret desires were leading her thoughts. She frowned.

'I. Am. Rebecca.'

He looked at her.

'Would. You. Like. Me. To. Recite. Verses. To. You?'

He lifted his hand and made a cupping shape, and tipped the invisible glass close to his face.

'Thirsty? Ale… Water?'

He grunted, disagreeing.

'So your mind works?'

The slightest shake of his head.

'You've lost your senses?'

He held up the hand again. This time the drinking motion was more forceful. He then moved to push himself up, but winced instead.

She ran to the shelf and pulled off the ale. She grabbed one of the three glasses and poured a fingerwidth in it, then grabbed the dipper from the bucket and poured in another two fingerwidths. Just like her father liked it.

Next, she stopped at the bedside.

He used both hands to nudge himself to a sitting position. But he didn't right himself fully. And then he looked at her and she could see thoughts. She didn't know if they were fully formed or if they only half made sense.

He looked towards her breasts and then her eyes, then he wilted a bit and pushed, but didn't move.

She realised she was going to have to help him sit. Well, if she had to, she would do it.

'Give me a moment.' She set the glass onto the table. 'Vicar.'

When she turned to help him, little sharp lines etched at the sides of his eyes. His expression had changed to darkness. She didn't move.

He made a flat, stopping motion with his hand and he stared at her as if she'd pinched his bruises.

Then he moved himself upwards even more, doing a fine job of righting himself, but the pillow was at an odd angle. She must correct it. It was impossible not to brush against him. She put a hand on his arm to steady herself. She'd never been so close to anyone except Mrs Greaves when she had her babies and needed an extra day or so of help.

She moved to pull the pillow up. 'I'm so sorry, Vicar,' she said. 'I don't want you to be sitting on a lump.'

When she pulled away, the stark lines at his eyes had increased even more.

Perhaps he had a mind problem that came and went. Old Mr Jeffers had been like that. She reached out and patted the back of his hand just as her mother had patted Rebecca's hand.

He didn't move his head, but his eyes moved to stare into her face.

She jerked her hand back and her thoughts scattered. Apparently, the injury had affected his mind. How sad.

The thought jostled her that perhaps she'd been sent a man who would never be clear in his mind and she would have to spend the rest of her days caring for him. A man with a disfigured face and thoughts just as jumbled.

Oh, it had been a mistake to wish for a husband.

She squeezed her hands into fists. Well, so be it. If that was her lot in life, then it was to be accepted. She didn't quite want to do thousands of little good works in a day and then try to fit in the needs of the villagers. *Blast it.*

Immediately, she thrust those thoughts away.

She put the happy look on her face that worked well for getting babies to do as she wished. She reached for the glass, lifted it, held it up, pointed to it and smiled.

His head tilted to one side and his eyes blackened even more. A flush warmed her from head to toe.

'I'm the one who can talk.' She smiled it away.

'For a moment I forgot. Are you ready for the drink?'

He took it from her hand, put it to his lips, leaned forward and barely tipped the glass into the sliver of open mouth. He couldn't seem to move his lower jaw. She took the cloth again, reaching to his face. He grasped her wrist with his free hand, stopping her.

His eyes tensed as he sipped, downing only a small amount. Then he sat it on the table at his bedside.

'Would you like me to get you some milk toast?'

One blinking glare hit her and she took a half step back. Her arm loose at her side, she knotted the fabric of her dress in her hand.

Remaining unwed might be her best choice. The village had a considerable number of spinsters and widows.

But then she shut her eyes, realising the truth. If someone else wed the vicar, then Rebecca would just be another spinster. It was prideful, she knew, but her role gave her a certain standing. Sometimes—most times—even the ladies twice her age and long married looked to her when they needed advice or a listening ear. After all, she lived in the vicarage.

The only way she could retain the role her

mother had left to her was to become the new vicar's wife.

And if that meant propping him up and taking on many of his responsibilities, then she could do it.

One didn't receive training to only reach to the edge of what the teacher taught.

She would do what was needed even if it meant yoking herself to a man who must be cajoled to take his milk toast.

She examined his face. With the swelling around his eyes and the turn of his nose, he looked more like a prisoner of himself than a true man.

Perhaps he was in pain. 'Would you like a sip of laudanum?'

He didn't want to take laudanum. He wanted to drink the fine wine and dance the best of dances. Not lie in a bed and have someone hovering about him. He tightened his jaw and a spear of pain spiked into him.

Anger warred with the pain, causing both to flare. He shut his eyes, forcing the pain back. He'd never been still in his waking moments. Never. He could not remain in a bed. He would speak and he would go and get his own damn brandy. He opened his mouth and a thousand spears shot into his jaw. He contracted in pain, arms locked on to the space in front of him. Someone spoke. Noise. Buzzing darkness.

'Vicar. Vicar.' A soft voice. A whisper of sound.

Pressure on his chest. Not pain. Just hands, pressing at him.

He opened his eyes enough to be aware her face was inches from his. Her eyes were wide. 'Let me go,' she whispered.

He realised he clutched her to his chest. Instantly, he released his grip, dropping his arms. She pushed herself away, taking the solace of warmth with her. But not every last bit of it. One little gem of softness remained in him. One little spot free of pain and filled with comfort.

He looked at her eyes. Wide. Staring at him.

He expelled a short breath. That made two of them who couldn't talk.

She was a rather bland woman. All saintly and hair pulled back tight. But she had the gentlest eyes he'd ever seen. Soft heart-shaped face. He reached out. He couldn't help himself. He took her hand again. But this time, he wasn't overwhelmed by pain as he had been when he held her hand before.

Her hand. It— His mouth stopped hurting and went dry.

Her hands contrasted with the softness of her face. He looked, reassuring himself that the hands were as they felt. She tried to pull away. But he had to see the truth. And he did. An abrasion. Redness. One fingernail torn past the quick.

She jerked back from his touch.

He couldn't apologise, but he tried to with his eyes. Not for holding her hand. But for the hardness of her life.

If she'd been a lady, sitting in her house, perfecting her pianoforte or her embroidery stitches, he would have died.

When he looked into her face, he remembered hearing her and her father talk about her finding him.

The weather had been so cold when he'd started on the trip to his father's estate. The night would have been even colder. He would have died if he'd stayed on the ground.

He remembered the jests he'd made in the past about his funeral being filled with weeping women. That would have turned out to be a lie. His death would have been mentioned at length in a scandal rag for people to recount the foolish jests he'd done and certainly his mother would have shed a tear and erected a shrine of some sort.

His cousins would have been sad for a day and gone on with their lives. Steven, Andrew and Edgeworth had all married and settled into boredom. When their children were of an age the children would have been told stories about him and an admonishment about how reckless rakish living led to an early end.

'...ank you,' he said.

'I did nothing.'

He looked at her hands and held out his. She paused, hesitated and put her hand on his palm. He moved to touch the rough, reddened knuckles.

How much would this woman be missed if she died? Her friends would talk in lowered voices and shake their heads. His friends would raise a glass to his memory and laugh at the silliness he'd provided them.

He pulled her hand close. He could not kiss away the roughened skin. He couldn't laugh it away.

He took her palm and placed it over his heart.

Her face cleared of all emotion. Her eyes widened.

'Re...ecca.' His throat didn't want to work around the words, but he had to say her name.

'Vicar,' she whispered.

He took in a breath and removed her hand from his chest, holding it out and gently letting go.

She was pure. Too pure. Too saintly. How odd.

Chapter Five

If this was her day of rest, he understood why her hands were rough. She'd taken a break from washing clothing outside to warm by the fire and write a letter. Apparently Rebecca penned letters for a lady with gnarled fingers to the woman's sister in Leeds.

Strands of Rebecca's hair worked free of the bun and wisped around her face, haloing it.

He should ask her for the pen. He needed to tell her who he truly was.

Foxworthy waved her to him, ignoring the pain caused by raising his arm.

'What do you need?' she asked. Wide eyes. Soft face.

He didn't really want to go to his father's, but he did need to tell her who he was. As soon as he did, he'd become the heir again. To be fussed over by his father's servants and witnessing their underlying air of disapproval would grate under his skin. He didn't know how the staff could be so helpful, so perfect in their jobs, and yet manage to point out better than his father did that he was unwelcome.

He indicated the chair beside him.

She put the pen down and stood.

He held out his hand again. Her eyes examined each finger. He waited. She glanced at him, then her lips moved up even as they pressed into firmness, fighting a battle with themselves.

His face naturally moved towards a smile. Even beaten, he still could charm a woman to his side. His jaw reacted from the agony of demon's claws affixing themselves onto both sides of his face and ripping downwards.

He gasped inwardly, not moving his face.

'Oh. Oh.' She bustled forward, and he used his eyes to tell her not to touch him for a moment, but she grabbed the thrust-out hand and put her other over it. They both gripped and squeezed until his breathing became measured and he opened his eyes.

He held her cupped fingers and relaxed, putting their hands on his chest.

'Re...ecca...' The words trailed away.

'Do you hurt?'

He shook his head. 'Talking hurts.' His voice croaked frog-like into the air he spoke from his throat, keeping his lips still.

''oving… 'outh…' he added.

'Who hurt you?' she asked.

'Not sure…' He paused.

'I'm so thankful you survived with so many attackers. It terrifies me to think so many wayward men are loose in the area.'

'…not hurt village.' He tapped his chest several times, letting her know they'd been after him.

There'd been four in all. That he was sure of. The gold-buttoned one had been the instigator. He knew that. And it wasn't Peabody. But the fourth one had told the others to hit Fox again. Saying he'd proposed his last time.

And for the life of him he couldn't remember proposing to that man's wife. He was young and Fox had thought about the faces of the young women he'd spoken with and they all had older husbands.

Innocents were not his bailiwick. He didn't wish to be bored.

'We must see them caught,' she said. 'Now that you are awake and can tell us who they are.'

He crossed his wrists in front of him and then, palms out, abruptly spread his arms.

'You don't want them caught.' Her eyes softened and her voice couldn't have reached the walls of the room, and her face reflected awe. 'You're so forgiving.'

No one had ever looked at him like that and for good reason. Well, except perhaps after love-making.

'Forgiveness is so divine.'

He pushed her statement from his mind. He'd not forgiven them. He might have done the same thing in their place. He understood. He understood revenge, too. It was best not to see it coming. He'd exact one slow squeeze at a time.

Perhaps he'd courted it. But that didn't mean he had qualms about revenge.

'They could have killed you. You would have frozen if you'd stayed out the night without your coat and boots,' she said.

The laugh was on them if they'd stolen that coat and that pair of boots. The coat had fattened a moth or two and he'd kept it to wear to his father's. He wasn't sure if it was to fit in with his father's wishes for austerity, or to jest at it. The clothes weren't good enough to wear anywhere but to the country.

He reached up, touching his skin. Puffed. Not where it should be. A nose like he'd seen once at Gentleman Jackson's boxing salon. His skin felt foreign—like touching another person. A bristly person. He had short whiskers. He always shaved. He could not risk scratching a woman's face.

'Mirr...?' He held a hand in front of his face and then with the other hand made movements shaving.

'You'll have to be careful.'

She took a looking glass from the wall and brought it to him. He jumped, startled, staring into the glass, feeling he dreamt. A monster stared back at him.

'Holy...' *Damn.* He looked more like something found in a butcher's shop. Something discarded from a butcher's shop. One side wasn't so bad and that made his face worse. He had an almost normal half of his face and then he looked like an ogre who'd stuffed himself on overripe damson pastries and the colour had leaked through to the skin.

She bustled away, preparing water.

He put the mirror down, shut his eyes and lowered his head just a bit.

'You've actually looked worse every day since I found you.' She spoke from across the room. 'The bruising has darkened. You look like plum pudding on one side and an apricot tart on the other. We can't leave you outside,' she said. 'My cat Ray Anna might think we'd tossed out a treat.'

Fox imagined how pleased Mr Peabody would feel when he saw the injuries.

But he'd have to wait. He was not going to be seen by anyone who knew him until his face looked better. It could not look worse.

He took the mirror and held it to his gaze again. Surely he could not be that mangled.

The gut kick of seeing his face caused a recoil that shot pain throughout him. They should have killed him. It would have been kinder.

He held the mirror, feeling like he'd been encased in an extra layer of skin that didn't want to move and didn't belong to him and was nothing but pain. One eye even had the white stained in blood.

He stared, anger tensing his hand.

He lifted a finger and jabbed it in the direction of his face. He stared at her. He didn't ask. He told. *Look at this.*

'You'll look so much better after you've shaved.' Her voice wavered, but the words still sung out from her.

Better? He stared at her, challenging.

'You have a good head of hair,' she said. 'Perhaps you could just grow it longer.'

He stared at her. He'd have to cover his whole damn face.

'A person's face isn't everything,' she said.

It was his. And his smile. *Oh, Foxworthy, you*

have a beautiful smile. He'd heard that a thousand or so times. A*nd those blue eyes...*

'You could...' Her voice fell away and the mirror moved closer to her body. 'A beard? Close-cropped beards can be quite...'

He stared at her. Waiting. *Close-cropped beards could be?*

'Quite...nice.'

It hurt. It hurt a lot, but he forced a short burst of air from his nostrils.

'Apostles had beards.'

He jerked his two hands to rest together over his heart. Pat. Pause. Pause. Pat.

'Vicars aren't supposed to be sarcastic.'

Well, he wasn't a vicar. He held up one finger, pointing heavenwards, and then ever so gently shook his head. He was not now nor would he ever be a vicar. He had to make her understand.

'Oh...' She rushed to his side and took the hand he'd pointed heavenwards, holding it in both hers.

'I've seen this before. You cannot. You cannot lose faith over this.' Eyes pleaded. Her fingers soothed, running over his knuckles.

He wasn't willing to pull from her touch. This woman, who wanted him to grow his hair over his face, was doing the best she could. She had a heart and some misguided goodness. Using his left hand, he pointed upwards. Then, with four fingers, he lightly tapped his chest and made a shaking-away movement.

'No. You mustn't feel that way.'

He tapped his chest again. Oh, well. He'd tell her the truth. '...ad.'

Her eyes puzzled over his word and she shook her head. He'd tried to tell her he was bad, although he was very good at it. He had a certain skill there, he had to admit. He tried again without moving his jaw. 'Not good.'

He motioned the movement of writing. Wanting the paper. He'd tell her now.

She clasped those rough fingers over his hand, stilling him. 'None of us are good enough. And you mustn't think your actions caused you to be punished. These men were the ones who are not good. You will forgive them in time.'

After revenge. He could forgive them after that. Forgiveness was so much easier when your enemies were dead. And he knew damn well his actions had caused this.

That was part of the game. Dancing along the edge of the precipice. Seeing how close he could get without tumbling over and losing his smile. Well, he'd lost his smile and dangled too far, but that didn't mean he couldn't play another game.

The game. The game he'd tired of, truth be known, and decided to visit his father. In part, he supposed, to pretend otherwise and needle his father a bit.

She expected *him* to be an example. Perhaps she should reconsider that.

He moved his hand from hers and made a jabbing motion towards his face.

'It is what is inside the man that counts and you should know that better than anyone.'

Well, he was under the dunghill on that one. Unless you counted gambling and his manhood still having a nice morning stretch.

'…'ish… I could…'ill…' He would kill whoever did this and he doubted he'd even be noticed for it. One look at his face and if they'd known him before they'd overlook a small thing like murder.

'It takes time to recover.'

He grunted.

He knew. He knew the truth very well. Without his face and his ready smile to charm people, he was nothing but the heir.

She released his hand, taking her warmth with her. She moved to the table and brought him the pen, paper and placed the ink on the table at his side. Then she dipped the pen for him.

He clasped the paper and looked into her eyes. Waiting. Gentle.

One sentence and his father's servants would whisk him away.

When his father returned, Fox would hear nothing but how his evil ways had led to his downfall. Every time he saw his father, this tale would be resurrected and pointed to and every bump on Fox's face would be examined by the earl as he spoke. Anger flared in his thoughts. He'd never visit his father again. Ever. The ridicule.

A bit of ink dripped on the page.

'Do you need help?' she asked, leaning so that a wisp of her hair tickled his cheek. The lilacs engulfed him.

All thoughts of revenge slid into the back of his mind.

She clasped the paper, holding it steady and unsteadying the rest of him.

Thank y... he wrote. The ink ended. He handed her the pen, hands touching. She dipped it in the ink again and leaned over him again, their shoulders together. He finished the word. *I suppose*...he wrote, inhaling, taking his time. She dipped the pen and returned to his side... *revenge is wrong.*

He didn't add, *but necessary.*

She smiled and it touched her eyes and even her feet as she took the pen and paper and put it on the table.

Looking into her eyes was much better than looking in any mirror. And if she was happiest seeing him as a vicar, then he would stay a vicar for the time being.

At the first hint of his father returning, he'd make his way to the estate, get Rusty back and return to London. She'd never know who he was.

Only a few moments later, Rebecca's father walked in the door. She quickly stepped back from Fox and put her hands behind her back.

He saw the glance her father gave them and the widened eyes, followed by a smile.

'You missed a good service today. One of my best.' He spoke to Rebecca as he set the boots in his hand on the floor and then he put his scarf and coat on a peg. 'It was on pride and boastfulness.'

'Father,' she admonished, then turned to Foxworthy. 'That's his favourite jest.'

'I told everyone that our guest is still recovering.' He picked up the boots. 'And I may have mentioned my plans to let a younger man take my place.'

Fox shook his head. 'No…vicar.'

'Very kind of you, Son.' His smile had a sadness at his eyes. 'But you'll do a fine job and it's time everyone knows that I'm going to step down. A high calling indeed.'

'…'ox…orthee.' He touched his chest.

'You're worthy, son. Or the earl wouldn't have chosen you.'

The vicar held the boots nearer Fox. They were of good quality and scuffed. Fox wondered where they came from, a little warning fluttering inside his head. He'd never realised such a thing existed inside him and he considered carefully, and decided not to ask what he didn't want to know.

Fox looked at the covers over his bare feet.

He tried not to think of it. Poor villagers did not just outgrow boots in that size.

'Now, Rebecca,' the vicar said. 'What delicious meal are you going to cook for us?'

Rebecca moved to go about her chores.

Then the vicar started talking about Rebecca's mother and how saintly she was and how blessed they were to have a daughter like Rebecca. He complimented Rebecca with every other word.

Fox settled in to the covers. He wondered if Rebecca knew that her father had exchanged his prayer book for a matchmaker's tally sheet.

The man erred on a grand scale, as all fathers seemed to do where their child was concerned. Faithfulness was only for vicars and simpletons. And perhaps for a man so scarred only a wife would touch him without pity.

Chapter Six

Her father, the not-so-subtle matchmaker, left after they'd eaten, hoping to get more men involved in the search for the criminals who had attacked a vicar.

A waste of time, Fox thought, unless they searched for men in London who had a jealous streak.

Fox stuffed the pillow tighter at his head and watched Rebecca.

Her bottom bustled nicely as she worked. It worked better than any laudanum to relieve his pain. His eyes drooped, watching each nuance. Each twist. Each whisper of movement.

He'd been wrong to think her drab. The sun sparkling in the window when she walked by the glass showed him otherwise.

In fact, the sun taunted him by showing him what he could not have. He looked at the ceiling again, trying to recall something in his past he'd wanted—something he'd wanted but not been able to have. Nothing came to mind except Mrs Lake. And he'd worked hard to get her from his mind—filling his world with all the beauty he could surround himself with. He'd determined never to let anyone else that deep into his thoughts again.

He'd even been able to talk Gillray into drawing a caricature. Gillray had created a picture of Fox surrounded by a bevy of ladies of all shapes and ages.

That had been before he'd turned twenty. It had been published. He'd been certain the former Mrs Lake would have seen it.

The bereaved Mrs Lake had been beyond beautiful, and twice his age at thirty-two when she'd dropped her fan onto his boot.

Seeing her tearful eyes as she had told of her loss had torn at his heart, but when she'd clutched at him for support—he'd been too green to understand that she had him by the pizzle. Unfortunately, his heart had been attached to it at that moment.

Within days he'd told her he loved her; she'd told him she would wait until he became old enough to wed.

Then the Duke of Marchwell's wife had died and Mrs Lake had told Foxworthy he was just infatuated with her. That he would forget her and that she was much too old for him.

It had been quite immature of him to propose to the elderly Countess Bolton the day after Mrs Lake had announced her betrothal to the seventy-year-old duke, but even Earl Bolton had caught the humour in that proposal and thumped Foxworthy on the back and congratulated him at realising what a gem the countess was.

He doubted Mrs Lake had enjoyed the print as much as he had. The caricaturists in London had become quite fond of Foxworthy over the years.

Now was when he needed Gillray's pen. Fox would like a sketch of Rebecca. One of her bustling about, hovering over the little needs of the village like a mother hen guarding the chicks.

Now the little mother hen faced him, and he waited for the sound of her voice.

'You've met the earl as he's chosen you for his vicar.'

He nodded, more with his eyes than his head.

'He's such a good-hearted man. Kind. Caring. We're all so lucky to have him.'

No need to let her know her hero wasn't perfect. His father *was* a kind man.

A boring but kind man. The most boring man on the face of the earth. Sanctimonious, too. Proud in his austere life. As if he thought the things he could turn his back on made him stronger. When his daughter had died, he'd even turned his back on the whole of London.

He'd not taken well to a son who didn't turn his back.

Rebecca's voice interrupted his thoughts. 'Oh, dear,' she said. 'You've a spot of blood on your nightshirt.'

'How can you stand to look at this?' He forced out the words, this time willing to ignore the pain.

Now she huffed out a breath. 'I've never seen you any other way. That's just how you look to me. And it's the inner person…' She paused. 'Yes. It is.'

He shut his eyes. At least his eyelids didn't hurt. And his inner person chuckled, stoked the irritation with a pitchfork and gave a spit shine to its horns.

'And all things happen for a reason. Perhaps this is meant to give you time to spend in contemplation. And compassion for others in similar circumstances. We can never have too much compassion. Think of what is important in life.'

At that point, Fox's inner person stuck out its tongue and made a fluttering noise. His outer person was older, however. 'Ale.' He held out his hand.

She stepped forward and softly slapped his fingers. 'That's not what is important.'

He pushed and threw one leg from the bed, and remembered he was in one of those night-dresses. He'd never worn such a garment in front of any woman. Ever. His inner person might have lacked modesty, but it did have some pride.

He reached up, flapping the neck of the night-shirt. 'Cose…'

He looked around the room, searching for his trousers.

'They're put away.'

As soon as he moved his arm to fling back the covers, her eyes squeezed shut and her mouth went so tight her lips almost disappeared. A hand went over her face and she whirled around, her back to him.

He jarred his face and the pain nearly knocked him back to the bed, but he shoved himself for-ward. 'Cose…'

'You don't know where they are.'

He grunted, three little grunts.

He swung his legs around. His head took a moment to catch up, so he sat while his view straightened again.

He could focus on the back of her head. Her elbows still stuck from the sides. They moved a bit. She reached for the basket. 'I'm going outside and I'm going to pray until Father returns. I need to gather some apples for tarts.'

'Uh-un.' He spoke softly. He was certain he could find them on his own. 'Cose…'

'Your clothes are in Father's room,' she said. 'On a peg. I washed them for you.'

'…'ank…'oo.'

And then she swirled out the door, scenting the air with lilacs.

He watched her leave. Miss Prim and Proper who believed the inside of a person mattered. Only when it had enough ale to sleep like a babe.

Holding the iron bed frame, he put his weight on his legs and stood. His head swam, but then strength returned to his legs. His feet burned in spots, like small, fierce coals jabbed at his soles. But the tingles felt good and strength shot into him.

He strode to the inner door. Inside the other room, his eyes stopped on the shirt hanging over the peg. Two garments on one peg. Under the shirt, his trousers. He shut his eyes, relieved.

He stripped the frippery of a nightshirt from his shoulders, taking deep breaths and moving slowly while he finessed it around his jaw. The pain angered him. He tossed the shirt to the floor.

He dressed, finishing by leaning against the wall, using his strength to control the pain.

Putting on the clothing wasn't too difficult, but the cravat was the loosest one he'd ever tied and his jaw ached afresh.

He might not be dressed well enough for callers, but he definitely preferred the apparel over the nightshirt. It lay under his feet. He scooped it up with one hand, crushed the cloth within his grasp and tossed it on the bed. No valet would be along behind him. The mistress of this house was also the housekeeper, cook and scullery maid.

The mirror on the wall had a crack running the length of it, but the nails at the edge held it together.

It beckoned him. The scarred mirror.

He walked to it. Even the eyes that stared back at him didn't seem his own. He had all the organs necessary to make a man. At least the appearance of a man.

These people thought him a vicar. A man with a caring heart. A person who fit in his father's world. The exact opposite of who he was.

Well, he could play that game. It was perhaps the only one he hadn't tried. They wanted him to be a vicar. Until the man his father chose arrived, then Fox would be the vicar. A pretence to see how it would be to live as a man who saw someone behind the soulless orbs.

If he wasn't going to be able to smile his

way into people's good graces, then perhaps he could… No, he couldn't. He could never go back among the people who knew him and be anything but Foxworthy.

Now he touched the swollen cheek, his skin feeling leathery. The left side of his jaw looked the most swollen and the thin cut line along it showed the remnants of the club's mark.

He moved his head to one side, and then the other, still not believing the image followed his movements.

He put his hand over the glass, feeling the coldness where the eyes stared back at him. He spread his palm, covering the image.

He could not smash every mirror in the world. He could not hide away for ever. But he could not let anyone see him. Some of the swelling would have to recede. The colour would have to return to a semblance of human skin.

Someone would answer for this.

He returned to the main room of the house. His conscience was not sitting in her sewing chair.

Chapter Seven

Rebecca walked into the house and instantly her eyes moved to the empty bed. She stilled, except her heart doubled in speed. She wanted to call out his name, but realised she didn't know it. 'Vicar,' she whispered.

He dipped his head to walk under the door frame from the bedroom. An unshaven man, dishevelled, except for his hair. In bed, he'd taken up the size of the mattress. In the doorway, he completely filled her eyes.

She didn't speak and she took a tiny step back.

'Th…ank you for washin…' he said. 'Shirt… 'aistcoat…'

She rushed to the table, putting her basket down, not looking his way, watching the apples.

She took one from the top and put it on the table. She reached for a knife to peel the apples.

'The boots.' She indicated the footwear her father had brought back.

He looked at them and nodded, but he didn't get them.

The man moved to the chair and sat at her table as if it was his own. All the men of the village did the same occasionally. Even the earl had once or twice. But the vicar sat with his bare feet apart, his mangled head high and his eyes staring straight ahead. And he sat on the wrong side.

She pressed her lips together hard, then she spoke softly. 'You're in my father's chair.'

His brows raised and he slowly turned his head to look at her. She couldn't read his thoughts.

Then he stood and moved to the other chair and sat.

She moved to the stove, but then he turned the chair slightly so she was in his direct line of vision and it was much more straightforward than before. The trousers and shirt seemed to make him into a real person, not an invalid. And not the same.

In the bed, he'd not taken up so much room, but in the chair at the table, she couldn't move without being closer to him.

Then she laughed at herself. She was being

foolish. She'd just not seen a man so undressed before. Not even her father. He was always very particular about how he looked because at any moment a parishioner might appear and need counsel.

She took in a deep breath. 'You look half—'

He waited.

She couldn't say naked, wild, or any of the first words that hit her mind. '—dressed. But more like a gentleman.'

He pointed two jabs to his face.

'You don't look that bad.'

He pointed to the sky, jabbing upwards, and then to his ear.

She let out a deep breath, looked down and spoke softly. 'You do look rather bad.'

He agreed with a rumble from his throat.

She would do her duty. She would be a good wife if they married. She would learn to love his misshapen face. If she could love a hissy, splotchy orange cat with a missing ear then she could love this man. It would be nice to care for someone in such a way. Marriage softened the harshness in life. She would no longer be a woman and he would no longer be a man. They would be one, together.

Although it would take some time. She could tell that by looking at him.

And he was a bit too concerned about his appearance, but she could help him get over his vanity, although at this point, he might need a smattering of it.

He did have elegant lashes. She could compliment him on his lashes. His hair. She wasn't certain of his teeth because he couldn't seem to open his mouth. But there would be a lot of things she could remind him of so that he would not feel so…lopsided. She tilted her head. Yes, he was just lopsided and in different hues than anyone else she'd ever seen. He did not quite look as good as Mr Tilton did when he was dead, but Mr Tilton had only been kicked in the face by a horse.

He caught her looking at him with her head tilted. He crossed his arms. One could believe in beasts when he looked at her like that.

Stopping a moment, she reminded herself that all creatures were beautiful. And he was handsome in his own way. He did have a nice colour of hair.

He leaned across, and took her knife from her hand, and he worked at peeling the apple skin into one thin and perfect ribbon. He looked her way briefly and continued, his concentration on his task.

With his thoughts on his task, he didn't intimidate her at all and with his head down, he could be endearing enough, this man with bare toes.

He finished the peeling, then deftly sliced the apple in half, cored it and made another slice. He held it out to her. She took it, their fingers brushing, and ate it. Then he cut the smallest sliver, put it in his mouth, shut his eyes, chewed carefully, and she could see him tasting, swallowing. He opened his eyes, cut another piece for her and held it high, to her lips.

She took a bite and shut her eyes.

His hand stilled, fingers straightened and rested on her cheek by the crease of her lips.

She opened her eyes, and whispered, 'What is your given name?'

His eyes tightened. 'Dam…' His hand jerked away from her face.

'Did you just say Adam?' she asked.

Then shook his head. 'Dam…nation.'

'The oath?'

He nodded with a flick of his brows.

'What are you…angry with yourself for…?' Her cheeks reddened.

He took one hand, putting it under her chin, and lifting so that her eyes aligned with his vision.

He shook his head. With his free hand, he reached to cup her face, but he stilled just before touching.

Neither moved.

* * *

He took a step back, letting his hand slide from her. This would not end well. Not for her at any rate.

He wanted to kiss her, but he could not. He could not let his face against hers. No woman should be touched by such ugliness. He reached out and rested his fingertips against her cheeks. Then he traced her perfect nose. Even her jaw-line was perfect.

He'd thought nothing fascinating about her face, but now he looked closer. In her plainness, she had a simple beauty. The wisps of hair framing her face enhanced the softness of her skin. Such a contrast to the rough hands—the work she did made the woman more delicate.

He grasped her shoulders and her eyes opened. She'd taken pity on a beaten man and helped her neighbours with whatever they needed. He could see purity. An unaware angel.

He must kiss her. He must.

But he brushed his hands along the sides of her neck and downwards, tracing the shoulder, brushing her dress aside to the limits of its closures, ignoring the texture of fabric while his mind told him what lay underneath.

Her lips parted.

'Kissed?' he asked.

She shook her head.

'Never?'

Her head wobbled a 'no'. Eyes begged him.

'Later.'

His right hand rested against her throat. Her pulse hammered. She swallowed.

'Promise?' she asked.

He traced the fullness of her lips and without words made a promise to both of them.

Chapter Eight

'Bran…ee…' he mumbled, turning away. Brandy. He needed the brandy he'd sent to his father's estate.

He should put some space between Rebecca and himself. A road. A town, even.

'Ale.' He changed his request. Anything to create movement—distance between them.

She whirled around, poured a swallow of ale and diluted it with enough water to make it tasteless. She handed it to him, moving so fast their fingers couldn't touch.

Then she dashed away to pick up her stitching.

He looked at the glass. He wanted to down it, but he couldn't. He drank, ignoring the pain. Finally, he thumped the empty glass on to the table, much like he did during the contest with Lady Havisham.

Then, he moved the chair beside Rebecca and sat.

After she did three more stitches, he leaned forward, tugging on the little dress.

Her eyes moved to his face.

'*Do* you need something?'

He gave a bump of his shoulders.

She started stitching again. Her words jumped one after the other. 'I do need to get this finished. The babe could arrive any day, or I could be called to care for the other children. And once she needs me I'll be busy for a time.'

He tugged at the little skirt, but she didn't stop stitching as she pulled it away. Surely she understood he could not kiss her.

'...and all the little boys she has are just like you. Except they are children and they have an excuse.'

He grasped the dress, held firm and pulled it slowly away from her. She had no choice but to tumble towards him or stop stitching.

She picked up her scissors and rapped his hand. Instantly, he released the fabric and touched the tapped spot. He glared at her. He felt worse about not being able to kiss her than she did. And he was certain that scissor tap was punishment. Punishment he didn't deserve. He deserved a sword-tap on each shoulder, not a clunk from a pair of dull scissors.

'Oh, my pardon,' she said, smug. 'Perhaps I did that harder than I meant. Forgive me.'

Then she looked at him, eyes wide. 'Oh, you must forgive me, mustn't you? You have no choice.' She chuckled softly and began sewing, pulling the last of the thread through the garment. 'I know how that feels.'

He didn't. Forgiveness was only for people unable to plot a good revenge.

He pushed himself up, leaned over and touched just where her sleeve ended on her arm. Making little swirls, he lightly ran his fingertip down to her right hand. She stilled. He kept his eye on the needle. When he reached the fabric, the whole garment and the threaded needle slipped from her hand. He moved it to the side. She kept her eyes on the cloth.

'Give that back,' she whispered.

He didn't answer. Instead, he straightened each of her fingers, one at a time, running his thumb down their length, pressing as if pushing out any aches or soreness. With his fingers on the back of her hand and his thumb inside the palm, he moved from the inside to the outside, creating a friction that eased away soreness and, on this occasion, reddened a woman's cheeks.

Her hands. They needed the calluses soothed away.

She jumped up, scraping the chair legs against the floor and staring. 'It's not good for a man to touch a woman.'

He made a scornful sound. That was what he thought of that.

'You had best—' She marched away, went to the tiny desk and picked up the pen and paper. 'You had best beg my pardon.' She held it out to him. He crossed his arms and made another noise in his throat.

Her jaw dropped. She clasped the pen tightly, closed her mouth, took a step sideways and slapped the paper against his arm.

She gasped and held the paper against her chest. 'Look what you made me do.' She stood over him, eyes narrowed. 'I have never, ever done anything like that before.'

And from the look on her face, he wasn't sure she wasn't about to do it again. Oh, well, it would probably hurt her conscience more than it would ever hurt him.

'…'ungry,' he said. He meant it in more ways than one. His eyes travelled over her dress. Perfect handfuls. Everywhere.

'You're always wanting something.' She clenched her hand.

He nodded. No argument there.

'It's as if you've been waited on hand and foot your whole life,' she said.

He nodded. Nothing wrong with that. '…'ungry.'

'You ate not long ago.'

'…eatin' is a…a 'abit I formed long ti… ago.'

'You eat like a horse.'

He held up two fingers.

'You will need more discipline than you have to be a good vicar,' she said.

He exercised the discipline of a saint at that very moment—as far as he was concerned that was much better than any vicar.

He looked at her and raised his brows just a bit. With his mottled face, the effect startled her into action.

She bustled to the shelf and his eyes feasted. The dress was full in the back, but even though she was every bit as tall as her father, Rebecca had a round derrière and round bosom. She was round and angular in height, but the roundness far overshadowed the rest for keeping his attention. She was the perfect shape.

She cut off a sliver of bread.

That would not feed a sparrow, but he didn't care.

She put the bread on top of the stove to warm

it and reached for the crock of butter. He stood, walking to her, but before he could get close, she stepped towards him and handed him the crock. He stared at it.

'Put it on the stove.'

He stared at her.

'Put it on the stove,' she repeated. 'Warm it a little. It'll spread easier.'

His thoughts had a mind of their own, but he wasn't complaining. He took in a breath.

She turned back to the bread loaf. 'You've made me hungry.' She cut herself an even tinier slice and put it on the stove, touching his.

Then she handed him the knife. Their fingers brushed when he took it. She paused.

He turned, putting the knife in the butter.

He put a hearty dollop onto the bread, spread it, then held it to her mouth. Her eyes widened. He kept the bread close to her lips.

'But you're the one who is hungry.' Her eyes watched his.

He didn't move. She reached both hands to take it from him, but he didn't release it and helped her guide it to her mouth before letting his hand drop.

She had the tiniest bit of butter on her lips and when her fingertip brushed it away, he watched.

* * *

Rebecca pressed down the sides of her skirt and then crossed her arms again. Her body felt as if it belonged to someone else. All jittery, and the parts of her that he'd touched tingled and burned. Her skin remembered every bit of that moment. And then he'd stopped.

The abominable man. He'd made her like his touch and feel good and want to be kissed and then he'd stopped. She wanted to slap him, but her hand would not dare hurt his already ravaged face.

'A person's honour is all that they are.' At that second, she felt dishonoured. How dare he begin and then just end it, leaving her frazzled on the inside and bumbling about and feeling like a hideous spinster that even a man with only a good head of hair to recommend him would turn his back on.

'You.' She slapped out the word. 'A man devoted to goodness must know how important it is to be honourable.'

'Re...ecca. 'ardon. Didn'...'ean to offend.'

She looked to the side. 'I'm not offended.' She raised her chin. 'But you must give me your word that you'll behave properly.' And he'd best not touch her again. It felt too good.

He pulled off a piece of the smallest bread

and slid it into his mouth and swallowed. His eyes tightened every time he swallowed. She knew it hurt.

He didn't look her way. 'I can't say I… I won't touch you. Only that I…I won't offend.' He tore another piece of the bread.

Her anger wafted away like the little dandelion seeds that disappeared in a puff. She calmed her voice. 'You must mind your manners… And what is your name?'

He shook his head.

'You aren't going to tell me?'

'No.'

'That's not very honourable.'

'No.'

'You have a lot to learn about being a vicar. A vicar has to be agreeable. Good. Responsible. He has to be an example of how people should act at all times.' She put a hand on her hip.

He brushed her words away with an upwards flick of his eyes.

'That will be unacceptable behaviour. You disgraceful man. You are not worthy to be a vicar.'

She whirled around. 'I said that without thinking.' She reached for a towel and rubbed the cloth over her hands. He wondered she wasn't taking off skin. 'Please forgive me.'

'…ease…'orgive…'ee. 'ease…'orgive…'ee…'

he mocked, waggling his head. If he'd heard that once he'd heard it a thousand times. If she jostled him... *Please forgive me.* If she shut a door just loud enough to hear... *Please forgive me. I didn't mean to wake you.* Her habit to be good. Ingrained since birth.

'I do not think you mean that,' she snapped.

'I don't.' He shot the words back, his chin jutting and sending pain all the way to his toes.

'Well. I did.'

'No. You say it without thinking.' He bit out the words, letting the pain stab through his temples.

'I do not.' Her chin rose. Her eyes pierced. 'I mean it.'

'It frees your conscience.' He noted how plain the sentence left his lips. That pleased him. 'It is a …abit. You say it too easy.'

The woman marched well. 'I do not know how you ever became a vicar.'

He didn't speak.

'You are not worthy to be one.'

'I…agree.'

'And you don't even care. The worthiest calling on earth and you are not giving it the due respect.'

'No.'

'For shame. I will ask my father to speak with you about this. Maybe he can shake out that rubbish clogging your mind. Perhaps when those men hit you they jarred your brain as well as your face. If anyone can straighten your thoughts, Father can. He can be quite stirring.'

He put one hand over his ear, telling her what he thought of that little speech.

'You are just hurt and not feeling well.'

'Just…honest.'

'You…heathen.' Her chin went higher and her eyes sparked and she gripped the towel with the force of a man testing a knot in a hangman's noose.

He touched his chest. 'Heathen.' He pointed to her. 'Saint.' Then he waggled his shoulders. 'Easy. No te…temptation.'

'Oh. Oh. Oh. There is plenty of temptation in this village. If you only knew.' And most of it in his fingertips. She thrust those thoughts aside. 'You will find that out later when you get to know the people.'

'Not for you. Te…temptation for them. Not you.'

A lot he knew.

'Na… when you last te…tempted to do anything…bad?' he asked. She could see the sincerity in his eyes. Well, the women of the village always had plenty to say about their husbands' inability to reason.

'This second.' She raised the cloth. 'I would like to throw this towel at you.'

'Ooh… Big…and evil.' He shrugged. 'Throw. I don't care. It's not even wrong.'

She hurled it. He caught the flung towel in one hand. 'B…best you can do for evil? I did more by…by time I was three.'

'That is not something to be proud of.'

'I'm not. Just fact.'

'Oh.' Her shoulders dropped. The tension in her face smoothed away. Her chest moved as she breathed. 'I see what you are doing. I see it now.' Her lips pushed up into a thin smile. 'You're right. We are all not worthy. And I have fallen into the routine of doing my good works without really thinking of it. It is merely a path I am on. Not considering my words and how I might improve them, and how asking for forgiveness comes so easily to me that perhaps it means nothing.'

He shook his head, stirring more pain, which irritated him even more. With his teeth still clamped, he said, 'I do not care if you are… 'erfect.'

'I cannot be perfect. No one can. But if we were, you wouldn't have had the injury.'

She stalked to the broom, grabbed it in both hands and walked to him.

He braced himself for a thwack, but instead she swept the floor, avoiding the area he stood. When she finished, she leaned down to a little piece of pasteboard by the door and brushed the dust into it and walked to the door, took a few steps out and hurled the dirt into the air.

Then she returned and put the stiffened paper back in its place.

She stood with her head down and her fingers clasped around the handle, using it for support. 'I do beg your pardon for being so hateful. Please forgive me.' She looked at him, brown eyes sad. 'I said it again. I didn't mean to. I don't mean to be so hateful today.'

He walked to her, put a finger along her chin and raised it higher.

'Not you. 'ee. I'm bad. You're good.'

She looked at him and didn't flinch. Something he wasn't sure he could have done.

He slipped the broom from her fingers, then put it by the pasteboard, before walking back to stop beside her.

Keeping his head pulled back and his jaw as far from her as he could, he reached out, grasped her, twisted her around and sat, pulling her onto on his lap.

'Vicar,' she gasped. 'This is not—'

He rested his forehead at the top clasp on the back of her dress and then pulled her back enough so his head went higher and the softness of her skin melted against his. The fragrance of her soap touched him. He loosened his grasp, aware of the corset just under her clothes and the woman under that.

Her hands locked on his where they rested at her stomach and she could have pulled away if she wished. Instead, she turned sideways, sitting half on his lap, and perched to leave. 'Your hair tickles.'

He pulled back and wobbled his head, letting his hair flutter against her skin.

'This is not acceptable,' she said, 'unless we are courting.'

Courting? How like a woman to think of that. Then he realised. *How unlike the women he knew to think of that.*

She whispered, '*Are* we courting?'

He raised his head forward, and then down, letting the tendrils of his hair trail over the skin at her neck. Saying no would hurt her. The little wobble in her voice told him that. He would let her be the one to reject him because when she found out who he truly was, she would want to throw the broom, the pasteboard and all the crumbles of dirt into his face.

'I've never courted before,' she said.

He shut his eyes and took in a breath. Neither had he.

She looked over her shoulder, but her eyes didn't meet his face. 'If it is acceptable to you…' She paused and the pressure on his hands tightened. 'If it is acceptable to you, I will tell Father we are courting.' The last words came out in a rush.

She took in a breath. 'Although, perhaps I should wait a while. I would not want him to think there are any improprieties.'

Her voice sounded wistful and, even though his mouth didn't move, he smiled inside himself. He would be more than happy to provide her with plenty of improprieties. But it would be wrong. For the first time since Mrs Lake, he would treat her carefully.

'I've thought…' She took in a breath. 'I've thought it must be nice to be courted.'

She studied his face. 'I don't think the earl will be bothered at all with us courting,' she said. 'He is kind and has told my father I would make someone a fine wife some day. But if you wish us to keep it secret while everyone gets to know you, I completely understand.'

Once the new vicar arrived, full of his own good works, Rebecca would happily move on. All she would have to do was discover who Foxworthy was and she would be attacking his face with the broom.

She'd discover an understanding of why the

people around her did the foolish things they did and have a better understanding of desire, loss and the foibles of humans who did not sit on perches above the rest. Only three people he knew managed to sit above the odour of imperfection.

His father. Her father and her.

Then he caught a glance of her profile. The profile framed by wisps of hair that had escaped and skin so delicate it should always be protected. He touched her hand. He could not be the one to cause her to doubt herself.

He glanced at the paper. The pen. The ink. But she was closer.

It felt so good just to hold her hand. He would not destroy her innocence. When she discovered who he was, he would spin one of the tales that came so easily to his lips and soothed all the feminine feathers. He would be mournful and sad and help her see she was not deserving of someone so reprobate as he. Her good works would override her momentary lapse. The man his father returned with would be standing at the side, ready to sweep her into that fairy tale of matrimony which only worked for people who had no other resources.

'I do think the earl will be happy with us courting,' she said. 'Once he said something about my making a fine wife for someone and he wished his son would find someone with my values.'

Fox could have choked on his own tongue. *No.*

'Except he said his son was not likely to value me. The earl's son is a bit of a rogue, according to the newspaper. And his father says he is beyond redemption.'

Fox gave a slight nod. Rogue? He had invented the best ways to be a rogue. The ways which brought humour, except sometimes if a jest was pointed, it took the prick of truth and jabbed into someone. He could not condemn himself for that. Sometimes vicars did the same with truth.

'I'm pleased I've never met him. Trudy, the barmaid, has.'

Fox tried to think back to a Trudy. Or a barmaid. He could only remember the woman whose hair hung at the sides of her face almost like puppy ears and who had sort of a panting way of speaking that did remind him of a friendly hound. Her head wagged, too.

'Trudy said he is the worst of sorts. He pinched her bottom and told a very bad story Trudy would not even repeat.'

He had perhaps told a story or a hundred that shouldn't be repeated, but he'd never pinched anyone's bottom. Ever. He shook his head and grunted dissent.

'I know,' she whispered. 'I shouldn't say such things. But that is why his father is so disappointed in him and I can certainly understand that. His father said he is thankful that I do not have to associate with men like his son. But he assures me that I wouldn't even like him.'

Instinctively, Fox pushed a snort of air from his lungs.

She stilled. 'I'm not passing judgement. Or at least, I don't mean to be.'

''ou…'ould…like…'im.'

She shook her head, then put her fingers on his shoulder and snuggled into him, her head resting near her hand. 'I'm sure I would like him in the same way I like all God's creatures, but I doubt I could like him very much. His father says he is so immoral.'

'Not…'erfec'…' Fox didn't move, savouring the caresses of her hand. The calluses proved the differences of their lives.

He would talk to his father and insist the earl see that a maid of all work could be hired for the vicarage. Rebecca's time could be freed to meet the village's needs. He realised the servant wouldn't work out the same for her as it would for the women of the *ton.* Rebecca would probably take her maid along on her treks and they'd both be scrubbing some widow's home.

He pulled her around and hated that she could see his face, but he wanted to watch her.

Her eyes widened and he waited, watching the awareness, and her knowledge of him flourished in her eyes when he touched her face.

Smooth. He'd never appreciated just being able to run a hand over healthy skin before. Untarnished. Just a face. A quite well-made one. He had his share of easy compliments to give, but he didn't speak. He could just think about her skin.

It felt selfish really. Touching her without that wordiness.

His hand slid to her neck. Her smooth skin intrigued him in a way he'd never valued before. The skin beneath his touch caressed into him, filling some dark place in him with the feeling of innocence.

He looked at her eyes and felt he could see into her heart. Into the goodness that made her the person she was.

And he knew. With more strength than the sun used he knew. If he only did one good thing in his life, one good thing, and it would be the biggest good thing he ever did—he needed to leave now and go to his father's house.

He had the physical strength. He could walk out the door. He could.

Then she kissed his mottled, misshapen, unshaved cheek.

Damn her.

He shut his eyes, forcing the anger to stay inside his body. How dare she be so good? How dare she? Did she not know that hypocrites were the rule? Even in this little village he'd sat at the tavern table and heard the tales and the lies and knew that when opportunity arose, morals plummeted.

He stood, unsettled, putting her on her feet. Her eyes widened. He tapped a finger on her nose, quickly, moving away without meaning to insult.

He walked to the table where the pen and ink were. He would choose his words.

He pulled out the chair, the feet scraping against the floor, and reached for the pen.

She put a hand on his shoulder and the touch travelled through him, stopping only where his bare feet pressed against the wooden floor.

Then she ruffled his hair, and ran her hand back over it, smoothing it.

Even his blood seemed to stop moving until he turned, taking her hand. He pulled her into his arms, holding her against his body, breathing in the essence of her with more than his lungs. He took her in, the pleasant curves melding against him.

He pressed her against the length of him, keeping his face out of her view, and surrounding her with his touch. He held her derrière in one hand, pulling her close, weaving their bodies in a stationary dance.

He heard it before she did. The touch of a hand on the door.

He grasped her waist, but there was no time for her to move, and even if she could have, her face would have given her away the moment she realised someone was at the door. He held her.

The door opened and her father walked in.

Her face reacted with a kicked-in-the-stomach look and she tried to jump back. He held her steady and, as if he took a step in a waltz, he moved to open the space between them.

In that second, her face looked worse than his.

Her father's mouth was open and his eyes darkened. He took a breath and Fox could see the condemnation on his lips.

'I was a…asking… Re…ecca a question.' Fox's words hit the air with the authority he would have used to quell a fight between two men.

Her father paused.

Fox gazed at Rebecca. Soft eyes, soft mouth and gentle heart, and perhaps tears just at the inside corners of her eyes.

''arry…'ee?'

Something he'd said over and over before. Only before, he'd always been jesting with a married woman.

Her eyes tightened and her lips thinned.

She nodded. 'Of course.' Then her lips thinned even more.

He took a step back.

The married women always beamed. He'd expected a little more joy on her face, but then he did look like a monster.

He touched his cheek. 'I'll look…'etter.'

'You already do. And it *is* what is on the inside that counts.'

'Not good.'

'We all fall short.'

'So…some…'ore dan udders…'

'Well,' her father said at the door. 'I'll give you two a few moments to settle this.' The door closed. Her father was gone.

She clasped her hands in front of her. The air around them kept her voice barely above a whisper. 'I knew you would ask me to marry you when you asked about courting.'

He raised his brows.

'You are an unmarried vicar. A wife is what you need to manage the duties of the parish and who would be better than I am?' She shook her head. 'That is not boastful. It is just that I have spent my life preparing for this. I will be a good vicar's wife.'

'What a…about…not vicar?'

She glanced down, a smile at her lips. 'My mother trained me well. She told me many times that a wife was the most noble thing to be. That the good works of a wife reflect on her husband, but even more importantly, it is what we are put on this earth to do. To help others. And I know that I can help more people as a vicar's wife than as a spinster.'

She smiled. 'And I rather think you look nice in your own way. You've nice hair and shoulders. And a pleasant height.' She patted the juncture of his shoulder and arms. 'I've grown accustomed to your face so I don't see that as a problem. You're a bit selfish, though.' She nodded at him. 'When I gave the nicest biscuit to Father, I could tell you expected it.'

''iscuit…?' He didn't remember a biscuit.

'Yes. I fear you will have to hide that until you are able to overcome it. You must have the respect of others.'

'No.' He shook his head. He'd lived a fine life with no respect. In fact, he had a good many people who didn't respect him and some of them were great fun. He didn't respect them either.

He reached, snaking an arm around the tiny

waist, and pulled her against his side as easily as he could have pulled a doll.

She looked at him and her eyes sparkled.

He owed her. He did. She'd saved his life. And as his wife, she could do more of those meaningless little things she thought made the world better. Her one truly helpful thing, saving his life, would be rewarded.

Besides, he should marry. The clock was ticking away on that, so to speak. Unless he wanted to be like the man who married Mrs Lake and marry a woman half his age. The young women he'd been noticing at the soirées were younger every year and the debutantes were practically children to him.

Rebecca was older, good and unlikely to cause grief in a marriage. That might be something not easily found anywhere else.

He would make it a point to stay out of the papers in the future. He'd be discreet.

They'd mostly tired of writing about him in the papers anyway. His revenge would be the exception. She'd seen what they'd done to his face. She'd understand.

The door rattled this time and the vicar opened it, taking his time to sweep it wide, and was smiling when he walked in the door.

'We're planning to marry.' Rebecca's words rushed out.

'Well.' The vicar stopped moving and his eyes locked on the floor. 'I am not surprised. I didn't expect it to be this soon, but when a thing is right, you go forward.'

That evening, the vicar laughed at the slightest attempt at a jest, and Rebecca beamed.

Fox attended the conversation the same as he would have at the club. He added some bantering quips to keep Rebecca and her father talking.

Then, he stepped outside to shave in the better light because he could not bear the whiskers any longer. Rebecca brought the mirror, bouncing on her toes as she moved to stand in front of him. He took his time, ignoring the pain. Only once did he look closely at his eyes.

Nothing. Whatever he had been before his sister died was gone. In all ways.

Rebecca chattered about Mrs Berryfield. He nodded.

After they married, he would make certain she had a lady's maid who could listen to the tales of her good works. He would also convince her to let others do the actual labour, as her time could be better spent instructing others.

He wouldn't batter her gentle nature. She was innocent. A bit too naive. He would shelter her, provide for her and see that she was respected and could keep her naivety.

He would make it known that no one dare speak ill of the marriage and, after he'd found the men who'd beaten him and taken care of them, everyone would know that his words carried the weight of the peerage—the heir's advantage—and the ability to fashion revenge into its finest point.

Chapter Nine

The next morning, at the table, the vicar mentioned finding somewhere else to live after the marriage. Rebecca's eyes darted to Fox and he reassured the older man that he would always have a home with them.

The vicar's chest doubled in size. 'If you're in agreement,' he said, looking at both of them, 'I have thought it would be nice to tell the congregation of the betrothal at the end of Sunday Services, with you both present.'

Fox nodded. He would go along with that, but only after everyone knew who he was. 'I don't want…seen like…his.' He indicated his face. 'No…p…pity for Re…ecca.'

'No one will pity her, but I understand.' The

vicar stood and, beaming, left to go about his morning visits.

Inwardly, Fox laughed at his pride. He didn't want to be back in his own world yet. His face would still recover, somewhat, he knew. And he didn't want anyone seeing just how decidedly he'd been thumped.

Rebecca flew around the room, chattering, more of the vicarage nonsense about Mrs Addlepate's ingrown toenail or Mrs Stumblebum's digestion. He didn't really pay attention, finding it little different than the chatter of any other woman caught up in her own world. And Rebecca was caught up. A bee buzzing around, focusing on one bit of pollen to the next. She only paused once, her eyes crinkling in worry.

'What's wrong?' he asked, his curiosity genuine.

'My mother. I wish she'd lived to see my marriage.'

He didn't brush the words aside. He understood. He would have liked to have had his sister still in his life. She'd made games of everything, dragging him along behind her like a puppy she was particularly fond of.

'The dress.' She looked at Fox as if that explained everything and perhaps it did.

'New dress… London?'

'No.' Her eyes widened. She stepped towards

him. 'I have it. Already. It was one of the last things she did before she died. She made my dress. A new dress to be married in. Just in case.' She forced her words slowly, controlling emotion behind them. 'In case I needed it.'

He nodded.

Rebecca moved to work on the little garment she'd started, averting her face.

'Ring?' he asked. 'Family...heirloom?'

She didn't raise her eyes. 'Oh. No. My mother's band was buried with her. A simple one will be best for me. Like hers.'

Fox shook his head. In time, she'd discover the lure of jewels and adornments, but it wouldn't matter to him if she did or didn't.

She wasn't plain, as he'd first thought. He just hadn't been used to seeing a woman without a bauble or two and fripperies.

He had to force his face still when he thought of how surprised she'd be to discover how many good works she could do once she married and had funds at her disposal.

When her father returned, his smile was broad. He and Rebecca chattered over dinner, but Foxworthy discouraged their attempts to include him in the conversation. Speaking made his jaw ache. The pain had only recently subsided completely when he didn't move.

He wasn't ready to go to the estate, though. In fact, perhaps he would be best to miss seeing his father altogether. The banns could be read to give his face time to heal. A Special Licence might take some of the pride in the marriage from her father.

The evening wasn't the kind Fox preferred. The quiet clatter of dishes being put away made him think he was in the servants' quarters. Rebecca would learn soon enough how to let others do the routine chores for her, but the setting sun put a nice glow on the end of the day.

A rumbling sound caught Fox's ear. Carriage wheels. Only the earl would have a carriage. Well, he supposed his father was old enough to handle the news that his son had had a misadventure. Fox just hated the smugness he would see showing from his father's face.

'Ree…ecca.' He put a smile in his voice. He clasped her elbow and walked outside with her. The vicar followed along behind.

In the darkness, he could see the outline of her grasping at a strand of hair and poking it back into the twist of pins.

'We're about to be visited by your patron,' she said.

The carriage wheels rumbled closer.

She laughed, the richness of the sound fading away with the approaching wheels.

Fox felt a chuckle inside himself and he reached to her hair and brushed it up, pretending to help. He mumbled an assent.

His father would be pleased. The heir was marrying and, yes, she wasn't a lady of station, but the earl was odd in that regard. He'd written Fox enough letters telling him to keep out of the papers and marry a decent woman. Rebecca had the gentle, wifely demeanour his father would appreciate. She wasn't one of the fallen women his father had written stacks of letters warning his son against. Her purity would please the Earl of Boredom.

The carriage was rumbling closer at a too-fast speed, but slowed as it neared the house, the hooves stirring up a choking dust. Before anyone could speak, the carriage stopped and the bundle of a man surged out. The earl first. Another man behind. The earl looked straight to Rebecca's father. The grooms rushed down from their perch—one grabbing the lantern and another two bounding from the back. The driver had a fowling piece and two had cudgels.

Fox's pleasure exploded into tiny bits, flittering away like gunpowder after a shot. *Not again.*

'I heard you have a man living here claiming to be the new vicar I hired. Where is he?' the earl asked, peering into the darkness. 'Mr Gallant and I decided to travel together.'

'But he's here,' the vicar said, arm waving to indicate Fox. 'He arrived early.'

'It's me.' Fox stepped forward.

The earl shouted, pointing a long finger at Fox, 'Apprehend the imposter.'

The air burst with activity as the men surged forward. Rebecca stumbled back. Two men with clubs lunged for Fox. He moved forward, diving for the nearest weapon. He grabbed before the man could react, swinging him into the other one charging forward. They tumbled like balls rolling down a hill.

The one with the gun aimed.

'Father,' Fox exclaimed. 'Shooting…e will not get you an heir any faster.'

The earl stepped closer, peering into the darkness, his head cocked. 'Fenton?' He took one more step. 'Fenton?'

Fox clenched his teeth. 'D…don't call…'ee… Fen…on.' He would have preferred to have been named Penelope.

'It's a good name,' his father grumbled. 'Your grandfather was named Fenton. I'm named Fenton.'

Fox heard the quick intake of breath from Rebecca's father.

The man with the gun didn't move, however.

'Are you…? Have…'im shoot…'ee?' Fox asked his father.

A small female voice whispered into the darkness, 'I might.' She ran past her father, into the house, and the door shut.

'I asked…'er to…'arry…'ee,' Fox said, tapping the ring finger of his left hand.

'I take it she declined.'

'She said yes.' His mouth easily formed the words.

The earl's eyes darted to the door. 'You might wish to ask her again to verify that.'

'…said yes.'

'Lantern.' The earl waved a hand.

The servant held the lantern so the light reflected from Fox's face.

The earl took a step closer, examining Fox. 'You could have been hurt.'

Fox took in a breath. 'I think I was.'

'But, *son,* you could have been killed.'

Fox shook his head. 'Wasn't…y time.'

'Who did this to you?' His father's chin jutted and his voice shook. 'I will have them hanged.'

'Don't bother,' Fox said. 'I will take care of the…in my own time.'

'No—' his father's voice reached the treetops '—I will have them hanged and their bodies sold to those who hack them apart to study.'

'That's harsh.'

He raised his hands, words sputtering. 'If you

could see your face. They have already done more to you.'

'…'ank you.'

'And now you wish to marry?' The earl took the lantern from the servant and held the light towards Fox's face. 'Rebecca?'

Fox waved the lamplight away from his eyes.

His father didn't move, rapt. 'I cannot believe this. *She agreed?*'

Foxworthy forced his mouth to work and looked at his father. 'Why not?'

The vicar's voice cut into the air, fluttering in rage. 'You sinful scoundrel.'

Fox turned. The vicar snarled, teeth bared. Fox moved just in time to dodge the vicar's fist.

Fox stepped back, staring at the man who hardly reached his chin and was old enough to be his grandfather.

Rebecca's father put up both fists and squared off. 'She's changed her mind. My daughter will not marry a—'

The earl stepped between them, his palms on the vicar's chest. 'Whitelow. Don't you think he looks bad enough?'

The vicar controlled his heaving chest. He softened his speech and his shoulders. 'We will just forget all about it.'

Fox stared at Whitelow.

'My daughter needs a man with—moral fortitude. You're much too highborn for my daughter. It's not that I don't think you'd make her a—husband. But you're so far above her in standing. She's Rebecca. She's not a lady.'

Fox breathed himself taller and broader, and pulled every bit of his heritage into his eyes. The vicar took a step back.

The earl waggled his head, oblivious to Fox. He gave the vicar a stern look. 'My son isn't perfect, but he's—going to be my heir. He needs a wife like Rebecca.' He looked down his nose. 'Do not forget who owns the vicarage.'

'Father.' He stepped to look in the man's eyes. 'They will not…'ee…'omeless.' Pain ripped through Fox's jaw.

'Well, she would have to have my permission to wed.' The vicar's jaw sounded bruised. 'I…of course would be happy…um…um…of course.' He looked at the earl as he spoke. Then he watched Fox. 'My daughter is just a country woman. Suitable for a vicar's daughter. Perfect, in fact. But for a *peer…*' His voice squeaked on the last word.

'You cannot…tell…'ee not to wed.' The spears of pain from speaking were nothing compared to the boiling heat inside Fox. He'd thought the vicar fond of him. He should be happy to discover Fox's status.

'I would have to admit that she's important in the village,' the earl said. 'She's quite a dedicated woman. And if my son could stay here and have you believe *he's* a *vicar*?' He shook his head. 'Then she's already had a strong influence on him.'

The vicar spoke softly, eyes moving back and forth between the men. His hands formed a prayer-like clasp. 'She's more than a help to me. She is the lifeblood of this village. She must remain with the village.'

Fox did not speak. His rage would control his words.

'He's got enough high-born blood to give to the offspring.' The earl indicated his son with a waggle of head. 'He's got every ounce of his grandfather's high-born views and airs enough for the both of them.' One brow and his nose went higher. 'My son's children might need a drop more purity bred into them. Some virtue. Becca could help there.'

'But she's unsuited to the peerage.' A whisper. A condemned man's hope for pardon.

The lantern light moved to the vicar. 'She could stay at the country estate once the grandchildren arrive.' The earl spoke. 'Nothing wrong with a man and his wife living in different houses. And I need time to train the next generation.'

'You've been ill.' The vicar's voice wavered as he looked at Fox. 'I would hate for you to make such a decision when you've been so close to your death bed.'

'Nonsense,' the earl blustered an answer. 'He's making a good decision. I'll go with him for the Special Licence. We don't even need to wait.'

His father thought Fox would change his mind if they waited for the banns to be read. And even though both the earl and the vicar argued different sides, they both did so for the same reason. Neither had an ounce of faith in Fox's capabilities as a husband.

Damnation and—in Rebecca's words—*dash it*.

He supposed he agreed with them. He should do the right thing for Rebecca and step aside. The new vicar who watched the conversation would soon be swayed into Rebecca's charms.

After all, she'd been taught the role of vicar's wife from birth.

'Well, if I may insert a word,' the upstart spoke.

Fox imagined Rebecca in the new vicar's arms and fought off the urge to choke the rapt attention from the man's face. The little mongrel. All the bones on his face were where they were supposed to be. He'd never done an honest night's drinking in his life. That pious little puddle of mud. He probably had his own flower press and embroidery needle.

'You. May. Not.' Fox heard his voice.

So did his father and the vicar. Both stared at him.

Fox turned and went to the house. Only Rebecca had any say in this discussion.

The earl's heir was worse than she'd realised. She walked over, looked at the bed he'd slept in and crossed her arms. The covers so neatly tucked in place. How dare he use that bed? Eat the food she cooked? Not only was he immoral, he was a liar as well. How he must have been laughing at the vicar's daughter's foolish plans to marry him. And her plans were foolish, but not as ridiculous as her hopes had been.

She was only fortunate that his father had returned before the immoral heir had had his immoral way with her. Not that she was going to do something so impure, but still, he had fed her a bit of bread and he'd kissed probably hundreds of women. Hundreds. All of them society women, both married and single. And then—

then he'd visited his father's estate to ruin even more women. At any moment he could have told her who he was and they would have whisked him to the estate. She would personally have dragged him every step of the way and over every rock she could find.

The door opened and closed. She turned her back to it. Footsteps sounded behind her. 'Re… ecca.' Words feather-soft.

'So I was another one of the proposals.' She could not look at him. She could not risk herself slapping his traitorous deceitful, ragged, fitting face.

'No. You're the first 'oman I've ever pro'osed to…wasn't 'arried.'

'How many married women have you proposed to?'

He didn't move. 'A fair number.'

'You can't even remember. Not only are you a liar, you're a proposer.'

'Lie, no. Pro'oser. In jest.'

'I thought you were the vicar. A near saint.'

'Never said that.'

'You lied, though.'

'No.'

'Not with words, but that makes it worse.'

'Worse?'

'You lied and you didn't speak the words, but your mind knew. You knew you were misleading me. That is what a lie is. To mislead. It isn't just done with words. It's done with the heart and mind. And to try to get out of it because you didn't say the exact words doesn't make it truth. It is lying with trickery worked into it, which is even worse than an honest lie. I count it double.'

'I count it as…'alf.'

Her legs tensed and she turned, taking a strong step to him. 'You cannot have half a lie. That is what is wrong with you. There is no such thing as half lies or half-truths. They are whole.' She held her thumb and forefinger with a space of air between them. 'No lie is small. A man who kills another believes he has a reason to kill a man or he would not do so. So if he tells a magistrate he is innocent, to him that is a small lie.' She pinched her fingers tight and her wrist moved with the emphasis of a snap.

'N…not…'erfect. Not vicar. Not vicar's child. Heir. We don't have lie rules.'

'Another reason not to wed you.' She held up one finger. 'Lies.' Two fingers. 'Proposals.' Three fingers. 'Disgrace.'

The words blew over the coals of anger in his stomach. 'You…'ish to call 'o…off 'arriage?'

'Absolutely.'

'…'ou made…'romise…'oo wed.'

'You surely would not hold me to that?' Her voice rose and shrilled. 'I made a promise to wed a vicar. You are not a vicar, therefore I did not promise to marry you.'

'…'ou made…'romise…'oo wed. I asked…'ou said…'

'Yes. To the man I thought a vicar. The man I thought honest. Decent. Good. None of those other women you asked held you to your request,' she practically shouted.

'No.' He quietened his words and raised the volume of his stare. 'They…they're not as devout as you so I did not ex…expect much.'

She sputtered, arms crossed again, her voice a normal tone. 'Do you think you can keep the vows?'

'No. Human. Do you think you can keep… 'ows?' he asked. 'Those…'ows are senseless.'

She uncrossed her arms and stalked to the Prayer Book. She clasped the book with both hands and held it like a shield. 'I know I can.' Her voice had the force of a sword. 'If I vow to obey and serve my husband, then I will. And that's why I can't marry you. You're not a man I could obey.'

At that moment he realised their words carried outside the walls of the house. He grunted and shrugged. 'I could not tell you what to do. You are a…a person. You have thoughts of your own.'

'A woman should only marry a man she can

obey. We have to be as one facing the trials of the world. A man is the head of the family.'

He snorted. That was something a man's boot would step into in a stable.

Marriage was to be between two adults. An arrangement of family. Nothing could make two people one. And she didn't think he was good enough for her either. Blast it. He was the heir. He'd had the finest of everything in his life. *Everything.*

'You agreed,' he said. He touched her wrist, one finger swirling in a calming gesture. 'Your word.'

'It doesn't count if—I agreed to wed a vicar, not a rake. There's a big difference.'

'Ru…ish… Your word,' he said. And she was talking rubbish. 'Twisted truth is not truth either.'

She sniffled. 'I've made promises to myself. Promises about virtue. Honour. Purity. Goodness.' She sniffed again. 'Until I met you I did not realise how much I wanted to be a vicar's wife. Now…now I will be quite happy to remain here… To remain unmarried now that I see we will be having someone worthy to take my father's place.'

His thoughts kicked him in the stomach. 'You are hoping to wed the new vicar.'

She turned her head as if she'd been slapped,

but her eyes had had a look of guilt. 'I am not hoping to marry a man who doesn't know what truth and goodness are. And, yes, I thought to marry a vicar, but it was all based on deceit. You did not tell me the truth.'

'I tried… You didn't want to…'ear. You… had…me all dressed in halos and goodness.'

'Oh.' She whirled around. Her shoulders shook. 'You blame me? Despicable. Doubly despicable. I would expect no less from a man such as you.'

He let her words fade into the night. 'Look at me,' he said.

'No.'

'Do you not care about the good you can do?' He took her shoulders and turned her to him. 'Good works all day instead of cooking and washing.' He lifted one hand from her and rubbed his fingers of one hand together as if holding coins. 'I will gam…le away in one night more money than you…'ave to…'elp others. I… 'ill toss away funds you could use for those in need. You are sniffing away your chance to do… 'ore and…'ore good.'

'But I would have to marry you.'

He tossed his head back. He bit out his next words, ignoring the pain gripping him with his careful formation of words. 'Do you think the martyrs had easy lives?'

'But you will not make a good husband.'

He spoke slowly again to protect the muscles of his jaw. 'I will…'ake the…'est kind. You will hardly see me.'

'That is the problem. I want a true husband.'

'Your father can…'arry us. Should be legal.'

'That's not what I meant. You have a reputation for scandal.'

He nodded. 'Earned it. And you have re… reputation for good.'

'And I earned it. Can you remain…faithful?'

'Such an easy promise to make.' He grasped her fingers and gave her the same look he'd given countless others, but then he slipped his hand from hers. *But to keep?*

How could a man survive with only one woman in his life? It would be a strange form of celibacy. Celibacy with a laugh on the man. To live in a world of banquets and only be able to savour one dish on the table. It didn't matter how well the food tasted or how perfectly it was prepared, but after a time of having only one confection, even the turnips might have a strong appeal. 'You ask 'ee to change who I am. You ask me to lie.'

Her eyes softened. She swallowed. 'Yes. So you see why we cannot marry.' She reached out, touching the air in front of his face as if she touched him. 'It would be wrong for you.'

She took her hand away, and he felt as if he'd been slapped. *How dare she tell him that?* What she really meant was that he was not good enough for her. Well, he wasn't in that moral garden of Eden she lived in.

He touched his face.

Rough whiskers, swollen skin. And she'd said yes to that. But not to an earl's son. She could look at his fortune and turn her back. He would always know she did not marry him for funds, a title or his easy smile. And her heart was kind. She'd refused to kill a lizard he would have stomped on and he'd watched her push it out the door with her broom while keeping her arms extended and walking on her toes.

He knew. If he were ever to remain faithful to a woman it would be to this one. Her good works that she took Sundays off from were genuine. Her foolish views of truth would make her words genuine.

Well, what was one more lie?

All the memories of his previous liaisons spun into one. He tried to remember a name or a face of a woman who had meant something to him, other than the first, or one he thought would have considered him above any other.

The closest he could come to pulling a woman from his memory into his thoughts was the old asp Lady Havisham. She truly liked him, in a spitting, biting form of friendship.

He looked into Rebecca's eyes, seeing beyond, he believed, into innocence. He knew she didn't love him. She might, in some corner of her heart, have an affection for him. But he doubted it went deep. She couldn't. She didn't truly know him, and if she did, he'd not be seeing the compassion in her gaze. He doubted she'd even like him as much as Lady Havisham if she knew his past.

The sound of the bone cracking resurfaced and the memory of how he'd fought the fog in his mind when he tried to wake churned through him.

He reached for her hand, pulled it up so that her palm covered the thin scar line on his cheek. She didn't pull away, and her eyes softened.

It would destroy her if he married her and didn't remain true. Much in the same way his parents' marriage had been destroyed by fidelity.

And she didn't even know it. He would be discreet, which was as good as faithful.

He didn't love her. He wasn't even sure why he had any fascination with her, except he believed her more genuine than any person he'd ever seen.

He forced his lips around the painful words

and his jaw to speak. She asked too much. And she asked what he did not know.

'I…I will be faithful.' How, he did not know, short of cutting off his pizzle. Damn. It would bleed.

Chapter Ten

Rebecca hadn't spoken much with her father after Fox had left. The relief on the older man's face had numbed her words. He thought she'd changed her mind. It wasn't deception exactly. She'd told him they must wait until morning because the night had been so fretful. And that night, through the walls she'd heard the murmur of her father's prayers.

But she'd also heard the words the earl had spoken when they'd shouted in front of the house. The earl owned the roof over her head and the place her mother was buried. Now she had time to think of that.

With one word, he could banish them. She'd never, ever thought his lordship capable of such a thing. But she'd heard him threaten her father with it. And the earl wanted her to wed his son.

Even if the earl accepted her wish not to wed, and had no problems with it, his son would inherit if the earl died. There was no way around it.

And how would his son feel about letting her live in his village? He was vengeful. He'd freely admitted that.

She curled into bed, shut her eyes and realised she was not going to be able to stay in her home. No matter what. And it was likely that her father would not either. She could ensure that her father would have a home as the earl's daughter-in-law. It would even be possible for both her and her father to live on the earl's estate.

Rebecca knew the servants that worked there. She'd grown up with them. Seen them at Sunday Services her whole life.

She had to reconsider her wish not to marry the heir.

And she had to be careful. She could not let her father know she was making the sacrifice for him. And she could not be certain the earl's son wouldn't change his mind.

He'd proposed so many times to women and not moved through with it once. She needed a ring on her finger to put a roof over her father's head. He'd devoted his life to others and he deserved the best she could do for him.

The next morning, she discovered porridge could be burned. The scent alerted her and she scraped off the charred part from inside the bottom of the pan and started over.

When someone knocked on the door, she looked out the window and recognised one of the maids from the earl's house.

After opening the door, they spoke a few pleasantries and the woman gave Rebecca the note she'd been sent from the earl.

Rebecca broke the seal and read the earl's happiness at welcoming her into the family, and he wanted to assure her that, as his son's wife, she could choose wherever her father would live on the earl's property. Rebecca would only have to ask and a servant would be provided for her father's needs.

She threw the paper into the stove, not wanting her father to see it when he returned from his walk. The earl wasn't a bad person, but he had the power to choose his tenants and one who'd displeased him simply by missing too many Sunday Services had had to leave.

When her father arrived home, he used the broom to brush the dirt from his boots, then stepped inside. In that moment of the morning sun streaming through the window, she saw red-rimmed eyes. Only when her mother had died and dear Mr Scroggins, her father's closest friend, had passed had she seen his face so drawn.

She couldn't bring herself to speak the truth. But he would have to know. The banns would have to be read.

'I must beg your forgiveness, Becca,' he said, spoon lifting the porridge and then dropping it back into the bowl. 'We are so fortunate that we discovered who he was before you wed him. I must beg your forgiveness for letting someone so unfit close to you. But he is at his father's now. I just cannot see how such a saintly man as the earl could have such offspring.'

'Father.' She took a bite. Apparently she hadn't quite managed to rid the food of the over-cooking. She swallowed. 'You did not know who he was.'

'I thought—' He took in a breath and the effort seemed to weaken him. 'I thought him a husband to you. I was selfish. I saw only what I wanted to see. I thought it a solution for us all.'

'You gave shelter to a man you thought a vicar who'd been injured. You were doing right.'

'I'd mentioned to the earl that I had prayed that the new vicar might be a suitable mate for my daughter. I knew he meant…to select an unmarried man for the post.'

'You only care about my future.' The porridge tasted like the inside of a stove. She looked at the bowl. 'I did ruin the meal.'

He took a bite. 'It's fine. Nothing wrong with it but a little strength in taste.'

She stared at the lumpy mess. 'There's something I must tell you.'

'And something I must tell you.' His chest expanded on a slow breath. 'Pride, Becca. I didn't want to lose my service to the village even as I was supposed to step aside for a younger man. The earl said it was time for my pension and that he would provide for both of us, yet I did not want to go. And it almost caused an irreparable—'

'Father…' She tried to halt his words, but her own lodged in her throat.

'I let my wishes override what the true plan was,' he continued. 'Now there is a new man of marriageable age moving into the village. The real vicar. There is no other home suitable but this one. It is within easy reach of all the people. A vicar needs to be close to his flock. You and I will move. It is the right thing to do.'

She looked at the mess in her bowl, and then at her father. 'I will marry the earl's son.'

He choked.

She jumped up, ran to the back of his chair and thumped him on the back.

'No, Becca.' He gasped out the words and looked up at her, eyes watery. 'No. You must *not*.' He coughed again, clearing his throat. 'You have been too sheltered here. You cannot know the evils of a man like that. You cannot yoke yourself to someone who will not cherish you.'

'Father. I must.'

'No.' He stood and waved his arm in the direction of the estate. 'He will destroy your goodness.'

'Then my goodness doesn't go very far into my heart.'

'It doesn't matter how far it goes if he destroys the whole organ.'

'Do you not think I have the fortitude to withstand the trials?' She asked the question for herself.

'You shouldn't put yourself in such a position of risk. The fortitude is what you must have now. If you put yourself in the middle of an ocean, you can't will yourself strong enough to walk out. You must understand the limits of yourself and never get close to the edge. You may feel you are strong enough to stand near a precipice and you may well be. But the ground under you may crumble and no one can stand when the earth falls away beneath them. I forbid the marriage, Becca.'

She waited for him to lower his arm. 'I made my decision. I made it earlier. A vow unto my heart and I must continue with it. Promises are no good if they're able to be excused away.'

'It isn't a real vow until the banns are read and the words are said.'

'Then we will go forward. I want you to perform the ceremony. I want to wear the last dress Mother made for me.'

He gave one slow sideways shake of his head. 'I cannot. The new vicar will have to do it.'

'I remember Mother telling you how proud she would be to know that you could some day perform my marriage.'

'Rebecca. You ask too much.' Both his hands fisted lightly.

'Mother asked it.'

'I cannot give you into a life with a man like that. I just cannot.'

'Father.' She took his gnarled hand, scarred from the work he did in the fields with the people he cared for. 'Please.'

Chapter Eleven

Fox stood in his room at his father's estate. His cousin Andrew had been gracious enough not to comment on Foxworthy's change in appearance.

'I can't believe you're getting married.' Andrew sat propped on the arm of an overstuffed chair.

'Oh, I can,' Fox answered, taking one extra moment to adjust the perfect cravat. He'd had the mirror removed on the first night after walking into the room when he'd seen his reflection. For an instant, he'd thought himself a stranger and the realisation that he saw his own image had sickened him.

He'd avoided every mirror in the house for the past three weeks and doing so had helped him feel immensely better. His life was over. He might as well marry.

'Leave your cravat alone unless you want to put it over your face,' Andrew said. 'You laughed at me for wearing the same colour waistcoat every day. Leave it to you to find a way to rearrange your face into the latest fashion.'

'Thank you for bringing my clothing. I feel like myself now.' And he did. Mostly. But the marriage part of the day was not at all something he felt familiar with. 'Did you bring the guest as I wrote in the letter?'

'Yes. You're daft.'

'The newsprint will convince everyone I'm truly married. A love match. That I've found happiness even though I am disfigured.'

'You really don't look any worse than usual, Fox.' Andrew studied his cousin's face. 'Women never concerned themselves about your appearance anyway. They overlooked it because you had money.'

'Your kind words are accepted in the spirit given.' Fox reached up, touching the turn of his nose. It didn't ache at all. The cut had healed over quite well, too.

'How's the earl holding up to three weeks in your presence?'

'He almost died.'

Andrew's brows moved up.

'Yes. The vicar brought back some pestilence from his travels. The physician who travelled with him has been sick, too. We were not allowed to leave the estate for fear of spreading it among the countryside.'

'You have been...contained with your father?'

'And other than it almost causing his death...' he paused '...neither of us continue to be quite so fond of the new vicar.'

'Well, I hope you are fond of your wife.' Andrew shook his head. 'You had to get away from London to find someone who had not heard of you, I suppose.'

'She has astoundingly good taste,' Fox said, moving away.

'My wife has a bit of your reckless spirit.' Andrew threw out the words carelessly and walked to the next room, whistling as he went to the main sitting room. 'She swore to me that those proposals were your way of ensuring a single state. I guess she was wrong. Perhaps you were courting death.'

Fox stilled. Perhaps he had courted death in all his gaiety and pursuits and reckless ways. Then he shook his head. No, he'd just not believed it possible for anyone to be willing to risk their neck damaging a peer.

He followed Andrew while still contemplating how many times he'd danced along the edge of a societal precipice or hovered around a woman whose husband had a murderous temperament. He pushed those thoughts away. The past would not do him any good and he had no reason to dwell in it.

His life was all about the future. Or it had always been. And now his future was to be married.

Walking into the room, he saw Beatrice with her hair amassed on her head. The woman had painted a heart under and to the side of her right eye. Well, that was Andrew's burden to bear.

He smiled inside himself. Rebecca would never do such a thing.

Beatrice stood, her mouth wide when she caught sight of him. Well, he must get used to that reaction.

'Life is not just,' Beatrice said. She walked closer, examining him like a child might examine a particularly unusual worm.

But Beatrice was Beatrice. She always spoke before the words had a chance to reach her brain and if one somehow did creep in, he doubted the detour delayed it. She was granted such leeway because she was an artist.

She shook her head and grimaced. She pounded her fist against her chest. 'I get one minute of no sleep and I look as if I've been rolling in a sack of unwashed potatoes. You get beaten and appear looking better than ever.'

'I would have said *as bad as always*,' Andrew grunted.

'Look at that nose.' She practically crossed her eyes in the process of gazing at his broken nose.

Fox took in a breath. He could not believe her lack of manners. His nose would never be the same.

'It's gorgeous,' she exclaimed. 'Utterly perfect.'

Andrew tilted his head to the side, examining Fox. 'That's not how I would describe it.'

'Beatrice,' Fox muttered. 'It will never be the same.'

'Thank goodness,' Bea said. 'That has added something. Without it you had no character to your face. Now... Now I must paint you.' She turned to stare at her husband. 'You must see the beauty of it. He now has facial character.'

'If so, that's his only character,' Andrew said, head still tilted, looking around Beatrice. 'You are sure you didn't merely crash into a tavern floor after swallowing too much brandy?' he asked Fox.

Fox moved to stand out of Beatrice's view. He put his hand in front of his face, tilted his head in the same direction Andrew did and made the same gesture they'd often given each other as teens.

And his cousin responded with a cheerful flick of the wrist, his way of swatting the gesture back to Fox.

Chapter Twelve

It had been three weeks since Rebecca had seen the earl's son. Every day she had expected to get word from him that it had been another jest. Every day she had looked at her father and noticed the shadows under his eyes and the wrinkles around them.

He could not be without a home. Not after devoting his life to helping others.

She pulled back the curtains, hoping the warmth from the sun's rays would brighten the room. Even cooking breakfast hadn't brought the temperature high enough to erase all the chill. She glanced from the window to see if Fox had arrived at the church. He hadn't.

Now she was to stand beside him and be his wife. In some secret part of herself she'd not really expected him to continue the idea of marriage. He'd not done so on his previous proposals.

Perhaps some spirit of spite had caused her to go forward with the marriage. He'd asked her and she'd called his bluff—now she wasn't sure what was to happen.

Her father had voiced aloud his hope that Foxworthy would abscond. He'd reassured her countless times that the new vicar might be the answer yet.

The vicar had visited earlier that morning. His voice whistled from his nose or somewhere even less appealing.

Her good work for the day had been easy to accomplish. She'd smiled at him, listened as much as she could tolerate and complimented him on his quick recovery. She couldn't have complimented him on his unflattering hairstyle, the cheeks that puffed when he smiled or the many times he talked with rapt awe about the woman who'd once been his patron.

A vicar who made her want to cover her ears wasn't quite the husband she would have chosen for herself, but after he left, her father looked at her, frowned and mentioned that health was important in a vicar.

'Do you think the earl really thought him suitable for someone's husband?' she asked.

'I think he—he sometimes errs.' His face brightened. 'But the vicar has good points. He follows instructions well and has good habits. You could teach him to be more interesting.'

It dismayed her that anyone would think that man a suitable a husband for her. She raised her brows.

'A less interesting husband can help soothe one into slumber.'

She sighed. 'I do not like to sleep that much.'

But the thing that worried her was that if Foxworthy hadn't arrived and the new vicar had, she might not have noticed the way his hair was cut straight across his brow. That could be easily changed. His voice lingered in the air like a bad scent, but she would have overlooked that, too, planning a good work to help him find something that could be of interest. And that smirk of a smile. She shuddered. She'd been ready to marry and fall in love with the first upright man of morals who stumbled across her path.

Perhaps she deserved what she received. She clasped her hands together. Tight. It somehow seemed to help her stay on her feet.

Relief burst inside her when her father told her that a carriage had arrived, but the well-being didn't quite reach her feet. She looked out the window and didn't recognise the vehicle, but knew Foxworthy's cousins planned to arrive with a carriage large enough to take them all to London.

'Are you ready, Becca?' her father asked, his face turned to the window. 'We must go greet the earl's family. I'm sure the earl and Foxworthy will be along shortly.'

She nodded.

He turned to her, and her father smelled of the same soap her mother had gifted him with not long before her death. He only used that soap on wedding and funeral days.

He paused. 'You are every bit as beautiful as your mother today and I thought her the most beautiful woman I'd ever seen,' her father said. 'Seeing you in the dress, and remembering her stitching it in her last moments, it's as if she is here with us today.'

'I know, Father.'

Rebecca stepped into the sunshine, feeling the warmth on her face.

She steeled herself when she saw the carriage draw closer. It wasn't as big as the church, but she didn't think she'd ever seen one so large. The coachmen were dressed in matching livery. Her father stopped, turned back and his grim-lipped smile didn't make her feet want to work any faster.

A woman descended after manoeuvring her hat to get it through the carriage doorway. She stopped beside a man wearing black. The woman's dress had tucks, trims and huge puffs of sleeves. She reached out and tapped the man on the shoulder who stood beside her. He'd said something. 'Andrew,' her shriek admonished him.

Low rumbles of laughter floated through the air and another man, also laughing, stepped into the sunshine.

These toffs were to be her relatives?

She suddenly realised the new vicar's cheeks weren't quite so round as she'd thought and one could make quite a huge change with a sideways part of the hair.

But perhaps Foxworthy wouldn't arrive. If he didn't, she was certain she could be quite gracious—quite gracious in her predicament. She might be the first woman jilted at the altar to fall upon her knees and give thanks.

Her father turned to her again. 'Rebecca,' he whispered. 'You had three weeks to change your mind. Now you only have a few moments, but it's still enough. And I know the new vicar would much love to have a wife such as you. He told me so three times when I walked him to the church and he asked if I thought there was a chance you would reconsider.'

'I just...' She tried to think of something to say to reassure him that she wasn't really slowing because she'd changed her mind. She couldn't say she'd been admiring the lady's dress—that would have been a lie—and she couldn't see anything else about the trio to compliment, except the men did look like she'd imagined royals would look. They wore lavish cravats and the flowery twists somehow contrasted in a way to make the men seem more masculine to be able to wear such things with confidence.

The cravats seemed to be the source of the woman's amusement. She was asking if she could have them later to be sewn around the hem of one of her dresses so it would look like she'd stepped into a garden of blooms.

The second man leaned towards her, flicked at the white on his neck, said something low and laughter again floated through the air.

Fox's cousins would laugh at her, too. She knew it.

Her father paused and turned back. 'You are happy in the vicarage, Rebecca. Happy. You can still change your mind, Becca,' her father whispered. 'We will make do. The earl will understand. Just faint dead away when he arrives. Hold your stomach. Moan and groan when you wake. Act addled from pain.'

'That would be deceit, Father.'

He sighed. 'I will put in a good word for you and I'm certain you'll be forgiven.'

Then Foxworthy's cousin who'd pointed to his cravat turned to her. She could feel his eyes taking her in more than she could see them because she simply could not meet the man's gaze.

She'd heard Foxworthy had a cousin who was a duke and perhaps he'd decided to attend the marriage. Her mouth became parched.

The trio moved closer.

'Father, I am feeling a bit faint.' The words fell away on the air. She would not have to have a good word put in for her. It was the truth.

'Rebecca. Are you all right?' The voice. She heard Fox's voice and looked around for him. Then she realised the man watching her wasn't the duke. It was Foxworthy.

Her knees truly buckled, but it wasn't her father who caught her. It was Fox. She looked into his eyes. 'I will…' her breath returned '… be fine.'

His face had healed. The bruising was mostly gone.

He cradled her and her strength returned. 'Just give me a moment,' she said. 'I've never been married before.'

A cackling female voice jarred her back into the present, and Fox released her.

'I have,' the woman stated. 'Twice. The trick is to outlive them.'

'Beatrice,' the man beside her said. 'I would hate to think you're not happy with me.'

'Oh, I'm supremely happy. I've brought out the beast in you.' She tapped his cheek, resting her hand against him, and swaggered her shoulders. 'And made it purr.'

He clasped her hand and removed it from his cheek. A look passed between them.

Rebecca looked at Fox, searching out his expression. 'Ignore them,' he said. 'They won't go away so that's all you can do.'

As Foxworthy completed the introductions, the earl's carriage rolled up. Rebecca turned around. Her father had vanished into the church.

Perhaps he wouldn't make good on his word to marry her.

Chapter Thirteen

Fox stood at Rebecca's side. So this was what one's wedding felt like. Much like a late night with the rising moon in a contented smile and stars glowing. A rare night that made him want to sit and gaze above, not thinking, not drinking, just looking at the grandeur.

Not unpleasant at all.

He felt at peace. Willing to stand and feel the world around him. This moment. An orchestra of happy notes fluttered about in his memory and, for once, he was certain he did the right thing. It didn't actually hurt.

In fact, this was the best he'd felt in quite some time.

The vicar didn't look so relaxed. Rebecca's

father appeared to be choking. His forehead glistened and he stammered the first words.

Foxworthy kept his grin tamped down. The vicar was more nervous than the groom.

At the third word from the man's lips, he paused, looking in Fox's direction. He stumbled over his next syllables. A smile edged Fox's lips. Really, Rebecca's father looked as if he might faint away at any moment. He didn't understand this was the right thing for her to do. Her children would have the heir's advantage. Fox gave a half wink of reassurance to his future father-in-law.

Something hardened in the vicar's face. He completely stopped speaking, staring at the smile on Fox's lips.

The man's eyes squeezed to half their size, reminding Fox of a raptor. Perhaps a grin hadn't been a good idea.

Fox stiffened his own facial muscles. The older man struggled to breathe. Colour infused the vicar's face.

Fox braced himself for the collapse. He'd catch the vicar if he tumbled. Fox had never heard of a cleric fainting at a wedding, but then, Rebecca was his only child.

Fox gave him another reassuring smile.

Her father's colour heightened. His chin

snapped low and he peered at Fox, and this time his words flowed smoothly.

'Wilt thou have this woman to be thy wedded wife? To live together under God's ordinance, in the holy state of matrimony? To love her. Comfort her. Honour and obey. In sickness and in health, and forsaking all others, keeping thee only unto her, for as long as ye both shall live?'

The muffled snort from the earl distracted Fox.

The vicar's eyes locked on Fox's face much the same way the husband's did when Fox had danced too closely with the wife. The vicar's digestion must be off. 'I will.' Fox nodded. He'd not realised that part about obey was in the man's marriage ceremony. No one had informed him of that.

The vicar turned to Rebecca.

'Will thou have this man to be thy wedded husband? To live together after God's ordinance, in the holy estate of matrimony? Wilt thou keep him, in sickness and in—in— Forsaking all others, keeping thee only unto him, for as long as ye both shall live?'

Rebecca gurgled. Her eyes widened. 'No—' she whispered. *'Father.'*

Fox stared. After all this? *She* was backing out?

'Rebecca,' the vicar snapped. He put his lips

around each word, pushing the sounds with force. 'Will thou have this man to be thy wedded husband? To live together after God's ordinance, in the holy estate of matrimony? Wilt thou keep him, in sickness and in health, forsaking all others, keeping thee only unto him for as long as ye both shall live?'

The vicar did all but sprout his own set of horns from his head after he looked at his daughter and then back to Fox.

Fox turned to her. If she'd changed her mind, the laugh would be on him, but he'd take the jest. In fact, he would run with it. The man who'd proposed a dozen times, jilted at the altar. This would be quite the tale. Perfect, in fact.

He looked at her, waited and shrugged.

Her eyes had that same surrounded-by-vultures look that her father had.

'Oh, well, then, I will.' She spoke with no inflection.

The moment had taken her thoughts and overwhelmed her, he decided.

Seconds later her father's words completed the ceremony. At the moment they were wed, a guffaw erupted at Fox's side, followed by a clap on his shoulder which jarred him from his reverie.

The earl walked to the vicar and clapped him on the back as well. 'Thank you. Thank you, my friend.' He crossed an arm over his stomach and bent, still clasping the vicar's shoulder, still chuckling, his body racked with laughter.

'You just vowed to obey her.' The earl gasped in air, unable to speak and control his words easily at the same time. 'You just vowed to obey her. And she gave you no such promise.' He snorted in, gasping air. Rising, he swept a hand over his face, wiping his eyes. 'Sweet Mother of Saffron, my son just vowed to obey his wife.'

Fox turned, appraising the vicar's face.

Rebecca's father's gloom left his eyes. His lips firmed and he nodded the smallest movement. 'I was nervous. I mixed the vows.' He winked, but his face jerked forward when he did it, more of a jab than anything else.

'You did that on purpose.'

'I was nervous about it, though, son. I didn't lie. I mixed the vows. Truth again.'

'It was wrong, Father,' Rebecca's words burst through the men's conversation. 'That was—'

'Can't take it back now,' the vicar said. 'And we're in a church and there's witnesses, and you're married. Besides—' he tilted his head to Fox '—this one won't be able to keep a vow of any sort.'

'From my view, most vows have been a waste of breath,' Fox said.

'You cannot say such a thing. Here. Today,' Rebecca said.

Fox stared at her. She thought to tell him what to say?

The vicar swayed, tumbling forward. Fox caught him as the book crashed to the ground. He knelt, lowering the older man, helping him to sit. Rebecca kneeled at his side.

'Father?' she whispered.

He looked at her. 'I'm fine, Becca. It just hit me. I just can't…just can't believe I did that.'

'It's fine that you mixed the vows, Father. I will be a good wife anyway.'

The man sniffed. 'That's not what I mean. I stood there and did nothing to stop you from marrying this—man. I spoke the words condemning your life. I will not be able to live with myself for letting you marry this—' He held his palm towards Fox. 'It is as if I put a noose round my own child's neck.'

'It was my choice.' She clasped his hand. 'Father. I will survive this.' Her voice pleaded. 'I survived Mother's death.'

Fox watched his wife sitting on her knees, consoling her father that he had not condemned her to death.

'Vicar. Becca.' The earl knelt, speaking softly. 'I have provided a generous marriage settlement for her. It's not truly a settlement, but more of an inheritance. Becca is my daughter now. And no matter what, if Fenton should pass on and she should marry again, I want her well cared for. She'll always be my child. Her children will be my grandchildren. My heirs to the extent the law allows.'

Fox reached out, taking Rebecca's elbow and helping her rise to her feet. 'I will take care of her now. I am her husband.'

'A…a…guh…' Her father collapsed back, falling completely to the floor.

She jumped forward, kneeling beside him. His eyes opened, a trickle of tear running to his cheek.

'Father…' Rebecca's eyes brimmed '…please do not take this so hard.'

'Andrew,' Fox said to his cousin. 'Help Father take care of the vicar.'

While his cousin moved in, Fox lifted Rebecca to her feet, his hands clasping around her arms. She weighed less than a winter's coat. He'd not noticed before how slender she'd become. She couldn't have eaten more than a bite since he'd seen her last.

She looked up. Her eyes didn't have the white circle of fear he'd seen in a hare's eyes before, but they were close.

He walked her towards the back of the church.

As he walked by the man sketching, Fox

spoke, a challenging upbeat tone in his voice. 'You'd best not put any of this in your paper.'

The man's eyes flickered, and Fox walked out the door.

In the air, away from the mourners inside, Fox looked at the carriages. Forget the wedding breakfast. Forget sitting around a table with the lovestruck Andrew and Beatrice, and the weeping father of the bride, and the father of the groom who'd managed to make his preference known.

Andrew would surely not miss his carriage for a day. Fox would send it back.

Fox walked to Andrew's conveyance and the driver opened the door. Fox lifted Rebecca onto the steps. She didn't move forward and he caught the ever-so-delicate scent of lilacs. He guided her in front of himself.

He met the driver's eyes and gave the man a broad smile. 'My cousin will be staying with my father a day or so, but he's loaned me the use of his vehicle to go to London.' It was true. Andrew was loaning the carriage. Perhaps unwittingly and unwillingly, but no matter.

Rebecca sat on the leather squabs and leaned back, shutting her eyes. *London.* He'd said something about going to London.

The seat squished down beside her when he sat. Way down.

He was going to take her to the marriage breakfast and then leave her at his father's and return to London. To his home. She'd heard him say that. Well, the marriage had started better than she'd expected. She interlaced her fingers and raised her lashes just enough to glance at him. He stared ahead, looking at the dark wall of the carriage as if he could see actors on a stage in a quite demanding performance.

She didn't know his face, this man sitting beside her. She needed to hear his voice to reassure herself that he was truly...well, not the vicar. The earl's son. She knew the earl fairly well at least. Had known him from a distance all her life. He was a dear friend to her father. But the earl rarely visited their house, except perhaps to stop for a moment on a travel.

And she... She'd thought she'd known the new vicar. But he wasn't quite the new vicar and he had a different face than she remembered.

Well, this wasn't the first mistake she'd made. Just the most far-reaching. And mistakes could not always be fixed, but they could be lived with. Except when they couldn't. Except this one could. She could manage. She'd put salve on Mrs Oldman's bottom and that had been rather discouraging.

'You're snarling,' he said. 'You'll like London.' He looked to the window. 'Shops. Soirées. And there's a museum that I've heard is good. I've been to the art exhibitions at Somerset House. Beatrice had a painting there. Kind of a self-portrait. Andrew had it removed because he doesn't appreciate art quite like I do. You would prefer his view, I fear.'

She turned her head just enough to see out the window. Then she straightened. She squinted. The carriage slowed. They were crossing the stream.

She turned to him. 'The coachman is lost. We're going the wrong direction.'

'London.' He spoke without inflection. Without smiling.

'London.' His voice sounded so smooth she didn't feel she looked at the same person who'd helped her into the carriage. We are supposed to go to the marriage breakfast. My father is ill.'

'It was just the shock of marriage.'

'My *father* is ill.'

'My father will take care of him…like a brother.'

She reached down, removed her slipper and rapped it against the top of the carriage. Instantly, the vehicle slowed.

'Rebecca.'

'I can't leave him when he's ill. I can't.'

'I would rather you wait until after the wedding night to leave me,' he said.

'Before works best for me.' She rapped the shoe on the roof again. 'My father is ill.'

He grasped the end of the shoe and lowered it with her holding the other end. With his free hand he gently removed her fingers from the other end of the slipper. He pulled her knuckles near his chest. 'Are you certain?'

'Positive.'

'Well…' his grin enveloped the lower half of his face, but didn't quite touch his eyes '…I can never resist a beautiful woman.'

She snapped the shoe from his hand and leaned forward. 'You'd best keep your distance from them then.'

The coach stopped. She dropped her shoe and slid her foot into it. The door opened on Rebecca's side. The coachman leaned inside. 'Yes?' he asked.

She reached out. The servant had no choice but to help her alight as she moved towards him. She stepped onto the ground.

'Rebecca.' Fox bundled out behind her. 'What are you doing?'

'I have to make certain my father is well. I will ask your father to see that I get to London later. I'm certain he will.'

'I'm certain he will not,' Fox said. He looked at the coachman. The man stepped back.

Fox lifted one brow and looked at her. She could see emotion flare in his eyes, then it turned inside out and a softness rounded his lips. He spoke to the coachman. 'We'll be taking my beautiful bride to my father's estate now. I couldn't bear to have her distressed on her wedding day.'

She would have preferred if he'd merely said distressed—not distressed *on her wedding day.*

She stood, staring, confusion bobbing around in her head. She did not have a mother to talk to. And she was standing beside a carriage on a road on her wedding day. No one had warned her about the day, only given her advice on the night. The only guidance she had was sermons and this man hadn't listened to those sermons.

The physical intimacies didn't concern her overmuch. The women of the village had each given her a different perspective on what to expect, so she knew a wide variety of tableaus on how the night was to proceed. But they all assured her that would be over by the next day. And then what?

'Rebecca.' His voice faded in the breeze. 'Rebecca?'

She reminded herself that the martyrs had had difficult lives. Which he had mentioned, which of course did not mean he was to be a bad husband.

He was watching her. As if he'd never seen her face.

She wanted the disfigured vicar back. She wanted the bruises and bumps and man who needed her help. The stranger who hardly moved much and couldn't speak much. That was the man whom she wanted to marry.

She blinked away the picture of her hiring several of the villager's sons to help with a terrible, terrible idea.

He touched her arm, leaving her to her own thoughts.

She climbed inside the vehicle.

Everything was clear now, but it was a day too late.

The real reason for her marriage. She'd wanted marriage. Wanted a life just like her mother and father and her prospects had been dismal. Her only true hope for marriage had been if one of the ladies of the village died and left a widower. And that was a particularly hideous and revolting thought. None of the men were as attractive to her as the mangled face of the stranger and then he'd had the audacity to go and change it.

And he did not even want to go to the marriage breakfast. Who had ever heard of such a thing? She'd married a complete and utter heathen. A heathen's heathen. A wife's burden.

Her words tumbled forward. 'I liked you better...before...' She put her hand over her mouth. Well, not really. She shut her eyes tight. She would have to be silent to be truthful.

Apparently he felt the same way.

The carriage interior wobbled as it manoeuvred to turnaround, and Fox moved as if one with the carriage, facing her.

'I completely understand that you're disappointed I didn't heal well.' He touched his cheek. 'It still aches a bit and I'll never look the same. The men whose wives I've danced with will have quite the laugh. But the last laugh will be on them.'

'You don't think to—'

'Just the same old dances,' he said. 'Nothing to concern yourself with. Enough to make them note I've returned. I've had my horse sent ahead. And I have had men searching for the man with the gold buttons on his coat.'

On the positive side, an enormous opportunity for good works sat very near her. 'Perhaps vengeance isn't something to contemplate.'

'Certainly.' He shrugged. 'No need in thinking about it.'

'Evil men have to live with their misdeeds.'

'Oh, yes. I agree.' He patted her hand. 'They

will have to live with their misdeeds. I'll see to that.'

'You plan revenge.' The words were flat to her ears.

'Of course. But leave it to me. I'll take care.'

She imagined the conversations she heard between her parents and their occasional disagreements. Her father had insisted that her mother would choose what would be selected and then her mother had insisted she wished for him to make the decision and the conversation had moved back and forth, with each stumbling over the other in their wish to give an agreement.

'You have no compunction with dishonesty.'

'I hate it in others.'

'Might they hate it in you?'

'If they wish. I don't mind either way.'

He leaned forward, studying her face. 'Did you catch the illness that is in the area?'

'I'm just a bit jittery about the wedding.' Her cheeks did feel warm, but not in the pleasant way. Feverish. Not ill from the body, but ill from the day. She glanced at her hands in her lap and noticed the skirt of the dress she wore. She'd had to almost starve herself to fit into it. But she'd so wanted to wear it. 'And the groom.'

The slow twist of Fox's head as he moved back and the look he gave her was the most direct she'd ever received from anyone in her life.

He spoke. 'I am fine with some untruthfulness, by the way. Dishonesty is a bit of sweetness that helps the truth taste better, not bitter.'

She'd not known before how strong his jawline was. Her fingers straightened. Tense. 'Vic—' She'd almost called him vicar.

'You look lovely today.' He changed the subject. Very well. Their conversation wasn't reassuring her.

She didn't raise her eyes. 'Do you truly like this dress? Or is it a bit of untruthfulness.'

'You are stunning in it.' She looked sideways. Sincerity shone from every last glimmer of his eyes. He'd not been nearly so direct when he'd been recovering and he'd grumbled. It was almost as though he worked harder to be sincere when he didn't care.

'What if we don't really like each other?'

'Thousands of marriages rock along quite well every day under such circumstances.'

'I'd always imagined…'

'A vicar.' He pulled her fist to his lips and dropped a kiss over the knuckles. He held her hand lightly. She kept her fingers closed. 'And no matter what happens, no matter what unfolds, you have my word that I'm more palatable than that arse of a half brain my father brought to the village.'

He shifted, pulling his coat closer to his middle and taking in a deep breath. 'I have just spent three weeks with the man. The first week, my father tired of the man being at his elbow and requested, very sincerely, that the vicar give me guidance. My father then proceeded to recite my sins aloud—and someone has kept him much better informed than I realised. For the next two weeks Dunderhead believed his loyalty to his patron depended on his pointing out the error of my ways. And the words, "Get the hell out" meant "Talk faster" to him.'

He shut his eyes and shook his head. 'In the past three weeks, were you praying that I be punished for my sins, sweet?'

'No, I was praying that I not have to suffer for them.'

Just the tiniest movement of his eyes answered her and then he ended the silence by saying, 'I will beg the guests pardon for going in the wrong direction and explain that I couldn't wait any longer for a moment alone with my bride.'

Fox had not a care on his face.

She looked into the blue eyes, considering his words and how he'd said them. 'They will believe you.'

'Of course.' He looked to the window.

The calm waters. No ripples. So much sincerity.

'The time spent with my father was interesting. His pitching the new vicar my way was clever. I tried to shoo the man back, but it took some effort and a bit of fear.'

'I love my father very much.'

'Of course, your father may visit us in London. You can even send a carriage for him from time to time.' He glanced at her. 'I did receive his note telling me you would graciously decline from marrying me.'

'He is concerned about my happiness.' And she was worried about him. Her father was getting older and he… He had never lived alone. Her heart cracked a little. She'd not given the marriage enough thought. Everything had seemed perfect when she'd thought she courted the new vicar.

He gave the tiniest perusal of her face and his voice flowed with sincerity. 'I believe we will get along quite well.'

She somehow doubted he believed that.

She unclenched her fingers, moving them from his. She had a gold band on her left ring finger. She didn't remember seeing it placed there, but she did remember most of the ceremony. Touching the ring, she said, 'I suppose you plan to obey me, then.'

Her words had fluttered into the air, out the

window, and probably meant as much to the horses as they did to him.

He didn't answer.

Chapter Fourteen

Rebecca looked around. Each time she'd visited the earl's estate, she'd always noticed how tall the ceiling was when she walked into the main entrance.

The butler opened the door for them. She'd never spoken with him before. According to the village, he wasn't one to speak, particularly with common folk. Her friend Mary had told her he deemed anyone who didn't play an accomplished chess game well beneath him and could not sleep if someone bested him at a competition.

Then they walked into a grand room with an even higher ceiling. One she'd never seen before. Strains of violin music wafted in the air, muffled by voices competing to be heard. The whole town was in the one room. She searched to find her father.

He stood at the side, a wilted figure. Mrs Berryfield spoke with him at his right. The earl leaned in at his left

Then the earl raised his face and saw her. At that moment her father looked up. His shoulders straightened and he snapped back into the man she knew.

'My apologies that we've started without you.' The earl lessened the distance between them, his movements parting the visitors. 'We didn't know where you'd decided to go.' His smile beamed at her, but then his eyes moved to his son. 'Your cousin Andrew says you are planning to live in London.'

Rebecca's ears heard the imaginary court give her the verdict of *Transported.*

Fox felt Rebecca becoming smaller at his side. She wasn't teetering, about to tumble as her father did, but she certainly wasn't bursting at the seams with happiness. She swallowed. Her face was the colour of his cravat.

Damn. He'd been half-jesting when he'd said that about the martyrs, but she looked as if she'd eaten rotten fruit.

Beside the earl, her father managed a smile

and his eyes melted at the sight of his daughter. 'I'm pleased you didn't leave.'

Fox could have tipped a sword blade against the vicar's neck and he doubted her father would have noticed unless the blade obstructed the view of Rebecca. He glanced to the earl's eyes and stared into the heat of a forged blade. Neither looked away.

'I had to see you again before I left, Father. To make sure you are well.' Rebecca's voice diverted their attention.

'I am.' Her father took her hand. 'I just wasn't prepared to lose my little girl.'

'You've gained a son,' the earl said and turned so that his view excluded Fox. 'We traded children.'

'Now you both have two,' Rebecca said, her voice wavering into the silence. 'Both your families increased.'

Her father didn't look convinced. Neither did the earl.

'I would hate to feel we're orphans.' Her voice held an ache. She felt like one.

Fox chuckled, his arm going around her back, giving a pat. 'London isn't so far away. Just the right distance.'

She caught the jab at his father.

The earl shut his eyes briefly and gave one

of those little groans that the dog did when his stomach got mashed by accident.

Rebecca heard the sound of Thomas Greene's violin in the distance. He wasn't a bad sort. His wife was sickly. She should have waited.

They all moved into the dining room.

The earl had hosted wedding breakfasts before. In fact, he often did. But this one was different. More elaborate. A prodigal-type feast.

At the sidebar, mounds of ham, tongue, rashers of bacon and eggs waited.

She sat, staring at the plates. Hand-painted roses graced the edges. She traced the gilt-trimmed edge and looked again at the food. She looked around for her friend Mary, whom her father had helped gain employment. But she wasn't surprised not to see Mary. Mary would be in the scullery, working.

At the side, all dressed in his fine clothes, hands gloved, Chester Berryfield stood at alert, dressed in footman's livery, and they shared a smile. He'd managed to work his way from the stables to the house and soon she expected to get the news he and Mary were going to wed.

A tiered plate in front of her had rows of pears circling the base, stems inward, and managed to fill the spaces, leading up to the top with a circle of chestnuts topped with a flower bloom. Another sat at the other end of the table and, in the middle of everything, no taller than her hand, a round cake with a frothy icing. She wasn't surprised by the cake because the cook had sent a note asking if she wanted orange or rosewater flavour for the icing, or had a different preference.

And it wasn't a Sunday and she didn't know how she'd find a single good work to do in a world of gold-rimmed plates.

Everyone talked around her, the voices swirling into one huge strand of gaiety. Foxworthy chuckled and laughed as if it were the happiest day of his life. He even glanced her way a few times and his eyes caressed. But she imagined that to be the exact same look he'd given each of the women he'd proposed to. A natural look. One that easily attached itself to his face and stuck there, not really connected to thoughts, but to a smile and whimsy. He laughed at some jest Beatrice had made and said something about being the most fortunate man alive and again looked at Rebecca with that lovely, all the world's a stage gaze.

Fox even reassured her father that Rebecca was indeed a rare jewel, and her father's face lightened in relief.

The lines on the earl's face increased with Fox's banter. When the earl's eyes met hers, he spoke quietly. 'Of course, you may visit at any moment you wish to.' For the first time, she saw their familial resemblance. Both could encourage with their face and words. But the earl always spoke the truth and his face didn't conceal it.

Fox stood at the side after the breakfast ended, watching the other guests mill around in the grand room—a room swathed in grey colours reminiscent of a harsh winter.

Her father and his own had their heads together, eyes downwards, talking.

The door opened and the sounds of others talking drowned the fiddle tune.

As soon as Rebecca stepped from the table, a lady rushed to her. 'Oh, you look so lovely in the lace cap Mrs Smith made for you.'

Rebecca raised the hem of the dress so that her satin slippers were visible. 'Thank you so much for my shoes,' she said.

'Oh, I only embroidered the flowers on them. Lottie did the border stitching. That way one of us could finish our part while the other worked and they would match up.'

'If I do say so myself, we did a fine job,' Lottie walked up beside the other woman.

'All of us wanted to contribute,' a spindly young woman with her hair piled on her head spoke.

'Do you have the handkerchiefs?' A woman with sprigs of grey hair sticking from her bun asked.

'Yes. They're in my new reticule. Thank you for that, Mrs Berryfield, and you, too, Amanda.' She bent to talk to a little girl. 'I have never seen one prettier.'

Little Amanda clasped her mother's hand and smiled brightly, teeth missing in front. She blushed, nodding.

The bees swarmed around the honey. Then one of the ladies handed Rebecca a bag tied with a string at the top. 'From all of us,' the older woman with sprigs of grey hair said.

Rebecca loosened the string and peered inside. Then she pulled out a fabric ball as big as her fist. Her cheeks reddened. The ladies cackled. She shoved the ball back into the bag.

'Promise you'll use it,' one of the ladies admonished.

Rebecca's cheeks brightened even more.

'We've all added one of our pins,' Mrs Berryfield said, then she reached out and patted Rebecca on the arm.

The blush. So different from his world. He'd not noticed her simple ways until she'd stood by his cousins.

She'd never fit into his world of the *ton*. His father knew it. Her father knew it. She didn't.

His father shunned society and the action had tamped down his influence among the people who made the decisions that shaped the world.

He'd somehow chosen the most unlikely, impossible prospect for a wife, then proposed to her just because he wanted her. Because she had a pure heart and now the care of that heart rested in his hands. He should have let her reject his proposal.

'I cannot believe you wanted the man from the papers here for such a private thing as your marriage.' His father spoke at his side.

'Don't worry about it, Father.' He'd actually hoped it would be the last time he'd appear in print. But he doubted it now.

'You must do the right thing,' his father commanded. 'You can't hurt someone as gentle as Rebecca. Even you should have some compassion for her.'

'What about your actions, Father? You hardly show up at Parliament.'

'I do. When I can.'

'You should stop by and visit Mother while you're in town. Or at least write to her more. It isn't as if you don't have the time.'

'She asked me not to visit. You know that.'

'Was the obey part in your vows also?' Fox asked, eyebrows up.

His father directed a stare at him. 'For some

reason, I don't like her mentioning that I'm living proof one shouldn't marry for money.'

'She's jesting.'

'No. She's not. She told me within days after she married that the highest bidder isn't always the best choice.' He frowned. 'Her parents raised her to be a pretty confection. I was of an age to think I liked confections.'

'Mother's not all fluff.'

'No. She's not. But she was in love with a footman and felt if she didn't marry me, she'd never get to see him again.'

He studied his father's face.

'Yes. She's not a bad sort, but we were both young and I wasn't used to coming in second behind the servants, and she wasn't used to anything but her way. Got us off to a bit of a bumbling start.' He chuckled. 'We were stumbling along with some semblance of truce and we both decided to make the best of it, and we did, for a while. When your sister died, it didn't seem worth it any more.'

'You both live apart to be contrary.'

'And what if we do? It keeps us from hating each other. There's something to be said for that.'

'A lot, I'd say.'

'I always thought you were smart, but that you'd never taken the time to explore that option. Now it's time to use your head to think of someone other than yourself. There will be children.' He laughed softly. 'Wouldn't it be ironic if they were like you and preferred their grandfather over their father?' He clapped Fox on the back and lowered his voice. 'I can hardly wait for your son to be born.'

'I thought you didn't particularly like children.'

'Not all children expect to have gold spoons and silver rattles.'

'Well, I will be happy to give such toys to my child.'

Laughter burst from his father's lips. 'You do that. And he'll visit with his grandfather and discover he prefers austere life.'

The earl nodded, eyes towards Rebecca. 'The deck is stacked against you ruining my grandson's life with frivolity and nonsense. The vicar's daughter will instil values in her children that you have no wish for. She cannot accept immoral worlds. Her whole life has been devoted to caring for others. My grandchildren will have the values I wish for them. Your grandfather is not getting the last laugh.'

Fox saw the truth in his father's eyes and their truce dissolved.

He turned his back.

'Duelling at dawn tomorrow?' Andrew walked up and asked.

'Think nothing of our volleys with words,' Fox answered. 'Father would think I did not care for him if I didn't annoy him.'

'He always insisted he must visit you,' Andrew said.

'You think he cares for me? That's a laugh,' the earl retorted.

Fox saw his father studying him.

A month before he would have said he visited his father just to annoy him. But then he'd just stayed with him while they waited to see if his father became ill. They'd talked about the weather at least once in the morning, once midday, and then again as the sun set. And one day, when the sun was disappearing from the sky, his father had begun to recall how he'd personally woken his father to tell him of the birth of a baby boy.

Fox heard stories he'd never even known to ask of.

Fox was certain everyone in the gardens kept talking, but he couldn't hear them. He could only hear the echo of his words in his head. 'Of course. I visited you every long holiday from school and twice yearly since then. Did you not notice?'

'I assumed your mother insisted you come.'

'No.'

Fox watched the words register in his father's eyes.

'Aunt couldn't keep him from visiting you,' Andrew said. 'She tried. She was afraid you'd not let him return to London.' Andrew gave a bow, and moved back to Beatrice's side.

'Is that true?' the earl asked Fox.

'I fear my cousin's memories are much better than mine. All I remember is that when I arrived you would tell me constantly how I disappointed you and I'd be so encouraged I'd leave to accomplish more.'

'That's not how I remember it. You blathered on about how I'd not enough ballocks to stay with your mother.'

'I don't remember that, but I've drunk since then. It tends to wash away so much.'

'Perhaps now that you are married you will be able to remember that drinking washes away the memories, but not the actions.'

'I shall not forget. No matter how much I try,' Fox said, nodding.

'I showed you how two moderately decent people can so easily learn to detest each other.' His father turned slightly. 'You've been a young fool.' Then he moved enough so that his face was hidden. 'Do not become an old fool like your grandfather. Or like me.'

'I have always been more like Grandfather than like you,' Fox said.

'That would not be something I'd be proud of.'

Rebecca sat beside Beatrice in the carriage. This time there would be no turning around. Her home was behind her and the thought of leaving clogged her throat, making breathing difficult and smiling impossible. She just wished not to cry in front of her new relatives.

Beatrice kept adjusting the bonnet, trying to make it fit in a space not designed to accommodate the whole ostrich on top of the woman's head. 'I dare say they could make the carriage tops a little higher without too much work. Why, I'm a little dumpling and the plumes I wear are constantly getting broken on carriage roofs.' She turned to Rebecca. 'Is that why you don't wear plumes? Your height? You don't want them mangled?'

'I... It's not...'

'Rebecca's father wished for her to not outshine his congregation,' Fox inserted. Then he looked at her. 'Beatrice and Cousin Lily will be able to guide you to some of the best shops and seamstresses. You'll have the world at your fingertips and all you wish at your disposal.'

She kept her hands still. Even in the dress

her mother made—that she'd struggled to fit into—Beatrice's everyday wear squashed Rebecca into a corner.

She could never wear the bright colours and feathers that Beatrice sported. And if her other new cousin, Lily, was of the same sort, she doubted either of them would be able to give her guidance on anything she might like.

Andrew studied her face. 'Don't misjudge my wife,' he said, giving Rebecca an encouraging glance. He touched the grey waistcoat under his black frock coat. 'She is quite content to keep the little flourishes of style that suit her so well minimalised on other people.'

Rebecca knew that more of her dismay must have shown on her face than she realised.

'It has taken me months to convince him to wear the tiniest splash of colour,' Beatrice said. 'Months.' She pursed her lips. 'I would love to shop with you, but don't expect that it will all be scarlet and red and vermilion. Vermilion. My favourite colour. While I pretend...' she dragged the word out '...to want my husband to brighten his clothing, I quite realise he is best suited in the more sombre colours.' She appraised Foxworthy and leaned forward. 'Foxworthy, on the other hand, has always favoured the bold.'

Beatrice leaned forward, almost touching Fox's cravat with a wave of her hand.

'You had on quite the bluest waistcoat once,' Beatrice said to Fox, 'and a pair of red riding gloves. Do you still have them?'

'I'm sure, dearest cousin. I think my valet has hidden them away.' He hardly seemed aware of his own words and his eyes had a bit of tiredness smudged under them.

'I should paint your portrait in them.'

'There is hope for me then.' A shimmer of lightness shone in his face. 'If you could fix this nose and make me look like I did before.'

'You are more distinguished now.' Beatrice studied him with the same glare of the vicar staring at a child who'd just pummelled another. 'And it would be a contrast. The waistcoat. The gloves. The eyes, and then the bit of scarring.'

'Would you have liked it quite better if they'd taken my nose completely off?' His words were even lighter than before, laced by a hint of laughter, but a hint of grit hid somewhere in them.

'Oh, I don't know.' Beatrice studied him. 'It might have been gory for a portrait, but still, a hint of shadow would have corrected that. It truly isn't your features I wish to capture, but what is beyond them.'

'Then I fear you will have quite the difficult portrait,' Fox said, the merest challenge in the tilt of his chin. 'A portrait of a few bones. A hank of hair and some smiling flesh.' He gave a whimsical shudder.

Andrew moved in the seat, pulling his coat into a more comfortable position. 'I'd really like to see how Beatrice's brush paints you, Fox.' He lowered his chin, staring across at his cousin. 'You know she sorts out her thoughts about a person as she daubs paint on canvas. You might...' he squinted at Fox '...be painted as a ferret with a broken nose.'

Fox raised one finger, twirling an imaginary whisker. 'My ferreting days are over. So I must pass on that considerate offer.' He leaned forward, took her gloved hand and dusted a kiss in the air above it before settling back into place. 'Besides, I will hardly have time to spare as I'm sure I'll have so much to catch up on when I return to London.'

'Oh, you could easily make time for a portrait sitting or two,' Beatrice chirped.

'I doubt it,' Fox said, 'though I would so much like to do so. I fear, because of my dashed charm, you might be inclined to make me even more charming than I am and I simply could not bear to have it in my mind that your picture of me outshines the one of your husband.'

He leaned forward. 'Do you still have that quaint little estate you owned before your marriage?'

She nodded. 'Yes. Ghastly Green is still mine. But Andrew gutted it. Completely altered it. It doesn't look like the inside of a nightmare now.'

Andrew sat straight, uncrossed his arms and stretched a bit. 'Only took a few superficial changes. You'd hardly recognise it now. As soon as the gardens are finished, we plan to sell it. Should make a tidy profit for Bea.'

'Let me lease it for half a year.' For a moment, his face darkened, but then the brightness returned. 'That will bring it into springtime and have a chance for the grounds to be complete.'

Beatrice smirked and leaned forward. 'How could I not—if you promise to pose for a portrait later?'

'How could I let you waste your time so? Consider that I'm newlywed and your dear new cousin Rebecca might wish not to be thrust into the hustle and bustle of my mother's world so quickly.'

'Well, when you put it that way, how could I possibly refuse?' Beatrice said. 'But later on I may insist on a portrait.'

'That you may,' he said. 'Although I may insist not to sit for it.'

'The house is not to your taste,' Andrew said. 'No gilt. No gold. No oversized mirrors.'

'What? No oversized mirrors? How will I survive?' Then a bit of tiredness returned to his eyes and he looked at Andrew. 'I'd rather no one around the *ton* knows I've moved.'

Andrew's pose didn't change, but his eyes left Fox and moved to Beatrice.

'Of course I can keep a secret,' she said. She crossed one arm over her chest and tapped her chin. 'Or I could at least find out if it's possible.'

'You'll have to let your mother know where you're living, though.' Andrew stretched to the confines of the carriage.

Fox's eyes locked on to the passing countryside and his answer was little more than a grunt of agreement. Then his eyes met and caught Rebecca's. No humour. No smile. Nothing.

In that moment, she decided the fake Foxworthy might be a lot easier to live with than the true one.

Chapter Fifteen

Andrew and Beatrice had invited them in. Foxworthy had refused nicely. Beatrice had started insisting, but Andrew had put a hand on her arm. That single touch had completely changed Beatrice's attention.

The couple had stepped out of the carriage at Andrew's home, their backs to the vehicle window. Andrew told the driver where to take Foxworthy and Rebecca. Just enough light remained in the day that Rebecca could see Beatrice lean into Andrew and touch her earrings before the carriage horses moved again.

Rebecca stared out the window while the carriage pulled away, not wanting to read in his thoughts that he didn't have his cousin's enthusiasm for marriage.

Fox watched her, smiled one of the polite smiles, but didn't speak. Only seconds before she'd thought it grand that a couple could communicate with only a glance, but now she wasn't so sure.

Rebecca moved tighter into the seat, trying not to think of anything but the bounces of the vehicle.

The carriage plodded along to the house Beatrice called Ghastly Green and each bounce jarred an ache inside her. She pulled the pelisse closer, wishing it blocked the night's chill.

Then they jolted to a stop in front of a house that stood in a shadow rising to the stars. Two murky lights shone in the very lowest window, and a light at one of the upper windows could have been the reflection of the moon.

She couldn't see Foxworthy's expression, but she could hear his silence as he helped her alight.

He held an arm out to her at the steps, and she paused, staring at it a moment before taking it, not quite understanding why he offered help. The extended elbow was more the surprise to her than anything else. And the few little steps into the house looked mountainous.

She took his arm, held herself tall and moved with him.

'We had an eventful Tuesday,' Fox said,

opening the door for her to precede him into the house.

She nodded, feeling like those feathers of Beatrice's after they'd been bumped on the carriage roof too many times.

Her head spun when she moved and she touched her stomach. She would never make it if she didn't have something to eat. A biscuit even. She didn't think she'd had any food all day, worried the dress would not fit.

They both stopped. The coachman had insisted they wait until he had stirred the staff enough to light the way.

Fox waited, rocking on his heels.

'Which way is the kitchen?' she asked.

'I have no idea.'

'I must find it.'

'We can go upstairs and find a way to ring for a servant. That will probably be quicker.'

She paused. The stairs loomed and she didn't even want to raise her head to view the top of them. She didn't move.

He put an arm around her waist. 'Come on, Rebeca. You can do this.' Even in her state, she could hear the rumbling caress of his voice, but she was so tired it hardly seemed she was in the same room with her body.

'I'll see to a meal in a few moments.' He tightened his arm, steadying her. He kept one arm on the stair rail and her snug at his side. If her feet gave way she wouldn't fall. He guided her up the dark stairs and into a tomb-dark house.

At the first floor they reached, he walked down the hallway. She could hear his hand sliding along a wall. A knob rattled.

He opened the door. 'We can wait here.'

'Yes,' she said, moving into the room as carefully as she would have crept into a crypt. Enough light shone in through the open window curtains that they could make out the shapes of furniture.

The rooms didn't smell of dust as she'd expected, but of paint and starch and newness.

Within moments, footsteps sounded in the hallway and a halo of light touched the entrance.

'In here,' Fox called out.

A servant, silver hair mussed, looking dazed and with a lamp in each hand, entered the room.

Fox took one of the lamps and held out his hand for her. The servant led them up another floor of stairs. 'The master and mistress's sitting room,' he said. 'On each end is a bedchamber and each has a dressing chamber with a stairway entrance so servants can enter and exit without disruption.'

'Bring us some refreshment,' Fox said, instructing the servant away. 'Whatever is quick.'

Then he walked to the door at one end of the

room and opened it. 'Ah,' he said. 'The private room for the mistress of the house.'

Curiosity giving her a burst of energy, she peered into the chamber.

He held the lamp and walked to the corners of the room, examining the wall. Her head turned, but her eyes followed his movements first, then focused on the furnishings.

A room with soft colours and a hint of blue in the ceiling bordered by a line of hand-painted swirls with one little angel dancing around at the corners. Another corner had an angel resting on his stomach with his hands on his cheeks.

He put down the lamp and guided her to a soft chair at the edge of the room. Then he pulled the top cover from the bed and wrapped it around her and the chair, tucking the covering close.

He left, and she relaxed.

When he returned, he brought a tray and put it on the bed. He left for a moment and then walked in with a table in one hand and a chair in the other and sat them in front of her. He put the tray closer and sat at her side, pouring her some wine, slicing cheese and putting it all at her fingertips, and then he sat.

She didn't move.

This was the same man she'd seen lying on the bed, battered and bruised. She turned away slightly and her shoes bumped his boots, and she pulled her body tighter.

'Excuse me,' he said.

'You take up more space than I remembered.' She spoke the first words in her mind.

His head dipped a half second and a smile edged on to his lips. 'I take up less than I expect.'

'I don't know what to call you. No name seems to fit you because I thought of you as Vicar. And that isn't right.'

'In time you will settle on something.' He studied her. '*Husband*, perhaps. Perhaps not.'

'That does not feel like you at all.'

His laugh soothed her ears in the way of a warm stove reaching cold fingers. 'You would think it would as many times as I've proposed.'

'I would think you wouldn't want to mention that.'

'My dear, I worked quite hard to gain that reputation.'

'Twenty-four hours a day?'

'I even worked harder on Sunday.'

'Never a day of rest from it?'

His breath flowed into the room. 'I didn't need one.'

'That doesn't bode well for me, then.'

She took a piece of cheese and held it towards him.

He shook his head, lifted the bottle to pour

more wine into her glass, and she moved the glass aside and held it. He set down the bottle with a whispering thud. 'You are quite fond of the truth, so I thought I would experiment with it.'

'Experiments have gained many advances in knowledge.'

'You're starting to sound like…my father.'

'He's most kind. Except…' Except when he threatened to toss her and her father out of their home. But he was the earl and determined to have his way.

She finished her wine and placed the empty glass on the table. He poured liquid into it and picked it up, sipping from it.

'Oddest thing,' he said. 'The quiet doesn't seem so loud when I am with you.'

'It's not quiet. We're talking.'

'But we're only two voices.'

'Isn't that enough?'

She wasn't quite sure if he smiled or stilled or what. But he leaned to her, taking his finger and trailing it down her cheek. Little bursts of warmth touched her. His finger sparked life in her body. Making her feel not so tired. Strong. She was awake again. Refreshed.

'I would hope it is enough,' he said.

He cupped her face in the way of holding delicate china and shut his eyes. Lashes dusted his cheeks and he didn't move, taking in the feel of her face. Then his eyes opened, serene and liquid.

'The reason I stayed from you for three weeks was not because I feared the illness in the household.' His words rumbled, but in a way to give security, as if the thunderstorm's strength was so far away that no lightning could ever touch near. 'I knew that I could not be with you without wanting to kiss you. And I thought that perhaps tonight would be the night for our first kiss.'

'It will be my first kiss,' she said.

'That is quite the responsibility on me then.' He touched her chin, holding it. 'Would you like to see how it feels?'

She didn't answer. She wasn't quite sure how, or what to do.

But she didn't have to move. His lips touched hers, feather-light, but alive, sending the feel of him throughout her body.

'That's not what I expected a kiss to be like,' she said.

'Better?'

'It's much better.'

'That was hardly worthwhile of the name,' he said.

Someone knocked on the door, but it wasn't the entrance door.

'Give me a moment,' he said, dipping his

hand to take the last bit of cheese and pop it in his mouth. Then he borrowed the lamp, going through the door to his bedchamber. She heard him speaking with someone and instructions on where to place the light and water.

When he returned the second time, he dotted a cloth against his chin. He'd left the coat and waistcoat behind. His shirt was loose from his trousers.

His jaw was smooth. 'You shaved.'

He tossed the towel onto the table beside the door. 'Absolutely.' He smiled and put his hand on the table near her, leaning so that his upper half surrounded her without touching.

A woodsy scent touched her nose. She felt that he'd wrapped himself completely around her.

'If you don't like my shaving soap, I can get a different scent.'

He then pushed himself away. His face was still, studious. If he had been a true vicar, she would have thought him beginning a prayer. 'Rebecca.'

The single word. He bathed her in it, and she absorbed it like nectar.

He held out his hand as if inviting her into a dance. She stood, and he walked them to her room.

With the slightest movement, he controlled

the air. She leaned forward, pulled in his direction by the strength of his gaze.

'So good.' He finished the words on a kiss, nestling against her, and the soap scent danced into the back of her mind, joined by warm male skin.

He held her and stilled. She reached up, trailing fingers along his face.

'I wanted to be able to feel you with my face and not worry about scratching you.'

'It does feel soft. Scrubbed. Different than I expected.'

'What did you expect?'

'I don't know, really.'

'I feel stronger than any army when I hold you. That to be allowed to hold you is to grant me the power of the sun.' He turned, resting the side of his face that hadn't been marred against hers.

She felt the sunshine he talked about. The warmth that grew with each movement he made to lessen the distance between them.

He picked her up, lifting her in the same method of lifting a bundle of flowers randomly gathered and not wanting to damage a single petal. Then he put her on the bed just as gently.

He moved, holding himself over her on his elbows.

'I was wrong.' His breath touched her lips.

All she could see was his eyes and he closed them, moving closer. 'Before. That was not a kiss. This is a kiss.'

Lips touched hers, but she didn't feel them because she felt so much more. Her senses captured every place his body rested against hers.

He lingered, his movements soft, delicate.

When he rolled to his side, he pulled her even closer, guiding her in the movements of helping remove his shirt.

Each touch of her fingertips against his skin released a sensation that closed away more and more of the world, until all that was left that she could see or feel was where their bodies joined or her eyes took him in.

Time changed when he removed her clothing. She could feel the garments being pulled away, but it was as if each stirring of air against her was from his breath and each cloth that slid away was imprinted with his hand.

When he held her breasts and the curves of her body, her fingers trailed his skin. She didn't have to tell herself what to do, or wonder if she did the right thing. Every movement brought them closer with the same unseen guidance that blooms used to grow closer to the sky.

His hands encircled her hips and he positioned his body even closer, running a hand over her leg and wrapping it around him, taking even more time to kiss and caress and give her an awareness of him.

Then his face was again above hers and his lips parted, and he somehow guided her with his eyes, making her aware of his movements, attentive to every nuance of her.

His lips brushed her face while he pulled her close for a moment and then moved back, watching her responses.

Her hands clenched at his back, pulling her against him tight—tighter than she would have believed possible.

When he rolled aside, she lay very still, trying to pull the pieces of her body back into herself.

Covers floated over her and she realised he'd stepped from the bed and gathered them from the floor. Then he slipped back into bed beside her and the room got very, very quiet.

He felt her slide just a bit from him. She pulled the covers tight against her body and didn't settle back against him. No part of her touched him.

The quiet in the air sounded different. Much like the first moments when waking in the middle of the morning in a strange room. Or when waking after thunder shook the house and not quite having a knowledge of what had just happened.

Fox rubbed the back of his neck, then rested

his head in his hand. A marriage alone. Just as he expected.

Then the covers at his side rustled and a pinch nipped into his arm.

He turned on his side and she pulled back into herself, snugged the covers close at her neck and looked at him.

'You just pinched me.'

She nodded, eyes wide. 'Yes. To wake you.'

'I was not asleep.'

'Well, Mrs Berryfield told me that it's natural for a man to fall asleep after the act and it is dangerous for his heart and can cause an apoplexy. She said a husband should be pinched awake after such an event to keep the blood flowing or it pools in his head and causes damage. She said it is advice all the women of the village give their daughters.'

'Any other advice I might need to watch for?' He propped himself on one elbow and put the other hand at her waist. The grip on the covers tightened.

'If a pinch doesn't work, I have the pin cushion to be kept at the bedside. She said to blame the pain on a spider bite when needed, but I couldn't do that—blame a spider. She said a man needs to hear the little love words.'

'Oh.' He leaned closer, brushing his nose briefly against hers. She even smelled like a home should smell. Maybe a bit of perfume, a bit of baking and a hint of husband.

'What little love words?' he asked.

'They didn't tell me what you would say.'

'Me?' He pulled his head back.

'Yes. She said a man has to say love words afterwards so he hears them from his lips. If he falls asleep afterwards without saying them, he forgets it is not all about himself. And then there is the risk of apoplexy to worry about.'

'Oh.'

'She said that is why some men die so young. They did not learn how to behave properly after the marriage act.'

'Do you believe that?' he asked.

'Well, she said it was important that men believe it.' She pulled the covers close. 'All the other women seemed to think she was right. I suppose there is some truth to it.'

He bent to kiss her again, and she scooted away.

'I would like to hear some love words.'

'I'm not good with speech after tender moments.'

'Do the best you can. They told me I might have to work with you on that.'

'Rebecca.' He chuckled and reached to pull her into his arms.

She tightened and averted her face.

He burrowed his face into the warmth of her neck, rotating a bit so he could feel more of her against his skin. 'You feel like happiness. Like fairy tales are true. Like being bathed in sunshine.'

He pulled back. 'And how do I feel to you?'

'Hairy.'

He grunted. 'Oh, Miss Rebecca. That does not work. You will not fall asleep without some love words to offer on your own.'

'I like hairy.' She loosened her grip on the covers enough to touch his cheek, sliding her hand back. 'It feels strong—even without the prickly whiskers growing. And then the hair on your head, soft, silken, straight. And then the bit on your chest, curling.'

'I think I shall have to work with you on love words as well.'

'Very well. You may begin.'

He moved, lips touching the side of hers, breathing his words against hers. 'The best are whispered against the skin.'

His lips lingered, feathering, whispering with movement, giving her the words silently, letting them flow between them through the brushes of touch.

Chapter Sixteen

Foxworthy didn't leave her bed in the night. No reason to traipse across the way to the master's chambers.

His jaw ached. He'd been trying to take such care in lovemaking that he'd almost injured himself holding back.

He propped himself on one elbow, watching her sleep. He reached out and with a thumb and forefinger circled her wrist. Perhaps too slender. But soon he'd have someone assembling a staff. Someone to hire a cook who could tempt her to enjoy the meals.

He slid back onto the bed, staring at the ceiling. She'd not have to clean or do any duties but pamper herself. He was thankful he'd not been born a female. That would be such a boring life.

Hair being curled into ringlets. Layers of clothing. Choosing meals and trying to pick out just the right cloth for the new dress and nattering on with the servants about this and that and then teas with friends and then more of the same.

What a pitiful way to spend the day. It sounded much like drinking the same wine, singing the same song, visiting the same clubs, and repeating the same story appearing in the same newsprint.

He was fortunate. He knew it. Extremely.

And extremely boring. True, he could make people laugh and sing, and that was a skill of sorts. A good work, if you will. But even as everyone around him laughed at his humour, he bored himself. Perhaps that was why he married.

It was and it wasn't.

That irritation that she and her father felt he wasn't good enough had festered during that three weeks. Even his own father had muttered that perhaps Fox should reconsider as Rebecca was a decent sort and the earl did not like feeling that he'd… And then he'd stopped grumbling and left the room.

Fox knew—to be told he couldn't have something only made him determined to have it. Perhaps that had more to do with those other proposals than he realised. The women were married, and he liked the half-second look in their eyes that told him more than they dared say aloud.

He rolled to look again at his sleeping bride. The innocent.

The vicar had once confided to the earl that Rebecca had awoken crying, upset she was not good enough to be the daughter of her parents. She'd dreamed that they had tossed her in a rubbish heap because she had been playing with her doll instead of giving the toy to a little girl who didn't have one.

Oh, he had reserved a front-row seat in hell. He only wished he had not brought her along with him.

Her hand lay sprawled on the covers, the gold ring on her finger invisible in the darkness. Already he felt it choking him.

Rebecca woke and stared up at the ceiling, trying to place it. It was the first time in her life she'd awoken not in her house.

She dressed in her second-best dress, but even the curtains mocked her clothing. The fleur-de-lis woven into the fabric seemed shaped like laughing faces.

Then she walked into the main sitting room.

'If you like this house, let me know and I will make an offer on it.' Foxworthy stood at the sofa, a pen in his hand and the ink open on the small table in front. Five pages lay scattered about. Words lined them. The chair was beside the table and looked more as if it had been kicked aside, rather than moved.

His shirt was on and buttoned and so was his waistcoat.

'I did not expect you to be an early riser,' Rebecca said.

'I am not.'

The charmer was gone. His unshaven face. His hollowed eyes. He reminded her of the person she'd found face down, only this time his hair was mussed.

'In fact,' he continued, 'I'm about to call it a night and go to bed. But I had to finish these first.' He pointed the pen nib at the papers.

'What is it?'

'Notes for the instructions I believe will need to be carried out to make this place comfortable within the next few days. Andrew said that only the barest of staff is here, but that is a beginning. I've listed the results I wish and have written instructions as I see fit. Do you have any suggestions before I give it to the butler?'

A butler. To have a maid of all work would be grand, but that was only one person. What did one do with only the *barest staff*?

He folded one page and put it in the pocket of his waistcoat. Then he handed her four pages.

She saw meals listed in a handwriting more scrambled than legible. She could make out: Brandy. Wine. His valet to be relocated. A list of items to be brought from his former home.

'If you would rather live at the family town house we can do so. It doesn't matter to me. But our rooms will be a distance apart. You will be sharing a sitting room with my mother. And while I believe she will learn to get on well with you, she's always expressed the deepest concerns about any woman I might marry.' He gave a silent chuckle and turned his back. 'She had reservations about my finding someone good enough for me.'

She didn't hold a lot of hope for getting along with her mother-in-law. The earl was a peaceable man and if he could not tolerate his wife, then it was likely Rebecca couldn't please her. Particularly as Rebecca had quickly wed the only child. But even if the woman hated her, Rebecca would give her the respect due.

'I care for my mother,' Foxworthy said, turning back. 'I know she sees me better sometimes than perhaps she should. If she expresses concern for my marriage, it has nothing to do with you.' Fox dropped the pen on to the table. 'It is just the way she talks.'

'I have heard the women in the village talk

about how a mother often has trouble accepting the woman her son marries.'

'She will love you, of course. But it has been an eventful few months and she wasn't expecting my marriage.'

'What is on the paper you kept?' she asked.

He patted his pocket. 'I'm putting another man on the task of asking about the man who has the gold buttons on his coat. Someone will remember seeing it. I will have my revenge.'

Her jaw dropped. He had been almost killed and now he wished to prod the villain into more action.

'Revenge is not for us to take.' She pulled the fabric of her skirt wide. 'And I gave away my mourning dress. Black is a very unhappy colour for me to wear.'

The edges of his lips moved upwards. His hand reached towards her. It was as if he directed her attention away from himself. 'You will look fetching in any colour. But don't expect to wear black any time soon.'

'Your spirit will be the one that pays for the revenge.'

'A price I am willing to be responsible for. And should you need new mourning dresses, please do not hesitate to select several. You may spare no expense. Have a grand time with it.'

'This is not something to laugh at.'

'I'm very serious.' He picked up the pen, grabbed another sheet of paper and wrote again. 'I'm instructing that you should have all the dresses you wish in the year following my death. I wouldn't want you to be limited in colour, though. Feel free to push the boundaries of good taste. It would be expected of my widow.'

She shuddered. 'I don't feel like a wife. Pushing me into widowhood is unkind. It makes me wonder if you are trying to find a way to get out of the marriage.'

His head moved back and his eyes opened a bit wider, but the rest of him stilled.

'You don't have to worry.' His voice flowed silken. He finished writing, put the cap on the ink and dropped the pen to the blotter again.

'I would like not to.'

His eyes caught hers with the strength of a vise. 'You had three weeks to change your mind.' His eyes held hers too long. 'It's a little late now.'

'Are you talking to me, or to yourself?'

'Both of us.'

'You were good. You were good when…'

'When I could not move and talk. That helped a lot.'

This time her fist rested against her chest. She opened her mouth, but no words would come.

Her stomach flattened against itself on the inside, squeezing into a ball.

He stared at her. 'Even my mother understands discretion.'

'Your discretion?'

'Her own.'

He went to his room and shut the door. She did not have the courage to follow, but knew it would only make things worse.

That afternoon, a maid brought her a ball of wool and knitting needles. The wool didn't pull over the knitting needles as easily as she would have liked, but the window light in her room was so much better than at the vicarage.

She disliked knitting, but there would always be a new baby needing new blanket, or another woman whose gnarled fingers couldn't knit herself a new shawl. And since she didn't enjoy it, it definitely counted as a good work.

Rustling noises from the other side of the sitting-room door alerted her that he woke. She even heard the low rumble of his voice and another person speaking, which let her know his room had the same design as hers. A dressing chamber attached and beyond it lay a narrow stairway for a maid or valet to ascend and descend.

She moved to a window facing the street. A carriage rumbled by, lanterns bobbing.

An hour after his room quietened, she went to it and knocked. When no one answered, she opened the door to a deserted room. He'd left down the servants' stairs.

A maid had even been in and straightened, she supposed. Each item lay exactly where it should and had nothing to tie it to the owner.

She walked into his dressing room. The scent of leather wafted and she noticed three pair of boots by a bootjack. Several hats rested on hatstands. A shaving kit lay in precise perfection.

A wardrobe stood in the corner. She opened it. Various folded waistcoats greeted her. She pulled one from the top, marvelling at the feel of silk. Threads, dyed the colour of the blue cloth, swirled at edges of the garment. Even the cloth-covered buttons had tiny, nonsensical designs on them. She lay the clothing aside and picked up another waistcoat and saw buttons with blue stones in the centre. She didn't know if the centre was glass, or true sapphires or some other kind of jewel.

Carefully, she folded them back, making them match the precise way the others were arranged. She trespassed into this man's world.

She was alone. Alone at a time when she should be with someone.

She wouldn't be able to live this way.

She rang for assistance, because she knew she would need it. She was on the wrong side of the pull.

Fox walked into Boodle's, the most likely place to find Peabody, even though he would have recognised the man had he attacked him. But Fox had heard Peabody's name and he wasn't certain he'd not hired the culprits. If he had, he'd pay.

His blasted head felt like it had been kicked by a horse. It had never ached so before the attack. He'd wanted to see the man who'd caused this.

He saw Lord Havisham sitting at a table, brandy in front of him. Havisham waved him over. 'You've been gone for a while. Hiding from a husband?'

'No. Found someone's.' He touched the crook of his nose.

The laughter swirled. Havisham stood, thumped Fox's back and put a drink in his hand.

'Well, it's not been the same since you've been gone,' Havisham said, sitting.

Dawson Davis put his club-sized hands interlaced at the back of his head. 'When you sent my wife the flowers before, I had the butler remove your note and replace it with one of my own. By the way, you got my wife's given name confused with her sister's.'

Fox turned to the reddish-faced man. 'Didn't I propose to your wife once?'

'That's what the paper said. She claimed you didn't, but she preened a bit. Now she thinks herself more beautiful than any siren and expects me to put her on one of them chair, chariot-type things and walk her from room to room.' He shut his eyes and shook his head. 'Even the children have to speak nicely to her now.'

The man next to Davis glared at Fox. 'You owe me.'

He turned to the disgruntled eyes. 'How do I owe you? I don't think I've ever proposed to your wife. I may have danced with her once, but...'

'No.' The word had the finality of both letters. 'You never danced with her. She was feeling quite ignored. I bought her some emeralds. And I've been telling her she's the centre of my heart.' He shrugged. 'If you'd danced with her, she might not have missed the proposal. I keep having to reassure her it was an oversight on your part.' His eyes narrowed. 'It was an oversight. Wasn't it?'

'Yes. Of course.' He nodded. He didn't remember the woman at all.

'Are you going to ask her now? There's a soirée coming up.'

'I can't propose now. It might hurt my—Rebecca.'

'And who might she be married to?' Havisham asked.

'Me.'

The man choked, snuff trickling down his jaw.

A high-pitched voice from behind Fox snarled out, 'The canine has been penned?'

Foxworthy turned to see Millicent Peabody's husband standing behind him. Peabody's white hair curled at his ears, The lace on his cuffs had length enough to cover both hands and accentuate the longish fingernails Peabody favoured.

Fox smiled, his attention completely focused on Peabody.

'Without the visit from your hired toughs, I would never have met Rebecca.'

Peabody's gaze didn't waver. 'I heard you were beaten, but I had nothing to do with it.'

'I know you did.'

Peabody's lip hooked up enough so that his smile almost touched his ear. 'Foxworthy. I didn't do it. So soon after you proposed to my wife? They would have looked to me first and asked no questions. I would likely have hanged for killing a peer's son. I'm a merchant and have few friends in society. It would have been a quick trial and a snap of the neck for me. I am fortunate you lived.' His lips straightened. 'Fortunate, but not happy to see the sight of you.' His eyes flicked over Foxworthy's face. 'I would have done a better job on that nose.'

'They said your name.'

'Would they say their own?' Peabody raised his hand, scratching his ear. 'You'll have to find someone else to congratulate for your meeting with your wife. I had nothing to do with it. In fact, I have you to thank for making me realise how much I dislike my wife. I sent her away the next day. I'd been thinking about separating from her and, when you proposed, it made the way easy for me. I accused her of carrying on behind my back. Now I have no one to please but myself.'

He bowed to Foxworthy. 'I was angry at first, but then I realised what a favour you did for me.' He smiled. 'Thank you.' Then he turned. 'Not that I mind one hair that you received a beating.' He snorted as he walked away. 'You did me such a favour, Foxworthy.'

Chapter Seventeen

The town house didn't look that elaborate from the outside in the night air, but when Rebecca stepped inside, the butler's eyebrows rose to his powdered wig. If the maid hadn't travelled with her, she doubted her word would have been trusted enough to be allowed inside the house.

In moments, she was shown to a sitting room where a woman held a dog so fluffy that it yelped before Rebecca realised it wasn't a pillow.

Foxworthy's mother rose and naturally assumed a portrait pose. Lamplight bathed her and she sparkled. Rebecca didn't know if glass beads were sewn into her dress or real jewels, but the woman's gown twinkled as she moved.

She glanced at the woman's head, expecting to see a tiara, and more lights winked back at her. As she moved closer, Rebecca counted five jewelled pins resting in the woman's hair, not truly holding it in place, but ornamenting it.

His mother's eyes dripped gratitude. 'Dearling,' she said. 'I will be for ever in your debt for saving my son. I want your happiness above my own and I welcome you into my heart. I did wish to be with my son on his wedding day, but...' She sighed. 'I could not leave London.' She shrugged. 'Not to mention that my husband did write and tell me it was to be a very simple affair as he didn't expect our son to attend.'

She raised her brows. 'He did. Didn't he? Fenton did show up?'

Rebecca nodded.

Air whooshed from her lips and she coughed. 'Forgive me for being a little ill. The maid says this sickness has visited each of the servants in turn and now they've all recovered, but I'm the one sniffling.'

The countess looked at Rebecca and took both Rebecca's arms in her cool hands. 'And you are the sainted girl who found my son and kept him alive. You will have my gratitude for ever.' She sighed deeply, stepped back and appraised Rebecca. 'My husband wrote that Fenton proposed to the vicar's daughter and that you're like a daughter to him.' Her eyes narrowed. 'I'm sure his father pushed the two of you together. He thinks he knows best for everyone.' She shut her eyes, shaking her head. 'I will always have a place in my heart for the earl and an oath or two.' She gauged Rebecca's response. 'Did he mention me?'

'The earl usually speaks with my father. I have hardly talked with him recently.'

'Well, I suppose that's good. I see him every other year or so. But we are getting to an age where I suppose we should be together more. Especially if there might be grandchildren about.' Her eyes lingered on Rebecca's stomach. 'Dare I get my hopes up that it is the reason you wed?'

'No.' Rebecca felt her cheeks warm. 'I'm not expecting a babe.'

Then her eyes turned to Rebecca. 'When my son married, I just assumed there would be a child on the way as I couldn't really see him marrying for any other reason.' She leaned her head towards Rebecca. 'For as many times as he's proposed I would have expected him to marry long before now.' Then her face brightened as much as her gown. 'He was waiting for you.'

Rebecca wasn't sure about that.

'If I had known you were going to arrive today, I would have planned a welcome. You must meet the entire family. Particularly my sister. She thinks her sons walk on clouds because they married while my Fenton was…well… proposing.' She held her chin held high. 'And he married a vicar's daughter. He always has to cut a bit of a splash. This will show my dear sister who is always boasting about her three sons being so perfect.' She shrugged. 'My nephews are boast-worthy, I admit. But I expect Fenton to outdo them and my nephews did marry suitable—well, mostly suitable women. That Beatrice is a bit unhinged in my opinion.'

'She's quite nice.'

'If you say so. Took a parasol or a cane or some sort of object to her first husband's carriage and nearly demolished it, I heard. She's a bit impetuous, like my Fenton—' Her eyes widened. 'Not that he owns a parasol or cane. But he does have some frightful-looking gloves.' Her brows furrowed. 'Have you seen them?'

'No.'

'Burn them if you do see them. I told him no one has ever died from wearing a pair of black or white gloves.'

Rebecca swallowed. She'd never seen any other colour of gloves on a man.

'You seem perfect for Fenton. Much better than that—that one tart who chased him round the room at his first soirée. She was fast on her feet and faster on her back.' Her mouth made a perfect bow and the whites of her eyes enlarged, then she lowered her face and her voice, but only to give emphasis. 'If not for the misfortune of the old duchess dying suddenly and leaving behind a very stirred-up widower, that scheming harlot would have lured my boy straight into marriage. I tried to tell him.'

Then she moved her head sideways almost to her own shoulder and wrinkled her nose. 'It's not as though I didn't do almost the exact same thing to his own father—though he wasn't my first choice—but I was much younger and prettier, and the earl was old enough to know better.' She sighed. 'Men.'

When her mother-in-law blinked, Rebecca knew she was to say something, but she wasn't sure quite what.

She grasped at the first words that she could find. 'I was hoping you might be able to give me advice on how I might do charitable works to help others.'

'Charity?' The countess paused and put the dog onto the sofa. He jumped to the floor. 'Charity? That's for less fortunate people.' Then she straightened her back and smiled. 'You really don't have to help others. It's not a requirement to be a countess.' Her nose pointed straight at Rebecca. 'The babies are necessary, though. Don't forget that. Very important. One must either produce them or accept responsibility for it.'

'Charity?' Rebecca repeated.

The countess paused. 'I do know a seamstress who would be grateful for extra work.' She tapped her chin.

'Perhaps…someone in need?' Rebecca asked.

Foxworthy's mother reached to a bowl on the side table and took out a biscuit and held it out. The dog jumped back to the sofa, sniffed, then crunched down the food.

'Well, my dear. I don't know of the seamstress's fortunes, but she is looking stooped.' She beamed. 'We cannot just let our funds sit around and grow dusty. Where is the charity in that?' The countess raised her head. 'I always told Fenton that whomever he married would not be good enough for him. But that was because I expected him to marry one of those…' She leaned forward and whispered a word Rebecca had never heard before. She straightened her back. 'I never expected him to marry an innocent. Not unless he was somehow trapped.' Her eyes narrowed. 'Tell me truthfully, did my husband somehow orchestrate this? It would be just like something he'd do.'

'The earl did rather wish for the marriage.'

'My husband does like to meddle. Goodness knows he's tried to interfere in my life enough times.' She picked up the dog and brushed her nose close to his.

'Charity?' She sniffed and waggled her head. 'I suppose you were raised by quite a strict mother.' She stood straight. She paused. 'Charity.' She shivered in happiness. 'The word does make one sound rather benevolent and would look good in the newspaper if one was not too incautious and did not help people of too-low quality.'

Rebecca nodded. 'I would be happy if you'd help me shop for a few things. I'm used to having neighbours and here I know no one.'

His mother looked at the dog, loosening her hold. 'If you're sure… Oh, I simply could not. I simply could not intrude so. Unless you really wished it.' Her eyes brightened in hope.

'I'm sure Foxworthy will be pleased.'

'Don't you call him Fenton?'

'I don't think he likes the name.'

She frowned. 'Well, I can understand that. When he misbehaved, he was called Fenton. His tutor called him Fenton. But that was only when he was young. Surely it can't matter now. And I'm sure he expects you to call him such in private.'

'No. He doesn't want me to.'

'Well, you know better than I on that. Most of what I know about him I've found out from the papers.' She indicated a portfolio on the table.

Foxworthy's mother paused, looking down

at her dog. 'Forgive me. I must take Squiggles outside. I don't think he can wait until the maid arrives.' She called over her shoulder, 'Please make yourself at home. And feel free to look at the book.' She nodded her head to the portfolio.

An oblong book took up most of the space on the wood. The book creaked when Rebecca pulled open the cover. Newspaper pages had been affixed to the paper.

The stories started with a yellowed page mentioning the earl's marriage. A few soirées were mentioned. The death of the earl and countess's daughter earned only a sentence. Rebecca's father had told her that the earl's daughter had died only days after birthing a babe that had been much too small to survive.

She turned the pages, seeing story after story of Fox's exploits.

A later clipping told of his cousin Andrew's father and of a child born outside the marriage.

More and more was written about Foxworthy proposing to married women. Stories of him racing horses, but riding backwards. Of a man having to be restrained from pummelling him after Fox proposed to the wife.

Then the stories turned to mentions of Beatrice and her painting of his cousin Andrew, including an engraving likeness of him with only a leaf for covering. A mention of Andrew and

Beatrice's wedding—only they called her the Beast. A caricature of her at the marriage, beautifully dressed, but with a handprint on her bottom. Andrew had tufts on his ears in that one. Stories of Beatrice selling her art to help people in need.

Yet another proposal by Foxworthy to a married woman.

The duke, Fox's cousin, marrying a woman he'd loved since his youth.

Another story about Fox proposing to a married woman.

Footsteps sounded and she looked up, and up, straight into the eyes of her husband.

She shut the portfolio, feeling as if she'd been caught stealing from the poor box.

His lips turned up. Her inner guilt turned instantly into the feeling of being misdirected. She wondered if it was really fair to count a smile as a lie.

'I see you found your way to my mother's house. How remiss of me not to bring you. Please accept my request for forgiveness.' He said the right things and perhaps he meant them, somehow. And his eyes did remain on her, but he wasn't looking at her the same way her parents had looked at each other.

'Of course. No need to even mention it.' She

heard her voice, but it didn't even sound right to her.

'I'm pleased you understand.'

'I've been reading about…you.' She hoped her eyes weren't the same as his, but that would be expecting a lot from two little brown dots above a nose.

That caused a flicker of something—she didn't quite know what.

'I've managed to keep my name in the papers.'

'When you proposed to me…was it habit?'

The charmer in him disappeared. 'Habits are not usually considered good things.' His face blocked further questions.

She opened the book again, turning a page. She didn't like the stories. She closed the book and stood. She might as well leave if they were going to stay in a room stuffed with silence.

Then his mother rushed in the doorway. She held out her arms, thin bangles glittering along her wrists. The dog scampered behind her, then stopped and barked at Foxworthy.

'Son. You're home. At last.' His mother rushed forward, taking his shoulders in her hands, holding him for a brief second. He stepped back, but his lips tilted up. The dog moved quickly into the space in front of the countess and padded at her skirt. She stepped back and lifted the ball of fluff into her arms.

'When you wrote to tell me that you'd been scarred, I was devastated. And now I see how truly bad it is. We will get through this, son.'

Rebecca took a swift step sideways, accidentally jostling Fox's side. He put a hand out, capturing her waist, steadying her with a quick pat. And just like that, he'd frozen her in place with a warmth she couldn't leave. And she wasn't even sure she liked him.

His mother gazed at Fox, then she swallowed. 'I'm so sorry that your face was damaged. You look so rough, but you are still so precious in my heart.' She clasped the dog closer and the little animal raised his chin at Fox and yipped before snuggling deeper into her arms.

Rebecca stole a glance at him and studied his face. He had silken lashes, a mouth so perfect she could not imagine better and she could have gazed at him all day. No wonder he did as he pleased.

'Yes,' his mother commiserated. 'Isn't it sad?' His mother sighed, looked at the dog and shook her head.

'But without it, I would never have met Rebecca,' Fox said. He moved closer to his mother.

'She has a generous heart and I can understand your father pressing her to marry you.'

She raised her head. 'For once he knew what he was doing.'

Something cracked. His face. Just a bit of the smile faded away.

Rebecca took that as a bad sign.

Rebecca watched him sweet-talk his mother into laughter, then he held out his arm for Rebecca to take and suggested they leave together.

His mother's eyes were so hopeful, and his with just a touch of command in them, that she couldn't say no.

He didn't speak again until after they reached the former Ghastly Green, a place which Rebecca could not even imagine ever deserving of the name. The oak glistened and the pale curtains hung like royal robes on the windows.

His footsteps were behind her when they walked into the main sitting room.

'So how did my father coerce you into this marriage?' he asked.

'He didn't.' She spun around. 'I overheard when he threatened to force my father out of our home and I already knew, if I didn't marry the new vicar, we would have to leave. We'd accepted it.'

He took off his black gloves and dropped them onto the sofa. 'He would never do such a thing.'

'I've not known him to lie.'

'Sweet...' he looked at her '...you bet on the wrong horse.'

'You could not throw me out without providing for me. Society would condemn you.'

'And my father would put you on a pedestal as proof that I had no worth whatsoever, except the funds my grandfather passed on to me.'

He took off his coat as he talked, then threw his coat over the gloves. 'Grandfather did that. He circumvented Father with all that he could and passed his wealth on to me. Father only received the entailment, but enough came with it that he can live well. And he cannot circumvent me, short of killing me. As much as we disagree at times, he wouldn't do such a thing. Though I can't say that for everyone.'

He touched his jaw. 'I still feel it, but not so badly.'

'Our own injuries always take longer to heal than others'.'

'And did you learn that on your jaunts to do good works?'

'My mother told me. She tried to tell me all she'd learned and all my grandmother had learned from tending others.'

'So your inheritance—your birthright—is to tend others.'

'Yes. I thought there would be more to do

here. But it's different when you've not known everyone their whole lives. They have no trust.' She took off her pelisse and draped it over her arm.

'Give them time,' he said. 'If anyone can earn such a thing, it is you.'

She walked to her room and put the coat away.

He followed.

'Half the time when I hear your voice and look towards you,' she said, 'I don't recognise you. Only if I close my eyes can I match you with the hurt man I found. You healed so differently, both on the outside and inside. I miss the way you looked. I miss the other person I knew.'

'There was no other person.'

'This person wants to smile and cajole and dance through the days. When I thought you were a vicar and I imagined all good thoughts, I put a person inside you that I conjured from the inside of me. Not what you truly were. Now, I see the clippings about you and I can't even imagine the hurt man and the well man are the same.'

'I couldn't smile. I hurt. I didn't care about anything but the pain stopping.'

'And now do you care about anything?'

His hand stopped. He'd unbuttoned three buttons down on his waistcoat.

'I care about many, many things.' He paused. 'Too numerous to mention.'

He finished unbuttoning the waistcoat. 'Another question for me?'

She shook her head.

'I would have expected you to ask if I care about you.' He slid the waistcoat off.

'And you would have answered with some flowery words. Some fluff. Perhaps true, but still… fluff.'

'Wouldn't they have made you happy, though… at least for the moment?'

'I think they might have made the emptiness inside me a little bigger. It almost swallows me now.'

He stepped nearer her, reached out, touched one of her arms, stilling her, and with his free hand brushed back a wisp of hair at her forehead. 'I must beg your pardon. You have caught that from me.'

'No. It is from the world around me. I know no one. Not even you. The servants trip over their own feet trying to please me and I don't even know what to ask them for.'

'Just be yourself.'

She raised her brows. 'I am. That is the problem. Everyone else is at home. I am not.'

'Give yourself time.'

'I'm giving you time,' she said. 'And it's not easy.'

'Time?'

'I always expected my husband would fall in love with me. Quickly. It happened to my parents. My mother's first husband had died and I was only a month old, and my father heard of her, and her big heart, and he wrote to her and asked if she would consider marriage.'

'They were fortunate.'

'And he was a vicar. They have hearts full of love.'

'You saved my life and that counts for a great deal.'

'I wish you had reciprocated some other way besides marriage. Perhaps a soirée for the villagers instead of a wedding breakfast.'

'You accepted.'

'You were the vicar, to me. Even though I had heard the words that you weren't, some small part of me could not believe otherwise.'

'Perhaps you find weakness in others comforting. Less threatening.'

'Perhaps.' The calm look stayed on her face, she was certain, because if he could see inside her, the charm would have burst from him.

'Don't love me.' He had no emotion she could detect. 'Let my care for you be enough.'

'I don't love you.' At the moment she was

having to remind herself that pretend kindness was a virtue, perhaps even bigger than true kindness because it had to be gripped from the insides and forced into place.

'My honest wife.'

'And your care is not enough, but it is all that I have.'

He drew her over to the edge of the bed and gently encouraged her to sit down on it.

She moved, shifting more to the other side of the bed. 'I miss the country.'

The bed depressed on his side. He pulled off a boot. 'I don't miss my father and I refuse to live in the country.' He dropped the boot, and she heard a thud and a bump. 'I have put my foot down.'

'Well, you're about to lift it again to climb into bed so I'm not worried.'

He took off his other boot, tossed it and the noises reoccurred. 'Other foot is down as well.'

'Keep them there.'

'Is that really how you feel?'

'I am a stranger living in a new world that I must learn to like or I'll be miserable.'

He turned around and pulled her, still sitting against him. Strong arms imprisoned her. His face rested against her hair.

He touched his cheek to the side of her face

and moved gently. The warmth soothed her, erasing some of the ragged edges inside her heart.

'You will. You'll find plenty of ways to help others.'

'And what about you?' she asked softly. 'How will you keep busy?'

He pulled her on to his lap. 'Don't worry about me.'

'I don't know if you love me more than your second-best pair of boots.'

'I lost my innocence about love when I was very young.'

'I even loved my cat, Ray Anna, and I miss her.'

'Send for her.'

'But Father needs her.'

'With my father, it's almost as though I only want to be with him to joust words with him. He is the man who insisted I be sent to university. I tell him I thank him because my joyous school days taught me to drink and wager, and to pursue new adventures.'

'And me? Do you want to be in the same room with me?'

'I do. Very much.'

His kiss was the touch she'd waited for and wanted, chasing all thoughts but one from her head. He did want to be in the same room with her, as long as it was the bedchamber.

She could feel the heat starting where he touched her arms and flowing into the rest of her body, but she didn't move.

He stopped, looked at her and left the room.

She listened closely, expecting to hear the loud crash of a door slamming and then silence. Instead, she heard little thuds and little slams. He didn't leave the house.

Rebecca stared at the darkened window, wishing she hadn't been so irritated with him.

But the marriage didn't feel right to her. It felt like having a large ring on her finger, made with gold, and having a bit of chipped glass for the jewel.

She stared at the band on her finger. She'd thought a wedding ring would feel comforting, not heavy.

And she had so little to do in her life now but be a wife and the only place she was to be a wife was the bedroom. And of course, later, the nursery.

She had no need to sew. That would be done for her. Her letters were all written. The maid had made certain each and every last flounce in the main sitting room had flounced just the right amount. Rebecca had told the maid she could take care of it, but the girl's eyes had widened in fear and she'd needed reassurance that she was doing a perfect job.

No wonder the women spent so much time and care on hair and appearance. They had to do something.

Her good works simply could not consist of telling others how well they did. She could not bear it.

Something thumped again in the main sitting room.

She crossed her arms. Marriage had not brought her more good works to do. It had ceased them. She stood.

She moved to the writing desk. Picking up the corner of the desk, she edged it askew. She let it crash to the rug.

She heard a muffled sound in the sitting room. He was making entirely too much noise.

Rebecca stared at the desk as she touched her forehead. She was giving herself a headache.

She slapped her left hand down on the desk, the ring giving a clunk when it met with the wood.

No answering thwack. She moved to the door and opened it.

Walking inside the main chamber, Rebecca locked her eyes with Foxworthy's. He stood by the writing table. Several books had been pulled from the bookcase and were at his feet.

Crumpled paper littered the floor around the wastebasket at the other side of the room. She didn't want to go near him. She would smell his shaving soap, or the leathery scent that always surrounded him, and she would forget how dangerous he could be to her heart. She mustn't love him. She mustn't love anything about her new life. It was all built on the shoulders of a man who blinked away everything she believed in.

Without a word, she walked over, picked up one wad and straightened it. The page was blank.

'Someone will get that,' Fox said.

'Yes.'

He walked over to the lamp and turned it up.

'Can you not be still?' she asked.

Fox looked over his shoulder for a few seconds, not commenting, then he moved to the fireplace. He lifted the fireplace poker and raked it through the bottom of the fireplace, moving the coals about, causing sparks.

She picked up the books and put them away.

A few minutes later, he moved to the window tapping his finger on the moisture condensation, causing little dots.

'Don't your friends have anything planned for tonight?' she asked.

He examined her face. 'I want to stay home. I have done that on rare occasion.'

'I suppose the newspaper will next say, "*Where was Foxworthy?*"'

'I'll just send someone out in the morning to give a tale of my exploits to the newspaper.'

She popped the cork from the ink bottle and looked at him. Picking up the quill, she flicked the tip of the feather along her jaw. 'I'm sure I could do that for you.'

She leaned forward and pretended to write on the crumpled paper. 'Foxworthy proposes to an unmarried woman. And marries her.'

Then she dipped the pen and wrote.

What was he thinking?

He stood behind her, reading over her shoulder.

'That she was beyond compare and the fairest in the land.'

Balderdash. She dipped the pen twice for enough ink to underscore it.

He took the pen from her, their fingers brushing, sending her insides fluttering. Until she looked at the writing.

It was time I married. I had tried everything else.

'Consider me your good work,' he said.

'I asked for good works to do, but you are not one of mine. You are your own.' She looked to the ceiling without moving her head much, then back at him. 'If I have learned one thing from my father, it is that you cannot deter people from the course they are determined to take.'

'You cannot possibly believe that. Your father is a vicar. It is his job to put people on the path to goodness.'

'It is his job to show them that it is an admirable path. It is their job to take the steps.'

He took the pen and splashed it into the ink.

I would think you would be happy to have me home.

She flipped her hand out, palm up. He put the feather flat across her palm. She collected it and wrote.

But you are not.

When he reached to take the quill from her hand, she used her other to put the cork in the ink bottle and left her hand resting on the cork. 'Perhaps you should say your thoughts to me.'

'I have none.'

'To repeat?'

'Rebecca, I have carefully and methodically wasted my education. I took no time with learning when I was in school. It is a wonder I can write my own name. I took no interest in politics, while knowing I would be expected to move in my father's footsteps at some point.'

'Why did you do such?' she asked. 'Waste your education?'

He put his hand over hers, bringing them closer. 'Why should I do more than enjoy my life? The path was chosen for me. I was to be the peer. It is my role. That is the education I needed. To be able to gather eyes to me. To bring attention to the events I attend. I never lack for invitations.'

'From the ladies? I bet their husbands are not so thrilled about that.'

'I have not been lonely.'

'I read every bit of writing I could get my hands on, then read it again. Your father loaned my father books and I read them and told him and my mother what they said as we ate our breakfast and dinner.'

'I have not read a book of my own free will in my entire life.'

'Well, I have not drunk an entire bottle of brandy in my life so I suppose we are both green in certain areas.' She paused. 'I plan to keep my inexperience. What of you?'

His lip turned up a bit at the side, then lost its humour. 'I see no need to change.'

'Truly?'

'No. I cannot live my life staring out a window, tossing paper into a basket or pulling books from the shelves and only seeing words that tire me, suffering the feeling that I am imprisoned. And while you are the most lovely gaol mate a man could ask for, I cannot be a different person. Just as I can't change my hair colour, I cannot change the feeling of imprisonment.'

If he continued the rituals of before, then in time their marriage would mean little more to him than an unfinished book. If he left the house alone at night, she couldn't imagine good coming of it. He would not be out helping a blacksmith shoe a horse.

'I cannot be your gaoler,' she said. She moved, pointing to the stairs. 'The door isn't locked. And I don't wish to be in close quarters with someone imprisoned.'

Little eruptions of anger, so foreign, began to bubble inside her and she didn't know if she'd ever felt that much irritation before.

He studied her, one quick perusal, and she could tell he knew exactly what she was thinking.

He stepped forward, but she stood her ground, arms crossed.

Then he ran one finger up the length of her arm, taking his time. He doused the anger, banishing it completely, causing an awareness of him that she didn't want to feel. An awareness that warred with her control, pushing aside everything but knowledge of the sensations of pleasure he could bring to her.

Which caused a second, different burst of anger. How dare he?

At that moment her body didn't care one speck that she was fuming. All it cared about was what his hand was doing and how he stood casually, black coat, simple cravat, and yet so different than anyone she'd ever seen before.

Then he reversed and retraced the path he'd made on her skin.

'I don't like you very much right now.' She used her willpower to keep herself immobile.

'I understand.'

She believed him.

He ran his finger up her arm again and tilted his head closer. His breath touched her lips, teasing her with the memory of his kisses.

'You know what you're doing.' She challenged him with her eyes, or at least tried to. Even her eyes were traitorous—as misguided as her body, which kept wanting to melt against him.

'You can be angry at me again afterwards,' he whispered, his voice rough, but softening her resistance. 'Let us just stop this moment for a time and find some joy in each other, and you can return to this exact moment of not liking me—later.'

'I don't want to leave it.' She needed to stand her ground with him. Very much. But the earth was crumbling under her feet.

'We should have some comfort from each other.' His face had the softness of someone lost. And she remembered how close he'd been to death.

'Comfort is important in a marriage. Step aside from your feelings and return to them tomorrow.' He caressed her waist with one hand, and she felt cherished and small and protected and all the things she'd hoped for. Just from that one touch.

'It might not be that easy.' She blinked, taking him in on the upsweep of her lashes. 'It's very hard to be angry when—'

'Not as difficult as you'd think, sweet.'

'For me, it would be.'

'You can sort it out later.' He took her hands, unfolding her arms, and his lips moved so near that she didn't know who closed the distance, him or her. 'You will have time.'

Their bodies pressed together, and he pulled her even closer. His hands at her back and then lower, guided her into the firmness of his body.

He wanted her. She could see it in his eyes and feel the proof of it.

She opened her mouth to speak, but she had nothing to say. The kiss at the edge of her lips erased the memory of everything except what his touches felt like.

'Unbutton me,' he whispered.

She reached to untie his cravat.

His laugher was silent against her face. 'That's not what I meant,' he whispered. 'Not at all.'

His hands clasped hers. 'I will show you.'

Chapter Eighteen

She'd dozed when he'd moved from the bed and he'd leaned down and kissed her. Whispers and caresses had lulled her back into half sleep. But somewhere between the dreams, she'd noticed he'd donned his boots.

She was right, she realised, when she woke fully the next morning. Anger rushed back into her, forcing her from the bed. He'd not needed boots to make the walk to his room.

She reached and grabbed the covers from the bed, wanting to remove all the scent of him from her world. She pulled them into a heap on the floor and threw the pillows on top, leaving the bed completely bare.

She dusted her hands against each other. Let the maid think what she wanted. Let the world think what it wanted.

A knock caused her to turn towards the door. 'Enter,' she called out.

The maid opened the door. The woman's eyes didn't flicker.

'Yes?' Rebecca spoke without inflection.

'The countess is here. She wishes to see if you might allow her to escape a bit of loneliness and have the joy of shopping with you.'

'Please let her know it would be grand.' Rebecca didn't move until the door closed. The servant had to have seen the bed and would have to know that Foxworthy wasn't in the house—or if she didn't now, she'd know when he returned. The villagers were not as close as the walls in this world made people and yet they could piece together every action around them.

She had a choice, whether to live in the world with her head up or down. She lifted her chin.

Ringing the bell to summon a servant for help, she began the task of readying herself for the day and for the rest of her life.

In moments, a different maid entered and Rebecca dressed to go shopping with her mother-in-law.

Fox's mother chatted constantly when they both sat in the vehicle and rode to the seamstress's shop.

The older woman's chatter was only interrupted by an occasional cough. 'The honey mixture my cook makes works wonders for soothing me, but I didn't take any this morning because I thought I was completely well,' she muttered. 'I do beg your pardon. I wouldn't have visited you this morning if I'd known I was ill.'

Rebecca reassured her mother-in-law that she'd often assisted with all sorts of illnesses in the village and was only sorry for the other woman's suffering.

Then the talk continued with mentions of what kind of dress Rebecca might like. Apparently the seamstress did not visit her customers often because she had small children she watched while she worked and her husband was a tailor who worked in an adjoining side of the shop.

After Rebecca and her mother-in-law had selected several fabrics for new dresses, she noticed another woman entering the shop. The husband stood at her side.

'Countess,' he greeted her with a tip of his hat and a bow.

Her mother-in-law turned. In moments she had introduced the older couple and her new daughter-in-law.

Both the man and woman's jaws dropped.

'Married?' the man, Mr Smothers, asked Rebecca. But the one word had many newspaper pages behind it.

She nodded.

'We would love to have the three of you to the soirée we're having tomorrow,' Mr Smothers said to the countess. 'I know you declined due to ill health, but you appear to be so much better now and we would be happy to share your joy.'

'Oh, I'd love to, but I can't answer for my son,' the countess sputtered the words out. 'I believe he is quite busy setting up his household. We are shopping for furnishings now.'

'Are you certain?' he asked.

The countess reached into her reticule. She pulled out a folded paper. 'My list. For fabrics. Yes. We've so much to do.'

He raised a brow.

'Their house is severely in need of curtains,' the countess inserted, putting the paper back into the reticule. 'Severely.'

'And how long have you known Foxworthy?' Mr Smothers asked Rebecca. She'd seen a serpent with a more friendly face, even though the man did smile. But it leaked a bit at the side.

'Long enough to wed him,' Rebecca answered.

'That could only be a day from what I've

seen of Foxworthy. He wastes no time asking a woman to the altar.'

She stared at him with the same look she'd given Mrs Oldman's bottom. She could do no better.

'True. The first day I met him, he was at my feet.' She paused, looking upwards and telling herself it was not true deception because he did propose rather quickly, but her conscience made her admit a bit more. 'Almost the first words he spoke to me were a proposal.'

'I wish you the best of luck.' The man chewed the words carefully and did all but use a fingernail to rake the last syllable from his teeth. 'Please do attend our soirée. We'd love to have you.'

'Thank you.' Her mother-in-law clutched Rebecca's arm. 'We must be going. We've many fabrics to select elsewhere.'

He lost the last of the sincerity in his smile, nodded to them and left.

'My dear,' the countess said. 'I believe my son may have proposed to Mr Smothers's wife.' She shook her head. 'Before he met you, of course. And always in jest. His proposals were all in jest.' Her eyes wavered when she realised what she'd said. 'Before you, of course. Before you. I'm sure he did just as I did and took one look at you and knew you'd be perfect for him.'

'I will just assume every woman I meet has been proposed to.'

'That isn't safe either. Some haven't and I've heard they felt left out.' She patted her reticule. 'The paper I have… Last night, I tried to make a list for you…but it was hard to separate the true proposals from the rumours. And I realised they were meaningless.'

'I'm sure they were meaningless.' Truth should have felt better and not so much like a bit of poison going deep.

'Well, you must have dinner with me tonight. No reason for us not to spend some time together.' The countess smiled, head moving forward in encouragement. 'I'm married to a man who likes to spend quiet evenings at home and I know what a pall that can be. My son is not one to sit at home and read.'

'He's more likely to be read about.'

'Yes.' The countess beamed. 'He's quite famous. And now the two of you can share that.'

A rosy glow illuminated the sky when Rebecca stepped inside her house. The butler opened the door for her. What did one say to a butler who seemed to have no inclination to speak but the barest syllables?

She walked into the sitting room. Foxworthy stood, an elbow on the mantel and lips in a grim line. She didn't think he knew she was in the room. This time, pages of newsprint littered the floor at his feet. He held one rolled sheaf in the hand at his side.

'Why do you drop things to the floor so easily?'

His head moved up quickly and he looked at her, then at his feet. He took a step away from the fireplace. 'I just wanted to tell you,' he said. 'It's nothing. I've been through it many, many times. You get used to it.'

'What was said?'

'Just the usual wedding nonsense.' He slapped the end of the paper against the mantel, but the lines at the edges of his mouth had fallen away. 'It does mention the mix-up with the vows, only it declares that was done at your request.'

'I would never have thought of it.'

'And the paper suggests I must have thought you were married or I would not have proposed.'

'I suppose you should save the clipping for your mother.' Rebecca walked forward and took the paper. 'For her memory book.'

Rebecca spread the print to read it. Her head moved forward when she saw the picture. The groom did have a shackle at his leg and the bride held the other end of the chain. And the bride did look like her and the groom like Foxworthy.

Foxworthy looked over her shoulder. 'They did not do you justice at all. I will speak to him about that.'

She turned. 'No need.' His eyes didn't have a care.

With his left hand, Fox snatched the paper from her fingers, wadded it and tossed it into the fireplace. The embers caught the paper alight and it blazed up before turning into ash.

'I wonder what he would make of the fact that Mr Smothers invited us to his house and that you have proposed to Mrs Smothers,' Rebecca said.

Foxworthy didn't speak, just examined her face.

'I saw him as we were visiting the seamstress,' she said. 'He invited us for a soirée, but the countess thought it best to decline.'

He still didn't speak, but now his face had returned to the expression he'd had when he didn't know she watched him, only darker.

She took a step back. 'You did start it, you know.'

Fox's smile returned. His face softened. He might have just stepped from the calming waters at Bath.

She gathered the papers where he'd stood and

wadded them. He had one boot on a page. She glanced at it and then at his face.

He reached down, picked it up and hurled the page to the fire.

'The paper has to sell copies. No harm done.' She added hers to the rest, standing back from the burst of heat.

His gaze seared into her, muddling her thoughts. Then her memory returned to the sight of him lying in the grass face down and her rolling him over. She missed that person. The one who couldn't talk and didn't leave the house.

She took in a breath that lodged in her throat. Was that what she'd wanted in a husband? It somehow didn't seem very noble.

She spoke quickly to push those thoughts aside.

'How long have your parents lived apart?' Rebecca moved to the fireplace. She appreciated the warmth from the grate because she could see so little in Foxworthy's eyes.

'After my older sister died, my parents never seemed to stay in the same house for very long.' He didn't move.

'Why? They both seem nice enough.' She touched the handle of the poker, feeling the warmth of the iron, and used it to push the rest of the paper into the flames.

'It's just the way it's always been. I was perhaps ten when my sister died.'

'It makes no sense to me. Your parents both have generous hearts. They would have needed each other for comfort.'

'No. That was not how it settled out. They grew wicked tempers with each other. It's best that they live where they are happiest. My mother's home was once owned by her own grandmother so I understand her connection. And the country estate has been in Father's family for even longer. They are close to their past memories.'

'A family should be together.'

'A husband and wife, you mean. Just because my parents aren't in the same room doesn't mean we aren't a family. We are.' He took one step closer. 'We are every bit as much a family as you and your father were. We just look to others for conversation.'

'That is not a family to me.'

'It is to us and, as it is our world, you should give it the same acceptance as you have for your own ways.' He moved towards her, brushing a lock from her cheek. 'They're happy apart. They are bound by marriage and even though they aren't in the same house, they are tied together for ever.'

'Tied together. You could not give Byron any views on writing.'

'Rebecca.' The shutters in his eyes faded, but even the small lines that had formed were better than the distance. 'Marriage is a vow. It means something to me. It is a lifelong connection. But it does not mean drinking out of the same tea-cup, or you trying to walk in my boots while I wear your slippers.'

She turned to him. 'Some day we will have children and I want them to have grandparents.'

'They will. My father will teach them how depriving oneself builds spirit and Mother will most likely spoil them senseless. And you will likely be thinking our children have too many grandparents once the tug of war begins.'

'Is that what happened with you?'

'My grandfather wanted me to follow in his footsteps and my father thought him senseless and too shallow.'

'So the tug of war?'

His lids half closed over his eyes. 'No. Grand-father made the rules as he controlled the allow-ances. Everyone answered to him, except me. I could make him laugh.'

'That wouldn't teach a child patience.'

His brows rose. 'I've never claimed to be patient.'

She took in a breath, but spoke softly. 'If you don't make claims of who you are, it is very easy to live up to your expectations.'

He waved a finger in the air, slowly, almost mocking. 'Ah, I do feel an obligation to have a good time. To make an event…an event.' A glimmer of challenge lit his eyes. 'And you should have more frivolous moments.' His voice lowered. 'But keep the patience. It's a virtue and something everyone always appreciates in the people nearby.'

'I think I should have worked harder on developing it.'

'Possibly. This town can be a bit trying at times.'

'I've already found that out.'

His blue eyes speared in her direction.

A pang of guilt hit her. She'd meant that barb and it was wrong of her.

She spoke softly, trying to erase the unkindness she'd just done. 'Secretly, I'd always thought London sounded pleasant on the few times people spoke of it. I just have yet to find the good works I need to do. At home, the people needed me. And if I couldn't help them I could pass the word along and help would be given.'

She straightened the hem of her sleeve. 'Everyone here has so much, or so very little, it doesn't feel like I belong among them.'

'We will go to the Smotherses' soirée. This would be a perfect opportunity for you to meet the ladies of the *ton*.'

'No.'

His eyes narrowed and the blue ice winked through. 'So a marriage of togetherness only is a consideration when you wish it?'

Her jaw tightened. 'I can understand married couples living apart much better now.'

She turned away—so angered at herself. She put her hands close to her body, hiding her fists from him. Her tongue had got away from her. That was wrong. A person who could not control her words could control nothing.

The door behind her shut. And this time no noises let her know he was in the house.

Fox sat at White's. The cards were stacked in square shapes, in tiers, three card-widths high. He'd declined the card game, making a wager that he could stack his cards twice as high as anyone else could, fully expecting to lose.

But the two men who challenged him expected to lose even more than he did and didn't give a valiant attempt to anything but having their glasses refilled.

He picked up a final card and rotated it within his fingers and placed it on top of the tower, which more than exceeded what he needed to win. 'I learned that at university.'

One of the other men reached over and tapped the base, and the cards tumbled. 'I learned that in the crib.'

The others laughed and Fox stood. 'I must be leaving to get ready for the soirée tonight. Besides, if I stay any longer the excitement here will be too overwhelming.' The men laughed again, and Fox left.

Rebecca needed to go out with him so people would know she wasn't a misprint.

When he stepped in the door, he noticed the silence.

He bounded up the stairs, wondering if Rebecca was at home.

She sat in an easy chair, her knitting needles at top speed. She looked up, nodded, smiled and appeared to return her concentration to her project.

'You aren't ready for the soirée.'

Tension formed at her eyes. 'No. I have nothing to wear. I can't go.'

'You need to attend some events with me so people will know you are not a misprint. The soirée will be a good event to introduce to you the *ton*. Especially since it is Smothers's.' And he wanted to see if he could find out if anyone might remember a servant or friend of a friend who had a gold-buttoned coat and who might be capable of an attack.

'I'll be sure to purchase something suitable to wear,' she said.

His head turned to the side. 'You've been shopping with Mother. I expected you to have plenty to wear.'

She nodded. 'I've ordered gowns, but only one has arrived and it's not right.'

'I'd like to see it.'

He stood, following her. She went to the clothes press in her room and pulled out the dress.

Her mother-in-law had asked the seamstress to complete it quickly. After all, this would be the garment the future countess would wear to her first event and everyone would be looking at her. And Rebecca had never seen a dress so elaborate.

A plain white gown underneath, overlaid with a pink silk more sheer than anything she'd ever seen. At the base of the puffed sleeves, an embroidered hem made the cuffs. Then a row of ribbon flowers climbed from the hem to the shoulder of the dress. A matching row of flowers swirled at the bottom of the skirt. She held it up and looked over her shoulder.

'It's beautiful.' His voice rolled into the air behind her.

She looked at it and didn't speak.

'Don't you like it?'

'It's lovely—more than I could have imagined.' She ran a hand over the fabric. 'I do think it's the most beautiful dress I've ever seen.'

'I'd like to see you in it. You'll need help with the corset.' He reached for the pull to summon her maid.

She shook her head. 'No.'

'Why?'

'It doesn't fit right.'

He stepped behind her. She could feel his breath at her neck. Smell the scent of leather and shaving soap.

The seamstress had made a sample top of muslin to make sure the pieces would fit. The sample garment had been perfect.

'It looks like it fits,' he said. 'Let me see you in it.' He rang for the maid.

Then he turned. 'I'll get ready while you're dressing.'

After she put on the garment, she walked into the sitting room, but had to slow because her head spun when she moved too fast.

The plain dress looked as if it had been made

for another woman. The puffed sleeves fell away from her shoulders.

When he walked out of his room, he paused. 'You're right. It doesn't quite fit.'

She shook her head, relieved. 'No.'

'Did it fit you when you purchased it?' he asked.

'I suppose so. The seamstress can alter it to fit.'

'You…are ill?' He leaned forward, watching her eyes.

She shook her head. 'I do have the sniffles your mother had, but I'm fine. I don't want to look too weighty. Your mother thought a babe was on the way when we married. I don't want that. And I'm really not hungry.'

Nothing tasted the same when the cook fixed it. Not like her own cooking. She'd tried to give gentle requests, but the woman couldn't seem to get the flavours quite right—besides, she'd been a cook for a quarter of a century and was quite proud of her skills.

'It's fine if everyone assumes you're going to have a baby. They can count later and figure out the truth. And it wouldn't be the end of the world to have a seven-month babe. Happens all the time.'

'I've always been a bit plump.' She held out the skirt, then dropped it, letting it flow back into place. 'I feel so much better now and the corset doesn't choke me like it did before. It's much more comfortable. I was just slow about sending the dress back to the seamstress.'

'Because you didn't really want to go to an event.'

'Everyone else will know everyone. And they'll be wondering why you proposed to me.'

'Don't worry about that.'

'I can't help it.'

'No.' He walked to her and took her chin, and pulled her face up to his. 'You truly have no need to worry. Sweet, I've pulled off many false proposals and many flirtations when I've only wished to be out the door.'

'I've not.' She wished he could have said it some other way. His being versed in false affection didn't make her feel better.

'You only have to follow my lead. And dance with me and look at my eyebrow or ear as if it's terribly fascinating. That's all you'll need and I'll do the rest.'

'So you'll stay home this time?'

He paused. 'I need to go. I'll let everyone know you're not feeling well.'

She didn't speak until she turned away from him. 'I hope you have a good time.'

'It would be better if you were with me. That is the one way to convince people we are married.'

'I can't tonight. I have no other dresses that

are even close to suitable and it's impossible to alter the one in time.'

'You planned this.'

He turned and left, and she knew he went to the soirée.

Chapter Nineteen

After brief greetings, Fox and Mr Smothers kept to opposite sides of the room during the event, and Fox watched the faces of the men, certain he would have known if it was someone from society who had ambushed him. But he was also certain someone at the event would know who might fit the description of the men.

The violins started and the couples formed for the dance, and Fox couldn't help watch his cousins with their wives.

Andrew chose another partner besides Beatrice and Bea danced with another man, but as the dancers moved, Fox caught the glances between the two. The Duke of Edgeworth danced with the duchess. Foxworthy was fairly certain the duchess hated to dance. Before she married, when the music started, she would attach herself to a frail woman and engage in conversation, and if Fox half looked her way, she darted to the other side of the room. Lily had even slapped him once when he'd not deserved it. Well, perhaps he had.

When the music stopped, Edgeworth and Lily walked to Fox.

'Your Grace,' Fox said to Lily. 'You are looking especially lovely this evening.' He bowed.

'Yes. She is quite lovely,' Edge said. 'I would advise against proposing to her.'

Fox locked eyes with Edgeworth. 'I was married a few weeks ago. Sorry you didn't get the news.'

'I thought we might see your wife tonight,' Lily said, putting a hand on Edge's sleeve.

Fox increased his smile. 'She didn't wish to be out.'

Edge's brows rose and his eyelashes flicked a bit of censure Fox's way.

Fox lowered his voice. 'I did ask her. She has no wish to attend any events yet. Claims she doesn't have anything suitable to wear.'

'Has she not had a chance to buy any new gowns?' Lily asked. 'Bea said she refused her offer of help.'

'She went out with Mother and says she is

waiting for the new clothing. The new gown she has wasn't right.'

'Perhaps Beatrice and I might take her about. Bea has some new paintings on display. We could look at them.'

'I'd like that,' Fox said, giving a bow to the duchess. 'Just please don't let her be around Edge too much. She frowns at me enough as it is. I'd hate her to learn that glare he has.'

Then Fox smiled and darted his eyes to Edgeworth. 'Yes. That one. Thank you for demonstrating, your Grace.'

Lily's fingers tightened on Edge's sleeve.

Fox stepped closer, moving to Edge's other side. 'I think I'm making your wife nervous.'

'No. She just doesn't like you.' Edge's eyes stayed straight ahead and his tone was non-committal.

'That's not true,' Lily burst out, moving her head to look around her husband at Fox. 'I have no dislike of you.'

Edge softly cleared his throat.

She looked at her husband's face. 'Foxworthy is a dear cousin.'

Edge shrugged. 'Yes. But if he ever proposes to you, he will be a dear, departed cousin.'

Fox laughed and moved closer so he could bump Edge's shoulder. 'Please do not get the rumour started that I've proposed to your wife. I doubt Rebecca would find those jests humorous.'

'So your days of proposing are over?'

Fox didn't answer. From the corner of his eye he'd seen a particularly drooping turban in a colour that simply could not match anything and he excused himself to ask Lady Havisham to dance. She paid a lot of attention to others and she would be the perfect person to ask about the man he wanted to find.

Their eyes met. Vultures had nothing on her. He walked to her and bowed.

'I guess you tired of waiting for dear old Havisham to die so we could wed,' she said as he whisked her into a contra dance.

'I would not want marriage to ruin our friendship,' he said as they met again.

'So you and your wife are not friends?'

The dance parted them.

'It seems I hardly know her,' he spoke when they met again. 'She should attend the next event with me. She is having new gowns made—eventually.'

'I heard she's a pious thing.'

'Very gentle of spirit,' he said. 'A lady after my own heart.'

'You *have* a heart?'

'Of course, Lady Havisham. I love you dearly.'

The words fell easily from his lips, but didn't rest so well at his ears.

Lady Havisham smiled. 'I love you every bit as much as you love me.'

Her eyes sparkled.

He swirled her back into the cluster of dancers. He'd told so many women he loved them. Not that it concerned him. Or that they concerned him.

He loved no one. He never had, after Mrs Lake.

Losing her had been even worse than losing his sister and he felt guilt for that. His sister, the stunning fair-haired girl who'd twirled him around in the air and called him Fenton Face, and told him that little boys were made mischievous because goblins sprinkled magic dust on the porridge, so he ate his porridge to get every last bit of the dust.

And then she married and told him she was going on a magnificent journey and he hardly ever saw her again. Then one day his grandfather sat him down and the old earl started talking and started crying. Not little tears. Heaving sobs. He'd not known men could do that.

Later, his grandfather had told him the only reason he'd been able to live was because of Fox. Fox knew it was true. His grandfather would laugh at Fox's jest when no one else could get him to do anything.

'What is love?' he asked Lady Havisham.

'It's a quick word to get people to do what you want.'

'You romantic,' he said.

'I am. For an evil old witch.'

'Perceptive, too?' His brows rose.

'Would you like to hear the secret of my attraction to men and your attraction to women?' she asked.

'You do not have to tell me your secret. It is your vast beauty and quick wit.'

She laughed and it ended with a snort. 'It is because I, like you, appear to be having the grandest adventure of all—life.'

'And are we not?'

'Of course we are. Appearing. Acting.' The dance ended, but she did not release his hand. 'You are newly wed and I am long wed and we both have spouses who are quite content to see the last of us or we are content to see the last of them.'

'And is your life not better for the joy you bring into Havisham's world?'

'Certainly. He is always glad to see the hem of my skirt as it slips from the door.'

'And I am glad to see you as you march into

the doorway. You have taught me more ways of swearing than any man I know.'

'And you, dear Foxworthy, have taught me nothing.' She reached up, her gloved hand patting his cheek. 'You are quite following in my footsteps. Like the son I never had.'

'You have four sons.'

'But it's not as if they are mine. I only gave birth to them. I parcelled them out to Havisham and their governess right away. They often visit the house. I see their carriages while they are talking with their father.'

She stared at his nose. 'You should thank the person who did that to you. Maybe…' Then she shook her head. 'No. Not possible. No one could knock sense into you. You'll always be a dolt. I do love you, but then, I've never claimed to be smart.'

'Do you happen to know a man who doesn't normally grace the social world with his presence, but has a coat with gold buttons?'

The dance ended and she nodded. 'Of course. That would be Peabody's son. He's living at his father's house now that he's been gambling heavily.'

She left him with the touch of her gloved pat on his face, but it burned with the sting of a slap.

The old witch. And he did like her. He could not really fathom why.

Fox left the dance. He knew the road to Peabody's house. But it was dark and he needed light to see the face of the man.

His cousin Andrew's home was across from the Peabody town house. Andrew's butler let him in without question, and agreed to have someone wake Fox if anyone entered or left the house opposite.

That morning, Fox sent a note to Rebecca, letting her know he was at his cousin's house and would be home when his business was finished. But while he waited, he thought about how drawn Rebecca's face had looked the last time he saw her and how he could have put a smile on her face if he had tried hard enough. And why something inside him had resisted when it would have taken so little time and effort to do one good thing.

Rebecca sat at the breakfast table in the formal dining room, looking at the plate. She smothered a cough.

She swirled her spoon around in the porridge. It didn't taste the same. She'd asked Cook not to put as much butter in it, but she should have asked her to put no butter. The woman had nodded and nodded after stammering a good morning, but the food hadn't changed enough. Rebecca pulled up the spoon, watching the porridge drip back into the bowl.

She didn't think plates could make a meal taste differently, but now she wasn't so sure. Perhaps it was the stove. But everything seemed a little off. Or a lot off. The tea was the only thing that agreed with her and the warmth soothed her stomach.

A maid entered the room, her curtsy perfect. 'His lordship's mother is here.'

Rebecca stood, putting the napkin aside. 'Please ask her to join me and if she would like something to eat, give the message to Cook.'

The servant whisked away.

Rebecca sighed and slipped the sleeve of her dress in place, tugging fabric closer to her neck. The bit of lace on the hem of her sleeve tickled her wrist. She didn't want the countess to notice that the day dress didn't fit properly. Nothing—in the new life—fit properly.

The countess swept into the room on an intake of breath, moving with the same steps of just finishing a grand dance. One person could hardly be worthy of such an entrance.

'My dear.' She nodded to Rebecca. 'So pleased to see you. So pleased.' Her bonnet stayed firmly in place, but small beads sticking straight from one side of the headgear bobbed with each movement.

'Thank you for visiting.'

'Where is Fenton?' she asked. 'I hoped I might see him. I must talk with him.'

'He is at his cousin Andrew's.'

The countess's movements froze. Her eyes locked on the porridge, squeezed at the sides and then studied Rebecca's face.

'Porridge?' The countess spoke, eyes wide, touching a glove to her lower lip. 'You're eating porridge?'

Rebecca glanced down to the food. 'I— My stomach was a bit unsettled.'

Her mother-in-law's eyes and smile took up all the space on her face. She took a few steps back, one hand at her heart. 'A child. An heir. And it will—'

'No.' Rebecca held out both hands, palms flat. 'No.'

Her mother-in-law's face resumed its normal proportions after the eyes and mouth shrank smaller than Rebecca had ever seen them. 'No?'

'I can't— I don't know. It's possible. But it's—' Then she looked at the bowl. 'It's porridge. Breakfast. My stomach has been unsettled since—' Since she found out she wasn't in love with a vicar.

'Well, it's not the end of the world. There's

still time.' She waved her hand, casting it spell-like in front of Rebecca's face. 'And if you never have a child I will be happy not to be a grandmother.' Her face lightened. 'It's much harder to lie about your age when the grandchildren start arriving. Unfortunately. And if you never have a child, that would certainly be a laugh on my husband.'

The countess's head wobbled in a superior fashion. 'He was not happy when it took so many years before Fenton was born.'

The countess sat across the table from her and leaned forward. 'I do know it's nearly impossible to live in close quarters with a husband, but I will speak to my son about staying home more, at least for the first few years. It is absurd he would not be here with you. His absence is only good for the talebearers.'

She straightened. 'Which is why I wanted to talk with him.' She rolled her eyes. 'He danced with Lady Havisham last night and she is old enough to be my mother—more or less.'

'Lady Havisham?' Rebecca repeated.

The countess's lips tightened, forming lines at the sides. 'She does not know how to dress. Always dresses much too young for her age.'

'And the Vic—and Foxworthy?' Rebecca gripped the back of the chair in front of her.

'Last night, one of my friends insisted he must

not care for you much, as he was dancing with Lady Havisham and speaking in hushed voices with her, and you were nowhere to be seen. I know my son doesn't listen to me much, but he will this time. He must go about with you.'

Air moved from Rebecca's lips. 'I had nothing to wear.'

'Nonsense. I helped you select the dresses myself.'

'I don't like the one I received as well as I thought.' She sniffed, trying to wish away the cough that wanted to erupt.

Her mother-in-law's head moved even closer. 'That porridge is not agreeing with you. I'll speak with your cook. I cannot believe my son is letting her get away with serving you such a peasant's meal. No wonder you look as if a good breeze could blow you away.'

The countess stared off into the distance. 'I know it might appear as if my son did not want to marry. I suppose that is my fault because I did not set an example and move to the estate with my husband, but I simply could not.'

Her head followed the upwards glance of her eyes. 'Fenton hardly has any of his father in him, except for his looks. I'm afraid on the inside he's a lot like I am.' She shook her head. 'Trust me. That's not always a good thing.'

'You seem quite nice—'

'Oh, I am. Everyone likes me.' Then her nose wrinkled. 'Well, except a chosen few like Lady Havisham and my husband.' She touched her chest. 'But Foxworthy does need to give the marriage a chance. He really must. Or he must at least appear to. That counts a lot in society.'

'Society will soon learn I'm not very used to attending large events.'

'You'll get into the habit easily enough.'

Rebecca nodded, but she couldn't see that happening.

'I'm sure Fenton went to his father's with the thought in the back of his mind that it was time to marry. He saw you and knew that you would fit into the family quite well. The Earl of Arrogance already knew you and liked you. The odds of Fox finding someone we could all three like were very difficult. But he did. And with a vicar's daughter he would know his heirs were not created without his help—so to speak. So he did the wise thing and married you.'

She let out a breath. 'I told him when he was a child that he must always be smarter than he lets on. People like you for wit and charm. They don't like you for…' She tapped her forehead. 'They all want to be smarter than you anyway. Makes it easier for them.' She tilted her head to the side. 'Now I told you that in strictest confidence as my daughter. It is a mother's wisdom and only to be passed from mother to child.'

She stood. 'I will speak to my son the next time I see him and explain that he should take you about regularly for a time.'

Pulling up her glove, she stretched her neck high. 'Remember, your mother-in-law is a countess and your cousin is the Duke of Edgeworth. You could spit on the floor in Almack's and you'd still be welcomed in the *ton*.' She stepped to the doorway. 'But, if the floor is to have such uncleanliness on it, let it be the drool of someone noticing how wonderfully we are attired.'

Then she swept out the door.

Rebecca stared at the porridge bowl and left it sitting. She supposed she could ask Cook what people like the countess preferred to eat in the morning.

Foxworthy waited in the shadows of tree across from Peabody's house, slapping his gloves against his palm and leaning against the trunk, tapping his heel against one of the roots that rain had washed free. He kept thinking of Rebecca and how she hadn't quite looked herself since she'd promised to wed him. And she was a new bride in a town where she hardly knew anyone and it wasn't as if she could walk into a club and build a house of cards.

Occasionally he would run his hand along the turn of his nose to remind himself why he waited.

Finally, he saw someone step out of the house, and his memory of the attack resurfaced. The turn of the head. The tilt of the hat. The one who'd stood by the horse with his face hidden and a cane in his hand. Now he wore a better hat, but it was the same person.

The feeling of being knocked from his horse fuelled his anger and the sound of his jaw cracking returned to his head.

Fox stepped forward, blocking the man's path. He saw the moment of recognition in the eyes.

'Pardon,' Fox said. 'I believe I owe you something.'

The man blocked the first fist. Fox sidestepped the answering punch and delivered a firm one, knocking the air from the man's stomach. Peabody's son stepped back, but righted himself, then lunged and connected a glancing blow to the cheek, but Fox moved aside, dodging the momentum, and slammed backwards with his elbow well enough to knock the attacker off balance.

The man jumped to his feet, but before he could get his balance, Fox gave a punch to the chin and knocked him to his backside.

'Get up five times, get knocked down six.'

Fox kept his fists ready. 'You can choose the numbers.'

The man swore, but he didn't stand. He touched his jaw.

'I know how that feels,' Fox said. 'And then some.' The face was rage-reddened, but hardly old enough to shave.

'Only the fact that I should not have proposed is keeping you alive,' Fox said. 'You nearly killed me.'

'I thought we did.'

Fox stared at him and, when he gritted his teeth, the pain of his jaw returned, fuelling his words. 'You must pay attention to details to be successful. I was most likely still breathing.'

'I thought you'd die. I heard the crack of your face. Your nose was a bloodied mess and it turned Robbie's stomach. No one had wanted to bash in your head again. We were just going to let you freeze. We were kind enough that we wanted your family to be able to recognise the body.'

'Well, that is a detail I wouldn't have considered.'

'You deserved to die.' He spat blood on the ground. 'You disgraced my family. My mother. Father sent her away and she'd done nothing wrong. People laughed at him and she had to leave her friends. My grandmother had to move, too. She cried. Mother, my sister and my grandmother have to stay in the country and my father has a *cousin* I never met before that keeps visiting and sitting in my mother's chair and drinking my mother's tea.'

Fox remembered how he'd felt when his father left and how he'd not liked the men who'd leered at his mother and acted like concerned gentlemen around her. She'd not cared. He'd gone to university then. It was the easiest thing to do.

'You'd proposed to my *mother*,' the one on the ground said. 'It was in the newspaper that she didn't say no and said she'd think about it. My sister can't have a coming out and she's sixteen.'

'My words meant nothing. And if your father had cared for your mother he wouldn't have sent her away.'

'I know he didn't care. Don't you think I see that when the woman is drinking her tea?'

He picked his hat up from the ground beside him. 'I don't care if they hang me or transport me for what I did. You insulted my family. It was worth it.'

Fox took that hit on the chin.

He saw the boy's footwear and recognised the boot. He tapped the toe of his new boot against it. 'Well-made. Not worth it, though.'

The boy turned his head, staring to the side.

'You won't do your mother any good…wearing someone else's boots.'

Fox smiled. 'But you can keep them with my blessings. You're disgracing her as badly as the rest of us did. Letting her down. Following in my footsteps. Yes. You're wearing my boots and making my footprints in the world.'

Peabody's son sneered.

'I'll see your name in the papers some day, too, and I'll know, every man in your mother's life let her down. Every one. Every single one. And how much more distressing it will be for her when the last hope she has fails.'

Fox turned, walking away. He had given Mr Peabody an easy excuse to walk away from his wife. Practically held the door open for him to shove her outside.

He could imagine the look on Rebecca's face if she heard what had happened to Mrs Peabody.

A flung boot hit his shoulder, but he didn't turn back. He couldn't change anything that lay behind him.

Sleep fogged Rebecca's mind, but she roused from her slumber, aware from the light filtering in that she'd fallen asleep in her chair. She coughed, wishing she had some of the honey tonic her mother-in-law had mentioned.

She sniffed, her head feeling stuffed. She stood up and reached for a handkerchief.

Then, the tickle in her nose grew. She coughed, holding the handkerchief over her face. And coughed again.

The door to the sitting room opened, and Foxworthy strode in. He had a fresh bruise on his cheek and that relieved her. It was unlikely a woman had put it there.

'Rebecca.' In a heartbeat, he stood in front of her.

'Are you ill?' he asked.

She stepped back so she could dot the handkerchief to her nose. Then she touched two fingers to her throat. 'It feels a little sore.'

'Is that why you don't fit your clothes? A sickness?'

'Just a little cough. Your mother had it. And my forehead… It feels warm.'

He reached to the pull and summoned a maid. 'Tell the maid you need a poultice. Some honey. An infusion of herbs. A physician.'

Almost at the same time someone knocked on the door.

'Enter,' he called out. A maid carried a lamp into the room. He took the lamp and held it to shine on Rebecca's face. 'Has she been acting sick?'

The maid looked at Rebecca. 'No.' She turned

to Foxworthy. 'No. She's healthy enough.' Then her eyes changed. She smiled and her voice softened. 'She's strong enough to have a healthy babe.'

Foxworthy's head snapped to Rebecca's face.

She used her full range of motion to shake her head in one definite movement.

No one moved, until Fox turned to the maid. 'Bring some tea. Brandy. Honey. Toast. And send for the physician.'

'No.' Rebecca's voice stopped the maid. The servant stared at them both.

He fixed a gaze on the maid. 'Get the honey. Send someone for the physician.'

'Wait outside,' Rebecca told the woman.

No one moved.

'I am not sick,' Rebecca said. 'I do not want any medicines and I will not see the physician.'

'Are you certain?' He brought the lamp close enough she could feel the heat.

'I am certain,' she said.

'You may go,' he told the maid. 'But tell the servant who can move the fastest to be prepared to go for a physician at a moment's notice.'

The servant dashed to the door and it shut with a click.

Rebecca strode away, the handkerchief in her hand. 'I have never had a physician attend me in my life. All I need is a handkerchief. I am sleepy and wish to go to bed.'

She stopped, kept her face from him and shut her eyes. 'Your mother was here. She wishes for us to appear together so the rumours will not swirl so greatly.'

She stepped into her room and with a flick of her wrist managed to reach up and undo the buttons of her dress. He followed her into her room. The shoulder of her gown slid down and bit into her skin as she managed the last fastening. She didn't feel right disrobing in front of him.

He didn't seem inclined to turn around so she did. The dress slid to the floor and she picked it up, put it across the foot of the bed and slid under the covers.

'Let me rest. Apparently I am ill.' She turned away, rolling to her side, and pulling the covers high over her neck and bundling down into them.

His footsteps sounded on the rug. He stood at the side of the bed, then sat on it. He rolled her over.

His finger trailed a lock of hair at the side of her face, brushing it into place. 'You must take care of yourself.'

'I do. I'm sleepy and I don't feel well.'

'But you're not sick?'

'No.' She corrected herself. 'No more than a

cough and my head is quite stuffed. Your mother has had this and she is over it. This is not sick. This is just a sniffle.'

He left the room and didn't close the door. Light remained. She heard his footsteps and muffled noises continued. When all was quiet, she slipped from the bed and peered into the sitting room. He lay on the sofa with a pillow under his head and his feet extended over the arm.

The coat could have been on the floor, but she didn't see it. His feet were bare. He wore trousers still.

His eyes didn't open. 'Go to sleep, Rebecca.'

Chapter Twenty

He walked in the entrance door of his house and one look at the butler and the man backed away without taking Foxworthy's hat. Fox had been to see his mother and let her know she was not to meddle in his marriage.

She'd agreed wholeheartedly, then began telling him a few thousand things he should do concerning him and Rebecca. It was not marriage talk, she assured him, she had so little experience in that.

He moved up the stairs and stood in the doorway. Rebecca sat by a lamp, reading. A wadded handkerchief was on the table beside her. He didn't think she'd heard him moving up the stairs.

The paper sounded crisp when she turned the page.

He settled against the door frame, twirling his hat, watching.

He couldn't wait long enough for her to read another page. 'Yesterday I spoke with the man who attacked me. It's over. I have no need for revenge. It wouldn't mean anything. My jest just went awry.'

'That's thoughtful of you.'

He put his hand inside the hat, holding it on one finger and spinning the hat. 'Not really. I realised I wouldn't gain anything from it.'

'It wasn't because it is the right action to take?'

'That is not how I choose what to do.'

'Perhaps you mislead yourself.'

'I do. Right to the brandy. Right to the soirées, the tasteless humour and the people who share the same sensibilities I do.'

'I doubt I have any of those.'

'I doubt you do. Odd, isn't it?'

'Why didn't you propose earlier and to someone else if you wanted someone so different from me?'

'Never said that.'

She coughed. 'I believe I should rest.' She picked up her book.

'You're escaping me. You don't wish to talk.'

'Not if I feel criticism from your words.'

'I don't mean them that way.' He didn't.

'Nor your actions, I'm sure.'

'I sent you a note letting you know I'd be out.'

'But I didn't know whether to believe it or not. And then your mother arrives telling me not to put stock in the tales that are going to be spread about concerning you and Lady Havisham.'

'I received a speech as well. But I had to see the person who ruined my face. I had to talk with him. And you had no clothes to go to the soirée. It is as if you purposely arranged so that you would not be on my arm.'

'Perhaps I did. Perhaps I wanted to see if you would find someone else for it.'

'I don't think that would count as a good work.'

She stood, not looking at him. 'My throat is hurting from all this talking.'

'Then don't talk.' In one step he was at her side. He smiled and leaned closer. 'We can go for a carriage ride and I will tell you about the best places in London.'

'That does sound grand.' She put a hand to her forehead. 'But I don't want to go about in the air. It will be dark soon and that's not healthful.'

'You would probably say the night air is not healthful for me either and I would have to agree. But I'm going out.'

He was out the door before he realised there was no place he wanted to go, except for a carriage ride. He didn't want to go alone either.

Even though he was certain Rebecca had the same sickness his mother had had, something about it concerned him.

He shook his head. He'd give her time to get some sleep, then he'd return home to make sure she was fine.

If anything happened to her, everyone he knew would hold him responsible. Even Lady Havisham. And even the part of him that remembered what it was like to be Fenton.

Rebecca woke when her bedroom door opened. She rose on her elbows to study his expression.

'How are you feeling?' She imagined the same look in his eyes when he proposed to someone who was married. He stood, shirt-sleeves dangling, legs muscled in the same way as a stallion's, his hair dark and his eyes light.

She touched her throat. 'Much better. It doesn't hurt at all.'

He moved closer, sat on the bed, leaned over and dropped a kiss on her lips. The flutters of warmth pushed away the uncertainty inside her.

'How are the good works faring?' he asked.

'I'm lost without them, but I'm sure I will get better at finding new ones as time goes one.'

'I'm sure you will also. One of your good works can be to go out with me. To dance with me. To show the world that I do know a woman named Rebecca and our marriage wasn't a misprint.'

'I have nothing to wear yet, but I will soon.'

'You've been to the seamstress. How many times?' His voice lilted, but his eyes studied.

'Some.'

'I stopped by the seamstress's shop and asked for the bills. I saw exactly how many dresses you ordered.'

She put her hand to her cheek. 'I'm sorry if I've spent too much.'

He frowned, shaking his head. 'You've not spent too much. But I can't think why the woman hasn't made you a dress to wear with all the charges she's included. Are you hiding them?'

In an instant, she saw past the charm and into the heart of him. He'd not happened into her bedroom for a few kisses.

'They just look hideous on me.' She'd tried the second one and it hadn't looked like the fashion plate and the seamstress had tucked a bit here and there and altered it. Still, the dress had felt heavy. Rebecca had even had some of the silk ribbons removed. 'I showed you the first one.'

'The first one. What about the other four?'

'I just would not want to be in the room when you court someone else. Or propose to someone.'

'One time cured you of that, I see.' He stood. His lips smiled, but his eyes didn't.

'I did not mean that. I saw the other ladies in the seamstress shop and I see how your mother dresses. And the seamstress has trouble making one my size. When she finishes a dress it does not fit.'

The covers fell away as she talked. The chemise concealed her well, but he could not see any problem with her size, except for the thinness.

'In order to be my wife, to be a countess, you will have to go about and visit and talk with people, much the same as you did in the country.'

The social world was his true home—no building or structure meant more than a roof to him. He saw that now. He didn't care what walls surrounded him, as long as people joined and the talk and laughter flowed. 'I will not hide in the country like my father did and I will fulfil my role. I must take up where my grandfather left off and follow in his dancing footsteps.'

'Then why did you marry me?' She crossed her arms again.

'You spent every moment searching about for a good work to do. I didn't give it much thought, but that would certainly be good in society.' He moved his head. 'And it might take some of the sting out of my actions when people do not get my jests.'

'I really don't see how proposing to women carried on your grandfather's good works, but I might have missed something.' She shook her head, causing her dishevelled hair to bob about. For a moment, it took his thoughts. He'd not noticed how narrow her face was.

Then he returned to the conversation.

'No. That wasn't particularly how my grandfather would handle things, but it did liven up the nights, for everyone. Most of the people who hate me forget the very next time I greet them with a swagger and a smile. It is a distinct advantage to have a broad smile and use it often.'

'And do you wish to be married?' She pushed back a strand of her hair. He wondered if the length of it reached her waist and he would wager it did.

He didn't want to feel married. But he did like the feeling of standing in her bedchamber and watching her.

But this wasn't the time to be thinking of the bed, no matter how she looked sitting in that white frock thing with her hair all about her shoulders.

They had to get past that. At least for a few moments. She could not hide behind a seamstress's errors for ever.

'I don't feel any more married today than I have on any other day of my life. But that doesn't matter,' he said. 'We are to be a couple working together. Some day I will be more involved in the political side of life and a trustworthy wife will be an advantage.'

'I will take that as a no.'

He didn't address it. 'My sister died and my father turned his back on his duties, though he does often stay in town when Parliament is meeting. He decided he needed that blasted, valuable quiet in the country. He tucked his tail between his legs and fled where he could be lord and master to all.'

'What if he was just grieving over the loss of your sister?'

'I know he grieved. We all did.' He turned his back to her. 'That's no excuse to stop living. Just as living in a larger house is no excuse to hide in it.'

Her eyes locked on his. 'If I had had somewhere to go to when my mother died, I might have moved there.'

'Let's both be truthful. You would never have left your father.'

'Perhaps not. He was hurt. Only faith helped us.'

'I do not have that. I have this. I have the clubs, the soirées, the dances, the proposals. The laughter. A different kind of faith.'

She blinked, and he stepped back to the bed and moved forward. In one move he could be holding her in his arms and the knowledge passed between them.

She let out a breath. 'I thought I loved you—when you could not speak and I didn't know who you were. I have heard so little good about you—'

'I think you expected a bit of clay already moulded into the shape you wished for.'

'Perhaps. That would be easiest. And what I asked for.'

'But not what you received.' He stared at her. 'And perhaps I have lived half of my years and became who I will always be. And have no wish to change.'

'I want your honesty. And if I hate your actions—' Her lips almost locked on the last word. 'You will have earned it.'

He took both of her hands and held them at his heart, pressing them into his shirt. 'If you truly wish for a marriage of truth, then I can attempt it. It feels like a new jest for me. But it may send us in different directions. But we've already started them and I do not like the feeling that my wife of only a few days is already preferring to stay home with a book or a knitting needle rather than be out with me.'

He dropped her hands and moved to his chamber. He heard her footsteps behind him.

She walked into his room. 'If you wish me to return to my father, I will as soon as a babe is on the way.'

He saw her from the corner of his eye. He didn't recognise her. He'd been concentrating on revenge so much that he'd not bothered to look at what was happening in front of him.

Fox turned and put his hand out, sliding the puff of sleeve back into place, but it slipped down again. Then he gripped her shoulders. He could feel the bones.

He took her hand and led her to the mirror and stood behind her. He reached up to brush her cheek. They both watched his hand move.

'You're fading away.' He dropped his hand from her face and gripped her shoulders so that she looked at her form in the mirror and couldn't turn away.

'See how thin you look. You do not need to think about your size. Are you eating at all?'

'Of course. It is just not the same as what I'm used to and I don't like it as well.'

He turned and stalked to the hallway. He didn't wait for the bell pull, but hit every other tread as he bounded down the stairs. He clasped the railing to stop his descent when he saw the wide eyes of the butler.

'Send for a physician. Do not let him stop until he is with my wife.'

He turned, moving up the stairs.

His mother had talked about her cough at length when they'd met and how almost every servant in the house had succumbed. And she sounded fine.

He remembered watching Rebecca's bottom while he lay in bed at the vicarage. A healthy one with a lot of movement. Then he thought of how she'd looked on the wedding day. This had started before the cough.

She'd changed while they waited for the banns to be read. He'd noted it, but understood that she would be the type of person to take those vows seriously, and marked it as the reason and forgotten about it.

That had been an error.

He stepped back into the bedroom. He didn't tell her the physician was on the way.

She still stood at the looking glass, but she

worked to corral the stray strands of hair that had escaped from the pins.

'You wed me to keep a roof over your father's head.'

Her eyes wavered a moment. 'I did not truly think your father would toss us out.'

'Have you ever known him not to make good on what he said?'

'No. He's very much in control of the village. But he had also promised my father another home, somewhere else. We did not know where.'

'You really did not wish to marry me.'

'It's— Well, you had proposed before and it had meant nothing. You'd lived through one scandal after another. But I didn't know what else to do. You seemed likeable enough and I knew very well that, as your wife, my father would be protected by the earl. He said he thinks of me as a daughter. And if nothing else, my father would be able to have a room at the earl's estate and still have the people around him he's known all his life.'

'You would sacrifice for him. By marrying me.'

She turned to him. 'What other options did I have? None. I could possibly marry the new vicar, but he looked a bit like a bland pickle and his voice grated on my ears.' She shrugged. 'And I liked you. You have a pleasant voice. And you seemed agreeable enough while you were healing. I just didn't realise it was all healing and you were too ill to move. I thought you were a quiet man who liked stillness.'

She put her hand on her cheek. 'Then I saw you get out of the carriage and I didn't recognise you. I'd never seen someone dressed so fine. You were there with the high hat on and the black clothing and I'd never seen such. Not even in portraits. And I could not change my mind then. Your father would have been so very angry and it was too late.'

He'd never expected someone to feel forced to marry him.

'I'll make it better for you, Rebecca.'

'You don't need to. I'm fine. I just haven't been very hungry.'

He held her until the physician arrived and he hoped she had not made herself so thin that she'd become ill.

Chapter Twenty-One

'The physician says you must return to your home in the village.' The doctor had said he truly wasn't quite sure what was wrong with her or what to do to treat her.

Fox walked to the bell in the sitting room and pulled it. He sat down at the desk, removed the topper from the ink and began to write.

'What are you writing?' she asked.

'Instructions for the servants for after I leave. I'm taking you to your father's.'

He heard her intake of breath and turned. For a half second, he saw concern.

'I want you to be happy,' he said. 'Simple as that. And starving yourself is not going to make anyone happy.'

'I'm not starving myself.'

He looked at the paper in front of him, but he thought about what he'd told her. No one in the world deserved happiness more than Rebecca. She'd spent her whole life thinking of what others might need.

'I need to live here,' she repeated. 'A wife should be with her husband.'

'Very well.' He tossed the pen aside. He used his smile and put all his sincerity into it. 'But a brief visit to your father would be good for him, and you could see your old friends.'

'I don't believe you.' She whirled around so he couldn't see her face. 'You're sending me away. My father and your father both will be hurt to think our marriage is already failing.'

He would try one good work. One very large good work. His lips curved up, but the movement was habit. He was too worried about Rebecca to feel the smile.

A maid arrived, with her mob cap sliding off her head. She straightened it. Fox returned to writing. 'I am going to the country.'

Rebecca gasped.

He looked at the maid. 'She's wasting away to nothing.' Fox stood. 'Did you not notice?'

He might as well have spoken the words to himself.

'Well, she did put her cake in the chamberpot.' He could hardly hear the servant's voice for the pounding in his head.

He folded the paper in half precisely. 'Have the carriage readied.' He folded the paper again. 'Send the valet to my room and tell him to pack a trunk for me. Be certain he packs my favourite wear, this time. Not the rags I usually wear to my father's. And not to pack lightly. Tell him to take the trunk to my father's house and bring his own clothing. We will be staying indefinitely.' He dropped the paper onto the table. 'These instructions are for later. The butler will know what to do. But wait a moment before you leave.'

He crossed the room and went into Rebecca's chamber and returned with her spencer folded over his arm.

He walked to Rebecca and put a hand at her waist. 'My wife and I are going for a walk to the east. Send her clothing along. Have the carriage catch up with us. My wife will be staying in the country with me indefinitely as well.'

He held the spencer for her to put her arms into it.

'I can't wear it.' She touched her chest. 'It doesn't match. At all. It's old and it's from my home.'

He lowered the cloth and looked at the drab brown, then shrugged and held it up again. 'So... You'll start a new style and you'll be warm.' He leaned closer. 'I once wore red gloves with a purple cravat. If someone sees you, they'll just think I chose your clothes.'

As soon as she had her arms in the clothing, he hustled her out the door and down the stairs.

'You hate the country,' she said.

'You did not think I'd let you go alone.'

'I am fine alone.'

He stopped and looked at her until she lowered her eyes. No one in the entire world had ever needed him as much as Rebecca did. Him, with his long list of bad deeds and her with the matching size of good works.

They'd walked for a mile before the carriage caught up with them.

She sat beside him in the vehicle, but after a distance leaned against the corner. Even talking seemed to take too much effort.

He reached over and pulled her into his lap sideways, and propped his arm high to cradle her. She could stretch her legs a bit.

'Try to sleep,' he said. 'It'll make the ride go quicker.'

She breathed in. His arms gave her a boost of strength. 'Do you want to spend time with your father?'

'Absolutely not. You smell much nicer than he does.'

'Lilacs. My mother's scent. My father would save all year to buy her the perfume and she would share it with me. After she died, it made me feel closer to her.'

'You must miss her.'

'Not every moment. She's still with me. In my heart. And I just know that she is aware of me.'

'That's not the way I feel about my sister. She's gone. I've never once felt she is with me. Or that any part of her remains or can touch us.'

'That must be sad.'

'It is, but that is just how it is.'

She snuggled against him. 'It would be beyond sad for me.'

'Then I am pleased you believe differently than I do. I just wish you liked London more.'

'Everyone moves so much faster. No one seems to have time to spare unless it is for buying something new. Even the servants. And they are quite particular about things.'

'The servants?'

'Yes. I saw ribbons that matched the maid's hair and bought them and gave them to her. She was in tears the next day because the housekeeper saw them and accused her of stealing. When I explained to the housekeeper that I had given them to the maid, her shoulders tightened, her lips pruned into a sour shape and she nodded. I had to tell her I'd been saving a shawl for her or her feelings would have been hurt. I had been—but for Boxing Day. I gave it to her and she wore it when she was cleaning the rug. The next day the maid noted the housekeeper was lording it over all the staff that her shawl was quite the thing. So then I bought ribbons for everyone, but I knew if I bought shawls, too… And then I overheard a footman ask another if he had received a vail of any kind.'

'Don't worry about the servants. They are of strong stock and they will survive some jealousy over ribbons. Get them all confections or teas or some such.'

'Oh.' She straightened. 'I must… I forgot. I had planned for the butler to have some spectacles. The housekeeper complained of him holding the list so far from his face… Would you mind? Would you mind—helping him get glasses?'

'I will tell him to see that he purchases himself some spectacles and I will see that it doesn't cause an uproar. I will tell him to let everyone know, if they will wear them, they may all have spectacles.'

'Oh, they will all be wearing spectacles. You wait and see. You have to give one exactly the same as the others. But in the village, we could never give everyone alike. Funds were too scarce. We all knew that sometimes one had good fortune, another time, someone else did.'

'Sounds simple.'

'It is. But nothing is simple now. The staff is trying hard to be so perfect and win my trust. They watch me so close to see what they might do to please me. Even my smiles are watched. The food I eat.'

'Only by me.'

'Ha.' She gave his waistcoat a tug. 'Leticia was concerned about my mind because my cake was in the chamberpot.'

'It seemed to me Cook has been preparing quite a lot of different dishes lately.'

'Yes. She was trying to please me with everything from cockscomb soup to rosewater biscuits. I don't want her to work so hard, particularly when it doesn't even taste good. I have been taking a walk and spiriting food for the neighbour's dogs. I pretend to be scratching their ears and I have oilcloth inside my reticule that the food is wrapped in.' She sighed. 'I like the dogs and I do not even know their names. They do not care what I say or do or how I look.'

'You need to stop caring.'

She turned in his arms and looked at his eyes.

'You care too much about what you say or how you look,' he explained.

She rested against his chest, and his arms

banded around her. Movable walls of comfort. A secure fortress. This just wasn't how she'd expected him to feel, not that she'd ever given it much thought. She'd not known he could be shelter.

His chin touched the top of her head. 'You must eat more.'

'I've been just a few days without feeling hungry. A leftover from the sniffles. I was a bit plump. My mother was a great bit plump.' She touched the cuff of the sleeve tip that hung from his coat, straightening with one movement, curling with the next. 'Father said it gave him more to love. But her knees pained her and she couldn't walk well.'

'Are you concerned that will happen to you?'

'I don't think about it much. I just miss my home.'

'It's the first home you ever had. I had my mother's home, my father's home and school. Plus I spent a lot of time at my uncle's house with my cousins. I stayed at Albany. The walls are just in different places.'

'Neither of us feels at home in the house.'

'A house is merely a place to keep the weather out and provide comfort. It isn't a being. Besides, if I want a house in London at a more convenient location, as soon as this lease is out, I can move.

I do not care what colour the walls are or where they are located within a residence.'

'You just need doorways.'

He put his hand over her fist and pulled it to his lips. 'To lead to you.'

'Easily said.' She touched the shoulder of his coat. 'Even though I can feel nothing of you beneath the fabric, I can still tell the strength of you beneath your clothing. And it is all strange to me. A person I do not know.'

'I would like it better if you could feel something of me.'

'I'm afraid of what I might find. You're so different. Down to the buttons on the clothing.' She touched the button on his waistcoat. 'The men in London have the nicest clothes.'

'The men?'

'Oh, yes. They're elegant. The ladies' dresses are fine beyond my imagination. And now I have them and I cannot get them to fit. The most costly dresses I could have imagined and yet…' She looked at her skirt. 'This dress. What if I spill something on it or get dirt on the hem?'

'Don't worry about something so trivial. Cloth is nothing compared to the person who wears it.' He touched his face to hers. 'Does that not sound like something you would say?'

'It does.'

'Then shut your eyes and go to sleep and see how long I can have the strength to hold you.'

'How long do you think you will manage?'

'As long as I need to.'

Chapter Twenty-Two

Foxworthy watched her sleep. Rebecca woke as the wheels of the carriage stopped and the cab bounced to stillness. She looked up.

She patted his chest. 'I believe we are at my father's house.'

He lifted her, helping her to sit beside him. He yawned. Then shut his eyes and shook his arms. 'Well, let us greet your father.'

He led her down from the steps and her father stepped out. In rumpled shirtsleeves and mussed hair, he appeared older than any other time Fox had seen him.

The cat rushed out and wound around Rebecca's skirt. She cooed, scratching its ears, patting the head and causing a huge purr to hit the air.

The vicar rushed to Rebecca. His cheeks had

sunk into his face and his skin reminded Fox of the way some leaves changed before they turned brown and fell to the earth.

'Becca. What's wrong? Your letter said you were well.' Her father's voice trembled. 'Have you seen the physician?'

'I'm fine.' Her laughter infused the air, moving across to her father and wiping away the added creases seeing her had caused.

Foxworthy took Rebecca's hand and lifted it. 'She misses her father.'

Her father took a half step forward and his cheeks reddened, contrasting the pallor. 'I miss her as well.'

Fox moved, stepping her to her father. 'I hoped she might stay with you for a bit.'

The vicar's eyes darkened.

'My precious wife…' Foxworthy raised his voice, overacting the moment, the same as the proposals which garnered him so much attention '…is missing her father beyond belief. If she were to stay away another minute, I might fear for her health.'

The words he said scraped him from the inside out, releasing something he'd never felt before. They took the feeling he'd had when his sister died and freshened it, strengthened it and cloaked him in it. His smile didn't falter.

Fox pulled up Rebecca's hand, putting his

lips to it, and then snugged Rebecca to his side. His free hand went around her waist from the back and when he hugged her to him, the clothes folded against her body. As Fox pulled her close, her father's smile grew.

'Well, I am missing her beyond belief,' her father said. 'I'd thought myself sensible until the days after she married and then I realised I am just an old man.'

'Father.' She rushed from Foxworthy's side, taking one of her father's hands in both hers and leaving a chill beside Fox. 'You are not just an old man. You are the vicar and a saint on earth.'

He ducked his head. 'You do my heart good to see you, Rebecca.'

'Then I trust you will need a few moments with her to share what she thinks of London,' Fox said. 'And I wish her to catch up on the things she has missed while she was away and I think she has missed most everything.'

'I'm glad I'm still here,' the vicar said. 'I didn't want to share it in a letter, but Vicar Gallant has been here almost every day and mentioned that he has a cabinet that will fit nice against my wall. The earl is certain he can find a house I will like better for my pension.'

'You will have this home as long as you wish it,' Fox said. Even though his eyes met her father's, his concentration was on her. She half stood on tiptoes and her eyes had more life than he remembered seeing since they'd married.

'I do not think it will be at all proper for Vicar Gallant to be living here while Rebecca is staying.' Fox bent his head. 'And I do believe I have some sway with the owner and, if I do not, I'll just toss Gallant out the door should he try to move in.'

The vicar's smile plumped his face, but then his face thinned again. He raised an eyebrow. 'How long will she be staying?'

'As long as she wishes.'

'Are you travelling back to London tonight?' the vicar asked, words low.

'No, I shall be staying at my father's,' Fox said. 'So you may expect me for breakfast in the morning, Rebecca.' He had to touch her once again. He took her hand and just held it. 'Your porridge will be delicious.'

He knew he had to let her go, so he pressed a kiss to the back of her hand. 'Do not forget to cook enough for me.'

She laughed, and he could not take his eyes from her.

'You'll be having breakfast here?' Her father studied Fox's face.

'If Rebecca will allow it. As I seem to remember *someone*...' he still watched Rebecca '...had the audacity to put that in my marriage vows.'

'You remembered.' The vicar's voice seemed to come from far away.

'That I remember is not the problem. That she remembers is.' He smiled, knowing the flippant manner served him well. He moved forward, aware he closed out her ability to see around or above him. 'Goodnight, Rebecca.' He stayed one second longer than necessary, his face so close to her that he was certain she could feel his breaths. Then he turned and strode away—because he had to leave quickly. If he lingered, he wouldn't be able to go.

He went to the carriage and jumped inside, then fell back against the seat—a man with the world at his fingertips and yet one wife so very, very far away.

He marched into his father's sitting room. His father looked up, took off his glasses and stared at Fox.

'What in blazes are you here for?' Strong words from his father.

'I missed you?' Fox pulled out his smile again, but twisted it a bit.

'Be wary. You might grow fond of me and where would that leave us?' His father put the glasses on the table with a sliding toss. He stood, stretching, and pointed to the pull at Fox's side. 'Ring for a servant. I'd like some tea.'

Fox looked at the pull, then back at his father. 'Why don't you try to mend things with Mother?'

His father stepped in front of him and gave a jerk of the rope. 'I have. We have. By letter. For us it is the best way to be married. We can write to each other and be friends. But within minutes of walking into the room with her, I want to leave. Even her perfume annoys me. And I know how much it costs. It shouldn't stink like that.'

'She can change her perfume.'

'I still wouldn't like it.'

'That's just an outward thing.'

His father's eyes met Fox's, and he smiled. Fox recognised the smile. For the first time ever, Fox saw himself in his father's actions. His father spoke.

'Your mother's inward things don't get on well with my outward things, either.'

'Father.' He used the word as a verbal slap. 'Can't you live under the same roof?'

'I'm sure we could, but there's no need. There is no peace for me in her house. It is like having a pet that will not stay away from your heels and keeps mewling on long after you've tried all you can do to get it to play with its shiny things. Her voice takes my thoughts and chops them away. And I cannot even care about Parliament or the bills that are passed or the way the world is changing when I have had to listen to her. I love her, but I do not want to be in the same town with her. It is all I can do to stay in the same country with her.' He paused and a softer smile drifted past his lips, but disappeared into his thoughts. 'I don't regret marrying her. I just like to be alone.'

'And Mother likes people.'

'And soirées, and chatter, and newspaper clippings and a flurry of life.'

'A bit like her son, she is.'

'Yes. But I try not to blame her for that. For that, I blame my father.'

'Don't.' Fox shook his head. 'Even if I'd never known him, I'm sure you and I wouldn't have liked each other that much.'

'The odds were against it from the beginning, I suppose. And don't be so harsh on your mother's and my marriage. Neither of us complain about it. I just prefer to read my books and write letters and have the peace of being with no one who disagrees with me.' His eyes jabbed.

Fox laughed. 'Well, that last one puts me out the door.'

His father nodded, moved forward and clapped him on the shoulder. 'You didn't lose the direction to the estate, though. I personally did not care at all to see my father the last years of his life.'

'Well, he was harsh on you.'

'I wasn't quite the son he wanted. But I certainly gave him the grandson he wanted. Irked me to please him so.' He laughed to take the ire from the words.

A maid arrived in the doorway, a tray in her hands. His father walked forward, took it and dismissed her with a nod.

'I used to stay here a day longer if you gritted your teeth when you spoke,' Fox added after the footsteps faded away on the stairway.

'When I guessed that, I did get more accepting of your visits.' His father's eyes half closed. 'What I really noticed is that if I grumbled more, you smiled more and jabbed more with your words. So I worked to tolerate you a bit easier. If you could get along with that old boot of my father then you should be able to get along with someone as peaceable as I am.'

'Grandfather was—'

'Exactly like his grandson.'

'One of the most intelligent, thoughtful and wise men I've ever met.'

'For an arse hat.'

His father put the tray by his glasses and poured a little cream in the cups, put the creamer down, then swirled each cup. Then he carefully poured the tea, taking a moment to savour the aroma.

He handed Fox a cup. Fox took it, looked at the contents and back at his father.

His father had the cup to his lips.

'I love you, Father.'

Tea spewed.

'Just jesting,' Fox said.

'Damn. You had me scared.' His father's head tilted. 'I thought for a moment you'd completely lost your mind.'

'I may have.' His lips turned up and he turned away from his father. 'I don't know what I'd do without Rebecca. I am fond of her. Attached beyond what I knew possible to feel.'

'She's likeable enough. Tries to find the good in everyone. So why are you here and she is in London?'

'She's not in London. She's at her father's.'

The earl's brows bumped together. 'So she left you?'

His father's face took on the look he'd had when Fox had bought the highest-priced stallion at Tattersall's by convincing his grandfather to buy the beast for Fox's thirteenth birthday. Geyser had been worth it. Rebecca was worth even more.

The world of uncertainty crashed into him and forced volume into his words. 'She's sick. She won't eat. I did not know what else to do. She thinks she is plump.'

'Rebecca?' Hardly louder than a puff of air, his father spoke. 'But I thought she had a cough. She wrote her father that she was well.'

Foxworthy turned his back to his father. He could not view the confusion in the eyes. He kept his own gaze straight ahead, focused on nothing. 'I noticed it then. How much her body was shrinking away. The physician said that since she is not coughing blood… He said I must get her to eat. He said if she does not eat, she will not live. I had figured that out before I sent for him. That's why I consulted him. But she doesn't know what he said.'

He turned. His father had collapsed into a chair. His head in his hands. 'I have known her since she was a child.'

Fox took in a breath, but didn't speak.

'Does she still have the nightmares?' the earl asked, raising his eyes.

'She's never mentioned them to me. But she doesn't feel she is doing enough good works.'

Foxworthy walked to the window, but he could not see beyond the glass. The remains of a spider's web had collapsed upon itself, leaving a few disjointed white threads without a pattern. Without purpose. The dregs of a home. A smear to be wiped away.

'You can learn, son. You can learn to live without someone you love. I thought I would never repair after your sister died. And I do well enough now.'

'That is when you left London and decided to live alone.' Fox nodded a circular movement. 'Doing well.' He paused. 'Doing well?'

'Yes. Then it's so much easier. Every object in the world stops conspiring to remind you of them. Your own beating heart doesn't mock you by its obsessive need to continue on.'

'There's no place that will give me peace without Rebecca.'

Sleep evaded him and Foxworthy dressed for breakfast as precisely as he would have for an evening with friends. His valet had arrived several hours after dark the night before. The man had dusted each speck from the fabric and Fox took a hat and gloves to step into the cold.

His father's eyes widened when he saw Foxworthy leaving so early. Foxworthy gave him a smile and walked out the door. He took the carriage, arrived at Rebecca's house, and told the driver to check back near twelve.

The door to the house opened before he finished speaking with the driver. Rebecca watched him, her lips parted, and eyes locked on him. At the entrance, he realised his hat would not make it under the doorway and took the hat off and put the gloves into it.

He bent forward so he could take her fingers, pull them up and kissed above her hand, then put his hat on the table by the bed. Rebecca still didn't move.

'You're dressed a bit fine for porridge,' her father said. 'Good thing she also cooked some bacon as well.'

'I'm hungry.' He looked around the room. 'Feels a bit strange to be able to talk while I'm here.'

'Feels a bit strange to see you all dandied up.'

'You're overdressed,' Rebecca said.

'Perhaps. But in the past, each time I came to my father's house I picked my oldest clothes and my plainest wear. This time, I thought I would wear what pleased me.'

'You have high taste in clothing.' The vicar tilted his head sideways and shook it. 'I definitely wouldn't connect you to the man Rebecca found.' His nose wrinkled and he snorted. 'Vicar.'

Foxworthy shrugged. 'An easily made conclusion.' Then he remember his truth. 'Easily made when I was unconscious, beaten and couldn't speak.'

'Why are you doing this?' Rebecca asked.

'We both have to be comfortable with each other if we're to be married. I have to be comfortable with who I am, anyway. Each time I visited my father, I changed what I wore to suit him. I met him more than halfway, I felt. It made me angry. I'm not going to be angry with him any more over something so senseless.'

'The same for me?' Rebecca asked.

'I will take you as you are. And shouldn't I?'

Before she could answer, her father stepped to the door. 'I believe I must make sure Mr Renfro's cow is better today. And he said he'd have some bones for Tommy Berryfield's new pup to gnaw on.' He slipped out, but glanced at Fox before he left. 'I do not know what we are going to do with the new vicar. He hardly knows what a plough looks like.'

Rebecca sat at the table and he sat across, his legs taking most of the space underneath. Their porridge sat in front of them and he warmed his hand on the side of the bowl, then he took a bite. The taste didn't truly appeal, but it wasn't bad.

She took a bite, her throat moved, and her lips turned down. 'It feels odd to be home. Not the same. I thought…'

'It is exactly the same. Only you have changed.'

'Did it feel the same to you at your father's?'

'Yes. And no. I suppose it was completely different. We are not adversaries for some reason. Perhaps you united us. That can be your good work for today.'

She clasped her right wrist and moved her

hand up the sleeve of her gown, pushing it higher on her shoulder.

'I wonder how my maid is faring without me.'

'I could send for her. She could stay here, or at my father's. Whatever is best for you.'

She shook her head. 'No. Her mother works in a house not too far away and she goes to see her mother when it is the mother's half-day off on Wednesday.'

'I saw her walking on the street on Tuesday with a basket. Did you send her on an errand?'

'Yes. To take some threads to her mother and some candles. They don't give the servants good candles below stairs at the Wilmare household. The scullery maid, Alice, showed me one and it smelled worse than any I had ever seen.' She stirred her porridge.

'I wouldn't have thought you would get used to beeswax here.' He had another bite of the porridge.

'Your father gifted them to us sometimes. But even when we used the others, they didn't smell rancid.'

She told him of Alice's family and her spoon never stilled. He finished his meal while she talked.

She stood to take his bowl. Out of habit, he stood as well and he could see the porridge inside her bowl.

'Finish your meal.' His tone hushed. 'I didn't mean to rush you.'

'I am finished.' She shook her head. 'The food doesn't taste...like I remembered it. And the cat is hungry and will like this.'

'I believe your father took the beast with him.' He took both bowls and put them back in their places and gently nudged her into her chair.

Sitting across from her, he studied her face. 'You did not sleep well.'

'Perhaps I'm ill. Or perhaps I am going to have a child.'

'If you are going to have a child, you will need to eat enough for the little one.'

'When I eat, I feel ill.'

'It doesn't matter. It's a good work for your body and you have to do it.'

She levelled her eyes at him. 'I believe I discussed this with the physician you sent. He told me to eat more.'

'I wouldn't be surprised.' He leaned forward, close. Touched her face as delicately as he could.

His hand slid down her cheek and he pulled the garment back on her shoulder. 'Let's bundle up and go for a walk. Perhaps that will make you hungry.'

'It's too cold.'

'Then we'll sit by the stove and you can read something to me. Anything but the prayer book.'

'I was touched that you liked it and held it close.'

He checked her eyes and saw the sincerity. 'Well, you may read it to me again if you wish.'

She rose to get the book. He watched her go into the next room. He kept all emotion from his face and blocked his thoughts from what could be.

Keeping his wrist near the edge of the table, Fox used his forefinger to trace circles on the table as she read. Her voice sounded strong. Not weakened.

He leaned back, watching. She believed the words she read. She read them with softness, different than he'd ever heard them read before. The others had directed the words into the air, putting a forcefulness into each one so that everyone could hear and realise just what they were hearing.

She read them in the same warm tone of a story book for a child who needed to rest.

'What's Cherubim and Seraphim?' he asked.

She paused, eyes meeting his, and shrugged.

'You don't know what you're reading means?'

'No.' She shook her head. 'It doesn't matter.'

'It doesn't matter?' He raised a brow.

'Well, no. I know what the parts mean that tell me to be a good person and since that's all

I have control over, that's all that matters.' She lowered her chin and pointed her nose like a derringer. 'I have known several vicars.' She looked at the book and turned a page. 'All but one of them have been extremely well versed in goodness. And he wasn't a real vicar.'

'Vicars need to know a lot about evil to fight it, I would assume.'

'No.'

She started to read again.

'No?' he interrupted.

'No.' That nose came forward again.

'I do not need to know anything about…' She looked around. 'Chopping a tree. But I can still tell you the wood will burn better after curing. And the aged wood certainly cooks my meals.'

'But you've seen a tree chopped. You know the process.'

'Precisely. And I didn't have to get blisters to know as much as I need.'

He spread his fingers and looked at his palm. 'Blisters. Doubt I've ever had one.'

Her eyes flicked to him. 'Not even from dancing in new boots?'

'Perhaps I should have said not from work. My life is never boring.'

Her fingers gripped the book and her body turned slightly away. 'I would have thought proposing would get tedious.'

He crossed his arms and looked across the top of her nose and into smug eyes. 'No. You wouldn't want to propose the same way over and over—a woman might not think you sincere.'

'And how sincere was your proposal to me?'

'Very. No one else could have said yes.'

'An error on your part? A habit that you were carried away with?'

'Could have been...but—' He squinted. 'Did you notice that I never proposed to an unmarried woman except for one time?'

'Truly?'

He shrugged, arms still crossed. 'What do you think? Do you really think I could propose to an unmarried woman I didn't wish to become married to?' He uncrossed his arms and leaned forward.

She blinked at him.

'Tell me. Do you?'

She almost closed the book, but then stopped. 'Perhaps you proposed before and the woman said no. Mrs Lake, for instance.'

His mouth opened, even though he couldn't keep it from tipping up at the sides. 'Are you suggesting a woman might say no to me? To a proposal?' He shook his head and his legs splayed under the table. He leaned back in his chair. 'Well, I never thought of that.'

'I assume that would be something the woman might think of, though.'

'No.' He shrugged. 'Except Mrs Lake. When she told me about the duke in her sights, I figured a proposal would fall flat with her.' He shrugged it away. 'I didn't realise how fortunate I was. Best thing…well, second-best thing that ever happened to me.' He looked at her. 'The best thing was the beating. It led me to you.'

Her cheeks reddened.

'Yes,' he said under his breath. 'I might not have stopped long enough to really look at you if I had not been forced to be still.'

She began reading again and after a few sentences she looked up. 'I cannot say that you only planned to ask simple-minded women to wed you. That would put me in a bad light.'

'I would never ask a simple-minded woman to wed.' He flicked his next words away with a toss of his head. 'Unless she was already married.'

'One person in the marriage should have some thoughts, I suppose.' She started reading again.

'Pardon?'

She paused. 'Don't you agree?'

'How could I not?'

She closed the book. 'You're smarter than you let on.'

'I would hope so.'

She slid the book across the table to him. 'Read to me.'

He took the book in his hands. The words were jumbled but he'd learned to switch them around well enough and make the funny f's an s. He read aloud and with precision until he finished the page, then he slid the book to her across the table.

'You said you can hardly read.'

'I can hardly stand to read.'

She looked at him. And he studied her and, in that moment, he saw something in her face he'd never seen before. Her lips tightened, then relaxed, in tandem with her eyes. 'I'm not very smart.'

'How do you know?'

'I know.'

'How many women in this village can read?'

Her lids dropped. 'All of them who wish to.'

'How?'

'How else can you write letters for your family if you cannot read? A wife needs to be able to read if her husband cannot. So we started a lending line. With your father's newspapers. And then books.'

'A lending line?'

'The newspaper is given to Mrs Renfro and then she knows it is to go to Mrs Berryfield who knows who it is to go to next. It travels around the village and everyone who wants to be in the lending line can be. Your father passes the books along to the lending line sometimes and they get back to him and he passes another along. Sometimes someone else will inherit a book or buy one.'

'And they travel right along the line?'

'After Sunday Services we met and made a provision that a newspaper can only be kept seven days and a book for two months. At first we wrote dates on the newspapers, but now we don't, but they move along the line fast, except with Mrs Greaves. She has to be reminded with every book, but that is just the way she is.'

'Who teaches them to read?'

'Their mothers teach the little girls and boys now. I help when the mother is busy and we take turns with the chores.' She bent her head forward. 'It takes hardly any time at all to teach a child to read. And it was going so quickly with the girls that the boys wanted to learn too. Your father bought Maria Edgeworth's *The Parent's Assistant*.'

'Who started it?'

'My mother.' She glanced at him. 'If you're trying to tell me I am smart because I can read, then you are not convincing me at all. My mother started the lending line and taught most of the women to read.'

'Was your mother smart?'

'Very. She could make medicines.'

'Can you not do the same?'

She pointed to a shelf. 'Because she wrote them all down for me. She wrote everything down. She said memories fade faster than ink.

'So do you keep records as well?'

'Memories fade faster than ink.'

'So you have your mother's knowledge?'

'Learned. From her.'

'Doesn't matter how you get knowledge. Only that you keep it.'

'I have little knowledge.'

'Doesn't mean you can't learn a lot more.'

'I will never live long enough to learn all the things that I would need to know to live in London.'

Someone knocked at the door.

She jumped to answer it, but he put a hand on her arm and stood. 'It's the carriage. I was hoping you might go with me to my father's house.'

Chapter Twenty-Three

Rebecca walked into the earl's sitting room, her arm tucked around Foxworthy's. Her fingers tightened on his sleeve.

His father's eyes wavered when he greeted them, but he looked at her with all the warmth her own father had.

She responded from habit. But the walls around her seemed higher and the sconces brighter.

'Father.' Foxworthy put his hand over hers. 'I'd like to show Rebecca the family portraits.'

'Haven't you seen them before?' The earl straightened his waistcoat. 'I definitely remember showing them to your father once.'

'Yes. Right before Christmas one year. I remember your housekeeper taking me about the rooms while we put greens out that the ladies had gathered.'

'Well.' Fox moved as he spoke, smiling at his father and whisking her along. 'Now they are family for Rebecca and I hope to test her afterwards to see if she can remember the names.'

'I added new nameplates.' The earl's grumbled words were directed at Foxworthy. 'After you couldn't remember any of them but your grandfather.'

They moved into a room she recognised, mostly for its armour standing in the corner. 'The helmet has returned.'

His eyes followed her. 'Yes. I borrowed it once to prove a point.'

'What was the point?'

He shrugged. 'That I could.'

'That's no reason.'

'It seemed one at the time. But it got annoying bumping against my horse's rump all the way to London. And I couldn't just toss it in a hedgerow, that would have been malicious. And I did like it and wanted to keep it in the family.'

They stopped in front of the first portrait. He stared at the man as if he needed to remember every detail from the pointed shoes to the plume in the vase behind him. 'Father sent a note with a servant demanding I hand it over immediately. I told the servant I absolutely did not have it.'

'You did.' She didn't release his arm. It gave her strength.

'I suppose the man could see it on the sofa. But I doubt he wished to go through me to get it as I told him I would put his head beside it.'

'The poor servant. Having to return to your father without accomplishing his errand.'

'I gave him a silver candlestick to take back, but I dare say he didn't tell my father what I said to do with it.'

'You should be ashamed.'

'I'm not. Not at all. That was who I was. Who a part of me still is and will always be. I can't take jests nearly as well as I can deal them out. But it just spurs me to improve with dealing them out.'

They walked along the path of portraits. She stopped in front of a picture of a woman in a golden dress. 'It's hard to believe she would have five sons survive and each of her daughters die.'

'Really?' he asked.

'Do you wish to tell me about any of your ancestors?'

'I do believe you know more of them than I do.' His eyes wandered along the portraits. 'I don't remember any stories of any of them.' He tilted his head to one, then stopped beside it. 'My grandfather, of course, because I remember him quite well. But none before him. I never liked this hallway. Never.' He ran a finger over the nameplate at the bottom of his grandfather's portrait.

'Why not?'

'When I was young, the eyes all seemed angry at me. They stared down, fierce. Hateful. Then Grandfather died and I hated to be reminded he wasn't here when I stood next to his portrait. I just didn't want to see the likeness when I couldn't hear his laughter. He laughed more than anyone I've ever seen.'

He turned her to face him. He took her chin in his hands. 'I didn't have any more wish to look at the portraits today than I did as a youth. I just wanted you to think of them as family.' His lips covered hers, bursting strength and weakness into her at the same time. The strength to stand alone and the weakness not to wish to.

He pulled back. 'And the tour continues.'

Moving towards a dark door panelled with narrow overlays, he opened it and indicated for her to precede him.

By the scent of leather and shaving soap, she could tell it was his room. She walked to the desk and opened the small box. Playing cards. 'No sitting room?' she asked.

'Just a dressing chamber. I tend not to sit long.'

She saw the windows. 'You chose it for the light?'

'The road. I can see the road leaving the estate.'

She met his eyes. 'I'm surprised your father ever let you visit.'

'I was sometimes as well.' He pointed to the bedside table.

The silver candlestick stood alone. 'This was here the next time I visited. I'd sent the helmet back to the servant, asking him to please replace it quietly. And saying if Father didn't know how it returned, I would reward him well. I rewarded him well.'

'Do you feel uncomfortable with routine? With things going along quite the same time after time. I feel a peace in sitting alone at night stitching, or reading or snapping peas.'

'I never think about how I feel except if I am not enjoying the day. Then I move somewhere else.' His eyes lightened. 'I think I would rather gnaw my fingers than sit quietly.'

'I think you do.' She touched his hand. His fingernails had a raggedness that didn't match the rest of him.

He glanced at the nails. 'Yes. My valet cannot truly complain of it, but he suggests over and over that he cannot fathom how the nails can break so.'

'And how is it to be with me?' she asked.

'The muscles in my legs want to move and

I tap my feet. I stretch my arms. Then I look at you, my body stills and I know I am in the right place.'

'Not the right place for you.'

'Yes.' He nodded. 'There is something I have to tell you and I hope you understand.' He put his hand on her shoulder. 'I won't let you out of my sight for my waking hours until you have returned to the woman I married. I've taken some of you away and I must see it return.'

'I don't think you have the constancy for it.'

'I have the constancy to be very annoying. Perhaps that will spur you forward to get me to leave your sight. Or perhaps you will find that I can bring laughter to your lips.' He scooped her up and deposited her on the bed with care. He put a knee on the bed and fell forward, his arms keeping him upright enough not to touch her. 'You do remember that I do not like boredom.' He leaned forward, swung his head from side to side so that his hair tickled the bridge of her nose. 'I don't like boredom and I have no intention of indulging in it because we can find so many other ways to spend our hours.' He stilled, let his lids drop, looked her in the eye and repeated. 'Hours.'

He made good on his promise, hugging, kissing and cuddling her for an hour, then he sat behind her to reach the buttons on the back of her dress. He unfastened them, moving aside the chemise as he worked and adding a kiss to the skin.

The strings of the corset weren't tight and he pulled the ties from their knots while he rested his face at her neck, reaching his hands around to remove the dress and encircle her waist, pulling her close.

Once he'd realised how slight she was, he noticed it with every brush over her and felt a pang inside. But each bit of pain soothed away with the touch of his lips against her skin. He wanted her to know how treasured her body was and he took his time, savouring every inch of it. Lingering longer when he could give her more pleasure and hoping the touches he gave her healed, in some way, the feeling that she didn't look the perfection he'd seen when he watched her bustle around the stove.

He touched her, bringing her to pleasure and holding himself back, hoping to let her know that, sometimes, she was the only one who had to feel good and the only one that mattered.

He pulled her fist near to drop a kiss on it as she lay beside him on the bed. 'I think I am beginning to see this house better now,' he said. 'Thick walls. Cosy bedrooms. I could learn to like it.' He tucked her into the crook of his arm and stared at the ceiling. 'And a magnificent view above to look at. Well crafted.'

All his life he had been able to walk the exact path he chose. If his father irritated him, he went to his mother's and she had him on such a high-reaching, wide-based pedestal he could never tumble from it. If she should irritate him, he moved to the Albany or visited his cousins. Only recently had their households grown to include wives.

Before marriage, when he showed up on their doorstep, his cousins had hardly given him more notice than a pair of boots in the corner or they spent time regaling each other with stories and insults. He liked tossing the insults.

He'd even liked opening the newspaper to see if his name would be in it. He didn't know why he liked that so much, but he did. The pompous criticisms ground his teeth, but somehow, they were erased with the next mention. He might remember the slashing words for ever, but blended with the good it let him know he breathed and lived in other people's eyes. The words gave him strength, notice and increased the swagger other people saw when they looked at him.

'What would you have me do for your happiness?' He meant the question. Even though he held her in his arms, he knew she held him just as firmly, yet in a different way.

'I'm happy.'

He saw her sinking into the horizon like the evening sun. His world fading into the darkness—not sputtering away, just dropping completely from view. Nothingness. Diminishing.

He pulled her tight for a second. The bones of her. Even her hair seemed different. Tired.

He opened his mouth, a lie on his lips to tell her how much he would enjoy staying at his father's, then paused. 'I am staying with you. You will think we are truly one.'

Lightly, he pulled her nearer his heart. He could not leave. Even if she promised to eat, he could not leave and not know for certain how she fared. He might die alongside her, but he could not live away from her.

She shuddered.

'What's wrong?' he asked.

'I just thought about— The first time you propose to one of the villagers, I will show you what we do to male calves who need to be gentled.'

'You have to do that before maturity is reached.'

'I've got time then.' An impish grin looked up at him.

She'd dozed, but woke when someone knocked at the door. His arms tightened, his skin pressed against hers.

'Your meal,' a servant called out.

'Leave it at the door,' Fox answered.

He donned a dressing gown and retrieved a tray. He put the silver in the centre of the table and pulled back a lid. The scent of roasted beef hit her and caused a shudder in her stomach. 'I'm not hungry.'

He looked at her and picked up the tray.

'I am.' He balanced the tray with one hand while he returned to bed and propped against the headboard, the tray on his lap.

'You cannot eat in bed. It is not done.' She pulled the covers to her chest as she sat.

'Neither is riding a horse backwards. Or so I've heard. And I don't recommend it. But eating in bed…' he paused '…no one ever has to know about that.'

'The marzipan looks good.' He pulled out a piece of white confection and offered it to her.

She took it and nibbled a tiny bite, forcing the sweetness not to overwhelm her. 'The Berryfield children would so love this. I should save it for them.' She put it back on the platter.

'It was gifted from my father to us. I wouldn't want to deceive him if he asks us how we enjoyed it.'

He took the small piece from her and popped it into his mouth. 'Very tasty.

'Beef,' he said. 'Boiled potatoes. Bread. The

cheese. The marzipan. A section of cake. Biscuits. Does any of it look good to you?'

'It's all very good, I'm sure.'

'But does any of it look good to you?'

'No.'

'What looks the least unappetising?'

'The potatoes.'

'Then have some with me. And I really do like the marzipan so I might eat Tommy Berryfield's.' He pulled up a piece and held it to her. When she shook her head, he put it in his mouth. Then he reached for a fork. He stuck it into a potato and held it her way.

She waved his wrist away. 'You will not be feeding me.'

'Rebecca. Your father needs you healthy. Did you see how frail he looks?'

She took the fork from his hand and sat up. 'I feel so… I didn't think I would mind leaving him alone. After all, he has the village to look after him and your father as well. But you're right. He's wasted away since I've gone. If it weren't for everyone else feeding him, I doubt he would eat at all.' She took in a breath. 'He says he cooks a little, but I believe it is very little.'

That was such a good thing about the village. They bickered with each other, but they banded together to help each other, too. When her mother had died, not a day went by without someone stopping by in the evening hours.

She paused. 'I just realised. The lending line.'

His brows rose.

'The lending line. After Mother died, someone always happened by in the late hours of the evening, but never two families on the same day. They would arrive with a question for Father, which wasn't at all unusual but…' She tapped her chin. 'They may have visited in the same order of the lending line. I'm not sure, but now that I think, it did seem odd that no two families ever arrived at the house on the same evening. Sometimes it would be a child, or the women bringing flowers or the men with a question. But…'

'You think they set up the same order for visiting you?'

She laughed. 'I am pretty certain that they did. Which is fairly astounding in this place because no one can keep a secret. No one told me. Not even the children.'

'They all shared in it—except you and your father.'

'Yes. Their ways may be troubling sometimes but they have golden hearts.'

'I see why you fit in so well here.' He pointed to the food.

She shook her head and put down the fork. 'You are not saying that to be pleasant.'

'That was not a lie.' He ran a finger over her hand and then reached for a biscuit, broke it in half and took one half and held the other to her lips.

She took a bite. 'I know what you're doing.'

'So do I.' He took a bit of the cheese, held it to her. She took a nibble from the edge, chewed and swallowed. Then he ate the last of the cheese he held and reached for the fork, spearing a potato.

She raised her hand, blocking the food.

He looked at her. 'Your father needs you. I did not realise how much until I saw him this time.'

'Will you say anything to get me to eat?'

He put his weight on an elbow, moved the utensil from between them and leaned into the air around her. 'It's my good work for today.' He brushed a kiss across her lips, then rested against the headboard. 'You cannot fault someone for doing a good work.' His eyes flicked from her to the food. 'Please. Try.'

When she finished, he put the tray to the side, took her hand and sat, his back against the wall, and pulled her into his arms, cradling her.

He brushed back the tendrils of hair that wisped at her face.

'You mustn't keep doing this. I will think you care for me.'

'Well. I do care for you.'

'Enough?'

'Of course.'

She sighed. 'More than the others?'

'Certainly. More than the others, the sun, the moon and the stars combined.'

'Pretty words.' She burrowed against him. 'For how long?'

'Until my eyes can no longer see the world around me, my heart no longer beats and my dust has been scattered in the wind. And if there is a bit of that dust that is floating in the air, and can think anything at all, then its first thought will be of you.'

She hugged him tight. 'I wish I could believe you.'

'You don't have to believe me. You just have to believe in yourself.'

'You've said so many words to so many others before. I'm not happy in the world you like. And you aren't happy in this world.'

'You can stay here.'

'But can you?'

He pulled the covers tight around them. He'd visited his father, time and time again, and each time he'd returned to London he'd felt he was riding back into a living, breathing world after leaving a tomb.

But she had broken down those walls of the tomb and made it a place of life.

'I don't think I can ever be strong enough to live in London. The ladies seem so different than I am.'

He shook his head. 'It doesn't matter what the other ladies are like. And some of them may be more like you than you realise. Including my mother.'

'We are not alike.'

'My mother is quite the gentle lady. A woman who has little thought in her head except for that yowling pup whose sole purpose is to cover everything inside with shedding hair and everything outside with excrement.'

'That's not a good thing to say of your mother. She loves you.'

'You asked for truth. And, yes, I know she loves me dearly. But she loves Piddles or Puddles, or whatever its name is, more than me.'

'You can't believe that.'

'Well, let me tell you about my dear, delicate mother. Mixed in with the nonsense—and it is her true nonsense—is a woman who will not let anything discourage her from her own wishes. She bends not a whisker. She likes flounces and surrounds herself with them. Don't try to take that from her or the dog, or you will have a fortress to crash against. Not to fight. But a wall of steel to face. Ask my father.'

'I'm not like that.'

'My father said you once tended a woman who died in your arms and you dressed her for burial. Would you care to tell me about that?'

She shook her head. 'Her children should not have had to do so. It was their mother and no child should have to see a mother's private sufferings.'

'The husband told my father. He told him about the blood and the stench and the fact that you shrugged it away as nothing. He suggested someone else do it, but you refused. You said you could not bear for your mother to walk so far as it would hurt her. Every other option he offered, you batted away.'

'Life is not all flowers. We must accept thorns, too.'

'And what nightmares do you have?'

She pulled the covers closer and didn't speak.

'When my father told me of how you took the duties of the village on when you were still in hair ribbons and your mother could not walk, I listened. And when he told of your nightmares and how you hid them from your mother so she would not worry, I listened. At that age—' she saw his teeth again, but the laughter was irony at himself '—I was learning to use a slingshot to hit my cousins with acorns. You were dreaming of the poultices you needed to put on a dying woman's skin.'

'I did what I had to do.'

'No one could have forced me to do that. That is how *my* strength would have been used. To resist. And when I heard of your nightmares—if I had had a doubt of standing at your side and saying those vows, then I knew I was honoured to stand at your side. I am honoured to have a wife who will clean feeding parasites off a dying woman's flesh and dream about it for years, and still walk about bouncing a basket on her arms and with a kind word on her lips.'

'I know how fast life can go and how cruel it can be.'

'And you do not turn your back on your belief in sunshine.'

'Of course not.'

'Show me your weakness then.'

She said nothing.

'But I know what your true weakness is.'

He nodded when she met his eyes.

'It is that you doubt your strength.'

He put his hands on her cheeks. 'Rebecca, I will give my life for you. I will spend every day seeing that you have food in your mouth and that you are eating. I will walk along beside you and make certain that food does not get put in the chamberpot. Because the good that you can do in the world is so much better than what I can do. I will make the world a better place simply by being at your side. So you can do that one good work a day. That one little good work that you mentioned. Like giving a child a treat, or caring for a dying woman so others will be spared. So those older or younger than you would not have to.'

Chapter Twenty-Four

The next day, Rebecca awoke in her father's home, in her old bed. Fox would be at her house soon, so she quickly dressed to begin breakfast. Fox had told her he thought he might try his hand at cooking porridge and preparing the bread and she wanted the meal finished by the time he arrived.

She believed him completely when he'd said he planned to cook and she imagined flour becoming a fascinating dust in his hands.

By the time they'd eaten, her father had convinced Foxworthy to help with chopping some wood for one of the vicarage's elderly widows. Fox and her father insisted she go along.

'Why don't we get the new vicar to help us?' Foxworthy asked.

Her father snorted. 'The man does not know which end of the axe to use.'

'All the more reason he will need to help us.'

Fox stepped quickly, before an answer could be formed, and moved in the direction of his father's house.

When they arrived, he insisted on having one of the stable hands prepare a donkey cart for them, gather all the axes around and then he went inside. Not long after, two sour-faced men followed him out. One the new vicar and one his father.

Her father's shoulder's tightened and he whispered to Rebecca, 'He cannot do this. The earl cannot work with us. It's unthinkable.'

Then two maids rushed out behind, carrying baskets.

'Are we all to go?' Rebecca asked.

Foxworthy nodded. 'Yes. My father and the vicar think it a grand idea that we have a brisk walk and make a quick morning's work of it.'

After they arrived at the trees to be cut, the men gathered around the first tree to be chopped, discussing how to make it fall in the correct direction.

'Vicar,' Fox said to her father, 'why don't

you build a fire and sit with my father while we work? Some quite good brandy is in—'

'Not the brandy from the—' the earl gasped.

'Yes, Father, I knew you were saving it for a special occasion and I thought an outing like this would be perfect.'

The earl frowned. 'You are so much my father's grandson.'

'I believe I am.' His lips turned up in a smile and he grasped the handle of the axe as if he'd been born with it in his hand. In moments he made quick work at the base of a tree.

'You've done this before,' Rebecca said to Foxworthy.

'My cousins and I used to play that we worked in the field and the woods. And how could we let the field hands see our weaknesses? We had to prove we had their grit.'

When the vicar took his turn at loading the chopped wood and the earl and her father supervised, Fox asked Rebecca if she would like to walk back to the estate. She nodded.

'I think I might enjoy this marriage,' he said, holding her in the crook of his arm. 'There are more pleasant ways to spend a night than drinking and moving from club to club and stitching my samplers.'

'Have you ever sewn a single thread?'

'Yes. And they were quite good stitches. I wish I had been there to see the results.'

'What did you sew?'

'My cousin Andrew had been rather pompous about how I was to be an earl and he was just plain Lord Andrew and we both put our pants on one leg at a time. He said it was only in disrobing that we differed. The barb was at me because I'd been too many sails to the wind the night before and I'd crashed into a chair when I took off my trousers. I'd woken the whole house and broken a chair leg.'

He slowed in his steps to let her keep up. 'So after he and his valet left that day, I sewed the bottom of his trouser leg closed. And his valet's as well because I heard the man chuckle when he was taking the broken chair leg to be mended.' He stopped, twirling her hair. 'I can imagine them hopping with the momentum of their foot hitting a stopping block.'

'You should be ashamed.'

'No. My stitches were well disguised.'

'Not for that. For drinking yourself insensible.'

'I have done that many times and I expect to do it a few more times before I hang up my needle.'

'Fox.' She did a quick press against his chest.

'Very well. The needle is put away. But I

can't promise I won't drink to excess from time to time.'

'I want to try again,' she said. 'To live in London. And I'd like my father to live with us, if he wishes.'

'I've already asked him if he would like to go with us if we return to London and he agreed.'

'That's wonderful,' she said.

'Not completely,' Fox admitted. 'He told my father of the request and now Father is assuming he will be able to live with us as well. He said the estate is getting too big for one person. I'm afraid Mother will start feeling left out and decide to join us. And bring the dog.' He stopped. 'I may not want to leave the village after all.'

'Well, you can manage them. A man is supposed to be the head of the family.'

'You think so?'

'Well, yes.' She spoke softly. 'And you are. The bumble head.' Her lids blinked, adding a quiet exclamation point to the words.

He leaned forward, eyes challenging. 'Still the head of the family.'

'Yes. But Mother said a woman is to be the backbone. To hold the head up because it would toddle to the ground on its own.' She shrugged.

'So I need you to keep me upright. But with you—' In a quick lunge he turned, grabbing her by the waist and lifting her up above him. 'With you, I am all I wish to be.'

Still in the air, and taking care not to press, she put her hands near his ears, holding his cheeks. She peered into his eyes and a bit beyond. 'I think I see a few cobwebs, a touch of something that smells of a barnyard and a lost earwax remover.'

His hands remained locked on to her waist, and he pulled her against him, the warmth of her causing a heat that soothed and rushed his blood.

He looked at her eyes. 'And I see tomes and tomes of rules and Thou Shalt Nots.'

'I did not know you paid attention to such things.'

'Have you ever thought about what my father-in-law says to me when you cannot hear us? The man who mixed the wedding vows.' He held her closer. 'He said the commandments had been printed with an error when they were transferred to written words.'

'He's never said such a thing to me.'

'No. I'm sure he would find no need to speak such to his daughter. He said we mostly hear the latter version and not the earlier, correct version of the nine commandments. Thou shalt not commit adultery and thou shalt not kill were miswritten because they were originally one sentence. He claims the true version went, *Thou shalt not commit adultery, and other than for a son-in-law who does that, thou shalt not kill.'*

'My father did not.'

'He most certainly did. He said he'd not heard of it until his father-in-law informed him of it.'

Then his words slowed. 'And he said something about a husband worshipping his wife's body as much as his own. And that I could never do. Yours deserves so much, much more than that. A thousand times more.' He finished the words with his lips less than a breath from hers.

Chapter Twenty-Five

Foxworthy and Rebecca had been in London a fortnight on the night of the Duke of Edgeworth's soirée, and Rebecca had had a gown made in every colour of the rainbow.

Fox took her into the ballroom and let them meld into the wall, but they both knew everyone was curious about Fox's bride.

When the music stopped, he took her hand and pulled her to the middle of the dance floor. She dug her heels in, but he kept her hand tight until she let out a breath and agreed with her eyes not to vanish.

He knelt on one knee, held her hands in his and looked up and into her eyes. 'My Rebecca,' he said.

For the first time, he understood the solemnity of a proposal. Of putting one's heart at a woman's feet.

'You have asked how many women I have proposed to. Many married women. So many women I cannot remember. But I have finally found the married woman that I wish to spend the rest of my life with. The one married woman who holds my heart in her hand, and the one woman, should she tell me no, that I will spend my life longing for.'

He took her hand and placed it against his chest, holding it so that she could feel his heart beating. 'My heart beats for you. I breathe for you. I love you. Rebecca, will you spend the rest of your days with me as your humble servant, put upon this earth to make you happy? Will you marry me?'

'It is a little late for me to change my mind,' she mumbled.

'Just as it is too late for me to change my mind. It is made up for ever. I must be the person you want to see reflected in your eyes. I can't go back to who I was. There is no future for me there. The only future I have is with you.'

'Is this a pretty speech for the others?'

'No. It is my heart speaking to you. And if you don't love me, you can have the freedom of your wishes. I would step into the shadows and be only a memory for you if you wish, but you will never be in the shadows of my heart. You are the last woman I will propose to.'

Silence.

'Rebecca...' He studied her eyes.

She leaned forward and the silence of the room gave volume to her whisper. 'I knew I would be the last when you asked me the first time.' She smiled.

His eyes opened wider. He stood. 'Well, then, I'll take that as a yes.' He spoke over his shoulder to the musicians. 'Music, please.'

When the song concealed their words from others, she asked. 'And would you marry me all over again?' She looked into his eyes.

'Is that a proposal?' He raised a brow.

'Oh, my. I do believe it is.'

'That is my first. And I accept.' He bowed to her and moved to shield her from the rest of the room.

'Don't be surprised if my proposal to you will make it to the newspapers,' Fox looked to the side. 'Agatha Crump is the biggest talker I know and she's watching every move we make.'

'Will you be disappointed if it doesn't?' she asked. 'We may never be mentioned again now that we are on the same page...so to speak.'

'Oh, I believe we will be,' Foxworthy said. 'I heard that the paper is considering an offer from someone who has no notion of how to run a newspaper and plans to cause all sorts of uproar. His man of affairs has been dangling a lot of coins in front of the publisher.'

Her mouth opened. She considered his words. 'Oh. That tale is already about. How unfortunate.'

She smoothed her skirt. 'I may have some private news for you later.' Then her voice softened. And she mumbled under her breath.

'An addition. An addition? Is there something...a babe?' His voice squeaked.

'No. No.' She rushed forward. 'I didn't say I'm looking forward to an addition. I said *edition*.'

'We did it.' Beatrice rushed over, shoes clattering on the floor in a way only Beatrice could manage. 'The duchess has the papers. The man of affairs just brought them over.'

'What papers?' Fox asked.

'Ours,' she almost growled.

He could certainly see how she'd been called Beatrice the Beast.

Edgeworth and Lily stepped behind Beatrice, a half-smile lighting Lily's face, and looking every bit the serene duchess. 'They will all find out sooner or later,' Lily said. 'I can't keep any secrets from Edge.'

'Andrew begs me to keep secrets from him.' Beatrice's lips went up at one side. 'He said he rests better when I do.' She looked around. 'I've lost him again. I'm sure he's hiding somewhere, drawing caricatures.' She shivered. 'He's almost as good at it as I am.'

'I was getting ready to tell Fox.' Rebecca glanced his way, eyes nervous, hands clasped. 'I just didn't want to until we were certain.'

'We are. Certain.' Lily gave one of the nods of a queen knighting a soldier. 'My father is so proud. He never thought he would be helping his daughter purchase a newspaper. I enjoy the accounting sheets as much as he does.'

'You purchased a newspaper?' Fox's brow furrowed.

'Yes. Printing press. Building. The entire newspaper. The publisher thinks he sold his business to Lily's father,' Rebecca said. 'But we're the true owners. Lily will work with the account books. I will edit and search out stories from ladies without standing because they are comfortable approaching me and realise I will tell their views fairly.'

'I will be providing lots to write about among the *ton*.' Beatrice raised her arm, bracelets sliding, and flared her gloved fingers to the ceiling. 'I'm skilled at that. Besides, I love being about in society. I adore...' the word rolled from her tongue with a husky purr '...the glitter of soirées.'

'Beatrice will be our eyes and ears of the social world,' Lily added. 'It's not as if we are changing who we are or who we want to be. We're each doing what we wish to.'

'And it can give me a way to help others every day—in the stories we share with the readers,' Rebecca added.

'Well, it's time for me to dance,' Beatrice said over her shoulder. 'Time to celebrate the new page of our lives.'

Beatrice bustled to the other side of the dance floor. Lily's steps floated along behind her.

Fox gazed at his wife, happy to see her wearing the new gown, pleased it fitted her so perfectly. 'You know I do not like to read.'

'Yes.' Her laugh reached higher than her gaze did. 'I think that might be good because we may have a story about you from time to time.'

He pulled her into a waltz, resting his face near her hair, scenting the floral that reminded him of love and contentment. 'It won't be the same as the other newspaper stories. I no longer feel I need to amuse everyone around me. Your smile is the only one I need.'

When the dance ended, he led her from the floor. Out of the corner of his eye, he saw a couple, much in love by the look of their faces.

He stopped, realising he saw the reflection

of Rebecca and himself in a mirror. He clasped her elbow.

'You have the most beautiful eyes I've ever seen and the most beautiful heart.' He stared into the glass. 'Until I met you, I thought people only did things to gain something for themselves. I didn't believe that someone really could care for strangers without getting something in return.'

She examined the mirror. 'I can't get over the fact that you're not bad-looking, Fenton.'

'I love you, but do not call me that.'

The woman in the mirror smiled, her eyebrows arched twice and he wasn't certain her inner person didn't give a polish to its horns.

* * * * *

MILLS & BOON

Coming next month

FROM GOVERNESS TO COUNTESS
Marguerite Kaye

'Surely there is some mistake?' the imposing figure said. His voice had a low timbre, his English accent soft and pleasing to the ear.

'I think there must be, Your—Your Illustrious Highness,' Allison mumbled. She looked up, past the skirts of his coat, which was fastened with a row of polished silver buttons across an impressive span of chest. The coat was braided with scarlet. A pair of epaulettes adorned a pair of very broad shoulders. Not court dress, but a uniform. A military man.

'Madam?' The hand extended was tanned, and though the nails were clean and neatly trimmed, the skin was much scarred and calloused. 'There really is no need to abase yourself as if I were royalty.'

His tone carried just a trace of amusement. He was not exactly an Adonis, there was nothing of the Cupid in that mouth, which was too wide, the top lip too thin, the bottom too full. This man looked like a sculpture, with high Slavic cheekbones, a very determined chin, and an even more determined nose. Close-cropped dark blond hair, darker brows. And his eyes. A deep artic blue, the blue of the Baltic Sea. Despite his extremely attractive exterior, there was something in those eyes that made her very certain she would not want to get on the wrong side of him. Whoever he was.

Belatedly, she realised she was still poised in her curtsy, and her knees were protesting. Rising shakily, refusing the extended hand, she tried to collect herself. 'My name is Miss Allison Galbraith and I have travelled here from England at the request of Count Aleksei Derevenko to take up the appointment of governess.'

His brows shot up and he muttered something under his breath. Clearly flustered, he ran his hand through his hair, before shaking his head. 'You are not what I was expecting. You do not look at all like a governess, and you most certainly don't look like a herbalist.'